The VALE
of
LAUGHTER

by Peter De Vries

The VALE
of
LAUGHTER

by Peter De Vries

Boston · Toronto

LITTLE, BROWN AND COMPANY

LIBRARY OF CONGRESS CATALOG CARD NO. 67-11236

FIRST EDITION

Sections of Chapters 5 and 9 of Part I, and of Chapters 5 and 7 of Part II,
originally appeared in *The New Yorker* in somewhat different form. Chapter
1 and a section of Chapter 2 of Part II appeared in *Harper's Magazine*.

Published simultaneously in Canada
by Little, Brown & Company (Canada) Limited

PRINTED IN THE UNITED STATES OF AMERICA

1
Joe Sandwich

one

CALL me, Ishmael. Feel absolutely free to. Call me any hour of the day or night at the office or at home and I'll be glad to give you the latest quotation with price-earnings ratio and estimated dividend of any security traded in those tirelessly tossing, deceptively shaded waters in which we pursue the elusive whale of Wealth, but from which we come away at last content to have hooked the twitching bluegill, solvency. And having got me call me anything you want, Ish baby. Tickled to death to be of service. Whether it's about a dog I recommended or a sweetheart I missed. It's all right. You know me. Everybody hates me because I'm so universally liked, and this is a beguiling work of great warmth and charm, whose effects will linger with you long after you have closed and put it by, to take up again in later years when seized with the hunger to renew the acquaintance of one well worth the knowing, and relive events of which time cannot dim the luster.

7

All that. I must succeed in setting myself down; I must manage to catch my own essence, that is the main problem. I don't want a million bucks, and don't let me handle your portfolio if that's all you're after. I want only to give pleasure, to spread sunshine whether people like it or not — a great leviathan of an ideal that will serve me for a lifetime, and that I pursue with a tenacity no one escapes.

What nationality I am I cannot say. My father would never tell me, always clamming up when the subject was broached. So I guess it is some race held in low esteem, which he deemed it just as well to keep from his offspring, who realized at an early age who did the deeming around the house. Still, one itches at times to know. Our name, Sandwich, is no clue, being the name of the English couple, both dead now, who adopted him. Learning his ethnic origin from them must have been a blow, judging from his decision to spare me, and my mother too (or to spare himself the possibility that she might break the engagement if she learned the truth). Mother was a mongrel but predominantly French, so at least I know what I am on that side. I would try to pry the facts out of my father with pleas, demands and finally outright threats of legal action, without effect. The discovery that he was illegitimate seemed to trouble him far less, so they must be pretty bad.

This aim to please is not by way of "compensation."

It's simply my nature, and would have been had I learned that I was pure Gallic, or descended clean down the paternal side from the Earl of Sandwich. People seem to like me. And the substructure, as I say, bears scrutiny. No mare's-nest will be uncovered, that I promise. And I think I can imagine your relief to learn that you are not to be ushered on yet another of those conducted tours of the sewermains of human nature, of which I do not possess a very interesting set, I fear, by yet another exponent of the fouler-than-thou school, of which I am not a member. If a man is the salt of the earth let him say so freely and openly, and without any tedious shilly-shallying.

So luckily some attempt can be made here to redress the character assassination now regarded as the proper study of mankind. As for spreading sunshine, that gets under way where least expected, in the very house of God — in my case St. Anthony's on the south side of Chicago — in whose confessionals some relief from the seamy side is sorely needed, judging from the greed and falsehood principally aired there by adults, as well as by their apple-thieving, parent-flouting young: my playmates. Oh, how I know them! Rather more encouraging food for thought can be gleaned there with my regular arrival bright and early Saturday morning.

"Father, I helped an old lady across the street, I found a home for a stray cat I found starving in an alley," I begin in one such typical appearance, in the shadowy arbor, at the age of eleven or twelve. "I did my homework without being told, and I returned a dime I found in the schoolyard to a boy I knew it belonged to. Instead of keeping it." That was the week that was.

There is a rustle beyond the latticework, as of the cloth getting a firm grip on itself. At last the whispered response: "And now you are puffed up about these things. Spiritually vain."

"I suppose. I put part of the dough I made at the parish bowling alley in the poor box, and let's see, what else? I don't have pimples from impure thoughts, even though I'm old enough to be thinking about girls. My complexion is clear. All that is pretty well under control, Father. Things are in pretty good shape. In fact apple-pie order."

Another rustle in the ecclesiastical half of the arbor, and this time the answer coming quickly and sharply.

"If you wish to confess the sin of pride, then do so without the commercial if you please. Because I'm busy and there are others waiting. Two Hail Marys."

This was Father Enright. I chose him when I could because I felt we were simpatico. I liked the characteristic wit about the "commercial," and was also amused by his making no bones about knowing who I was, thus scorning the sacred pretense of anonymity. The way the culprit greeted me on the street a few days later left no doubt of that.

"Well, if it isn't my old friend Joe Sandwich," he said with a laugh, as though in the mere act of greeting you by name lay already some contribution to the gaiety of nations. "On our way to Boy Scouts to report some good deeds, are we? Or just out scattering sunshine wherever possible, on a free lance sort of basis?"

I would pretend he was a Jewish rabbi who had blundered into the confessional by mistake, or been assigned there due to some terrible denominational mixup. "Op to wronk deeds again?" he would say then. "So Ah'll demend you should right now make ah good ect contrition. Get on de ball, pliz. Ah'm waitink, odders are waitink, so commence pliz mit de ect contrition." I once pulled a prank on him in the form of a "clerical error." On stationery stolen from Green's haberdashery when momentarily left alone near the back desk, I sent a lot of "bills" out to friends and acquaintances, Father Enright among them. He received one for a hundred and some dollars for a houndstooth jacket, several bright cravats, and a porkpie hat. I could see his expression when he got Mr. Green on the phone, and Mr. Green's too as he said, "Cravats? Wot's dat? I don't hendle merchandise like dat. Just shoits, neckties and a hendful jackets. *Cravats?* Dot some kind fency item for de feet, like spets?" I like people. Call me a people buff.

And as for resentment and rebellion toward parents, rubbish! I always loved mine, wanted only to please them too. I can remember as a child in my high chair

11

grasping my spoon by the wrong end and shoveling cereal into my mouth with the handle while they shrieked with laughter. That was when they were still alive. Since their departure I can remember many attempts to amuse them equally. When I once told them that in their absence from the house I had sliced my fingers off in the electric fan which they had imprudently left running, sliced them into pieces like so many bananas, my chief reward was not their expressions of anguished guilt — clapped brows, cries of self-reproach — but the ones of joy to which they changed when I unwound the stained cloth wrapped around my hand to resemble a bloody stump. How they hugged and kissed me, and nothing would do but that we all go out and have an ice cream. I am told that such antics are now regarded as having secret roots in hostility, but there is no evidence of this in my case. Introspection fails to yield a single clue to rancor, a single malicious bone in my body, only a natural love of fun when, say, I steal over a neighbor's rooftop to lay a plank across his chimney.

But back to Father Enright buttonholing me on Halsted Street.

"No, I'm on my way to the drugstore to get some medicine for my father," I said, looking him square in the tiny yellow citron-in-a-plum-pudding eye.

"Without being told no doubt."

It was a typical enough week, as I was able to state without qualification on my next visit to the arbor.

"Father, I sit up every evening with my father, doing my homework in his bedroom. He's been quite sick, you know. And I try to lighten the burden for my mother as much as I can, as all this is very hard on her."

It was Father Enright all right. He popped from his lair with more than a rustle this time and, grasping my ear, marched me toward the door of the church.

"I suppose we're just the salt of the earth, eh, Sandwich?" (It was the first time I heard the term used in a believable human context, and not just as an empty Scriptural abstraction.) "Heart of gold, have we, an example to all? Just one of the finest things going? Well, in that case we need the time and space for poor wretched sinners. Out!"

I did not leave without protest.

"I was only joking," I said as I was hustled out.

"Well, you'll have to do better than that here. You're a card, but not the Juggler of Notre Dame yet, by a long chalk!"

He was alluding of course to the itinerant entertainer of French legend who put on his act for the Blessed Virgin, and when the horrified monks broke into the chapel to put a stop to the sacrilege, they saw the Holy Mother descend the altar steps and wipe the sweat from his brow with the folds of her robe. You probably remember the story in its most familiar form as related by Anatole France.

My relations with the other priests soon came to much the same thing as they too became familiar with my intention to take literally what Our Lord said about being perfect even as our Father in heaven is perfect. If he hadn't thought we could be, he would not have bothered to issue the exhortation, is my idea. Not for him this Isaiah stuff about all our righteousness being as filthy rags, and bully for him! My mother's wasn't, neither was that of a lot of other people I could name, myself included. While I might not have been perfect, neither could I for the life of me think of any great faults to report, with the possible exception of a tendency illustrated by my remark that Christ and the Jews of his time were working at cross-purposes. But then that just slipped out. I later learned, from a college teacher named Hines, Freud's belief that all the work of the wit is done by the unconscious.

Well, we were expected to go to confession, and so like a good Christian I went. But no matter who was on duty I had only another string of good deeds to rattle off, and so I was at last warned that I must mend my ways or be barred from the house of the Lord. But the next week it was the same story. Model conduct again and nothing I could do about it.

"I have fed the hungry and clothed the naked," I quietly persisted.

"Ten Hail Marys and as many Our Fathers."

"And I have never neglected my devotionals."

"Well, you can hop to them now. Make it the entire rosary."

This abuse of the confessional I should have put past Father Enright, or whoever was peering through the gloom to get a good look at me now (I have forgotten who exactly it was in this instance), but, as I say, my fame as a saint had spread and they were all laying for me. A priest named Father Reardon, who had had some training in psychology, kept threatening to tell me what I was like.

I think I was handled very poorly, all in all. It was no doubt Father Enright's own obstinacy that prolonged my own. And though it wasn't to pull anybody's leg that I had originally taken the tack I did, it soon very subtly became my motive. I *was* clowning in the house of God.

I suppose the contest of wills would have gone on forever if it hadn't been for Father Enright's own rather perverse fancy coming into play — and here we do have the element of malice showing up. One day after hearing out another week's stellar deportment he said, "Swell. You're just the kind we want around here, Sandwich. We want to see more of you. Go over to the rectory and beat the rugs. Then wash the windows. And when you've

15

finished that we'll think of something else. Because you're a credit to the neighborhood, and we want you around just as much as possible."

It was then the tide turned. My inherent wish to please won the day. Feeling that I had made my point, and not wishing to labor it, I began reporting a few peccadilloes just to help them save face. I never liked to be a troublemaker. Quite the contrary. If a man ask me to walk with him one mile, I will go with him twain, like a good sort.

two

MY FATHER was recovering from a heart attack in those days. He had never been in any grave danger, but he thought he was, and his pessimism communicated itself to us — my mother and me, and an uncle, her brother, who was staying with us at the time. We took turns sitting with him, and in the course of my watches (by no means exaggerated to Father Enright) I became aware of a peculiar obsession.

My father was worried about precisely how he would go, in particular what his last words would be. He seemed eager to make an exit that would do him credit, especially since he was an unbeliever and had to show the church this sort of thing could be done without them. He prided himself on his worldliness, in short, and would like to have it said that he went as he had lived, with urbanity, even extreme unction! My mother was the devout one, whose efforts to give me some sort of religious background he did not resist, since he was no bigot on the other side, and perfectly willing that I be let make up my own mind in my own good time.

So he had been reading this recently published book, *How They Went*, which was a collection, with commentary, of the last words of great men. It told how Beethoven lay shaking his fist at the storm, how Thoreau when asked whether he had made his peace with God retorted, "We have never quarreled," and so on. All that was in this confounded book, you see, and whether his fascination with it was the cause or the result of his fixation, it came to the same thing.

"It makes a man wonder what his own last words will be," he said, when we were alone one evening.

"What difference does it make?" I said, my impatience a little more justified than might have seemed the case had he not been pronounced out of danger. It was hard enough trying to do your homework beside a sickbed without being continually interrupted by the contents of an anthology of death rattles.

"A lot of difference. It's a statement. It characterizes a man, and it's something to leave behind for others to remember him by," he said, his resemblance to a dachshund suddenly depressing. "A sort of summing up."

While he dilated in this vein, I rose and drifted toward the wardrobe mirror to check again whether my resemblance to him, and therefore to a hound dog, was increasing or decreasing with the onset of adolescence.

It was increasing. There was no doubt about it. The nose does not attain full growth till adulthood, but even now I was headed for the tapering snout he was going to leave me, whatever else I was to inherit in the way of mortuary memories and valedictory mots. Up to now I had clung to hopes of escaping this family cross. But when I tilted the cheval glass down to get a better joint view of us, my heart sank at the result.

There was no doubt that my pointed nose was lengthening like my stride, and that with time it would only accentuate the canine conformation of the chops, with the wide mouth circling far back into the cheeks, and the undershot lower jaw. Even as I took in the scene my father executed the mannerism that wrapped the whole thing up. He chucked back the corners of his mouth still farther, as we do to express exasperation or worry. The more "human" one's expression or activity under such circumstances, the greater the sense of caricature. If a man resembling a dog puts a cigar in his mouth or a derby on his head, he will only look like a dog smoking a cigar or wearing a derby, thereby pushing the lampoon to its limits. I sometimes had a dream about my father and me drinking water from a pan, on all fours.

Depressed by this train of thought, I said as I turned back, "Let's pull a trick on the people who just moved into the house next door."

"What kind of trick?"

"We'll make a nuisance call. Watch."

Their name was Upjohn, I had noticed on the mailbox. Getting their number from Information, I gave my father a wink and dialed it.

"Hello," I said when a man answered. "Are you Upjohn?"

"Yes."

"At this hour?" I said, and hung up, choking with laughter.

This is the sort of thing that makes new neighbors feel at home, but when I saw that it was too rich for my father's blood, put it that way, I decided to get out my collection of funny names and amuse him by reading aloud from it.

Funny names are my hobby. I collect them the way other people collect coins or stamps. Some I take from real life, some I make up — the former of course the wildly more improbable. Ima Nutt, for example, I saw with my own eyes on the window of a hairdresser's while passing through Kansas on a train. It is entered in a section of my collection devoted to Paronomastic Names that form phrases or thoughts: Justin Case, Miles Long, Brighton Early, Curt Manner, O. B. Still and the like (to which could now be added R. U. Upjohn, for that matter). It was I who first coined the name Herbie Hind, now, of course, part of American folklore. This sort of thing seems to me so much more rewarding, not to add creative, than the passive accumulation of pieces of pewter or milk glass over whose construction one has had no say. It is a challenge to your ingenuity, not merely your diligence. It's like first creating a butterfly and then going out to catch it. I am on the lookout, for example, for a Factor with the initials R. H., and comb the telephone directory of any new town I stop in, doggedly watching for this specimen, knowing that some day, somewhere, it will flutter into my ken.

Tonight I just read to my father from the general Open Section of names simply funny for their own sakes without any of the fine points that are of interest chiefly to the connoisseur (but from which entries are sometimes drawn for reclassification in Paronomastic or other special categories). I hitched the armchair up closer beside the bed, so the light from the nightstand fell across the large looseleaf notebook in which the entire collection is housed.

"Penelope Splatter," I began softly, "Gretchen Klobber, Mr. and Mrs. Ezekiel Gumthanks, Ernie Butterwar, Bill and Bessie Poolump, Aubrey Durt, Dr. McClinic, Fifi Brochure, Vladimir Vestoff, Lotta Noyes, O. Lord . . ."

Glancing at my father as I paused to take a suck of my Coke, I saw that his lids were lowered, and I thought that he was asleep, though the possibility that he might be dead was not entirely to be dismissed. I often read

21

him to sleep, with a volume of his choosing or mine. I therefore now turned out the light preparatory to stealing from the room. He checked my departure, however, by clearing his throat in a manner leaving no doubt that he was far from through with this life, or this evening. With a frown, and in the light still coming in from the corridor, he watched the play of his thumbs coming together on the counterpane as he said:

"What if a man goes in the middle of the night and says something there's nobody to hear?"

"Oh, my God."

It seems odd that what is plain as the nose on my face now eluded me then: that since he was not well born he wanted to die creditably. How obvious! But I never put two and two together until long afterward, and therefore remained puzzled by his obsession as well as irritated with it, seeing no reasonable motive for it at all except the desire to strut your stuff to the end.

"It might be something completely trite and worthless, and lucky nobody did hear it," I said, to cheer him up. But the observation failed of its intended soothing effect. I still think the book was an unfortunate influence, whether it actually put the bee in his bonnet or no, since he simply did not bat in the same league with Thoreau, Heine and all the other heavyweight perishers.

I tried to tell him as much as discreetly as possible, without success. It only reactivated the sense of challenge, while bringing out attendant apprehensions.

What if it turned out he really did say something memorable and there was no witness, or if there was, he was nodding himself and didn't hear it, or if awake, not sufficiently attentive to catch the words? They would then be forever lost. The family would be cheated of an inheritance better than gold, and the departed of the deserved enshrinement in their hearts. Einstein evidently said something in German, a language the nurse with him at the time didn't understand.

"I'll tell you what I'll do," I said.

I began to pace the floor again, my hands in my pockets and my eyes lowered in thought.

"Let's work it out this way. You settle in your own mind what you'd like best to be remembered by, and I'll just tell the others that you said it after you do go."

"That would be cheating."

"Why? It would be typical of you — it would be *you*. Something you want to pass on. And you might very well say it if you drilled it into your head enough. So we'll leave it that way. Just before I turn out the lights here and we go to sleep, you say it, and if anything happens during the night, why, that will be the thing people will report. I'll see to it that they do and no nonsense. Now what could be fairer than that?"

He shook his head in dissatisfaction with the plan, chucking back his dog's chops. "It would be too contrived. Not extemporaneous."

Which caused me to break out impatiently, "That's

not necessarily any guarantee! What does Lord Nelson blurt out? 'Kiss me, Hardy.' He wants a smack from his flag captain! What's so hot about that? And another thing. A lot of these official last words that have become famous weren't their last words at all. That remark of Thoreau's — oh, there's another attributed to him. That when a visitor wanted to discuss the hereafter Thoreau said, 'One world at a time, please.' The fact is that neither one was his last words. According to the book, he sank into unconsciousness and just before the end whispered, 'Moose,' and then, 'Indians.' What's so great about that? A man can plan to say something memorable, say it, and then sink into incoherent babbling, like nine tenths of the public."

Momentarily stymied by my point, my father again twitched back the corners of his mouth, inspiring fresh pangs of concern about one's future appearance. Perhaps in dwelling on it I was cultivating the very expression I wanted to avoid. Far better to develop a habit of pursing the lips slightly forward so as to strike a musing, or whimsical, note, advantageous for both physical appearance and social airs. I stood at the mirror experimenting with various modifications of this expression while continuing to chat with my father about his own primary concern.

"All Shaw managed," I remarked, pursing my lips into the half-smile of gently wry amusement, "was 'I'm going to die.' It's hardly worth the breath. One of the greatest wits of the century, and that was all he had to say. And even then it was two days before he made good on it. So in effect the greatest dramatist since Shakespeare had no curtain line at all."

We were occupied with these divergent themes when my uncle sauntered in.

There was a dreamboat! My mother's only brother, he always felt it incumbent on him to hurry down from Canada where he lived, and bred horses, for any family crisis, to "be on hand and help out." All his presence amounted to was an extra plate for my mother to set and an extra bed for her to make, since he did little for the duration of any stay but stroll the streets and go to the movies, so as "not to be underfoot." He had been to see a picture tonight.

We are all fed up with reminiscences about childhood relatives each of whom is more picturesque than the last. How refreshing, therefore, to be able to offer in my Uncle Hamilton an absolute miracle of colorlessness. My father couldn't stand him around. He was so dim and bland and bumbling that these qualities, or lack of them, became in themselves an irritant of a positive sort. For example, he was always lost in the shuffle conversationally, so that in any group discussion all you heard from him were the beginnings of statements, the rest being trampled or drowned out by more definite types, such as we all were here. So that in memory now I can hear him saying "If you ask my opinion," but not the opinion; "what the whole thing boils down to," but not what it boiled down to; "experience has taught me," but not what it did — and so on. Perhaps he finally didn't even bother to complete his thoughts, knowing there would have been no point.

Paradoxically, he started many a brisk dispute by irking people into the responses in which he himself vanished without a trace. Tonight he started an argument on foreign films, having just been to see a French one.

"I simply don't see how people enjoy something in a language they don't understand," my father said, forgetting for the moment that Uncle Hamilton knew at least enough Canadian French to follow a Parisian farce. "And I don't think they do. I don't believe it for a minute. I think it's all something of an affectation." This time he gave a curt nod as he drew back his chops.

"The trouble with Hollywood," Uncle Hamilton said.

"I have to follow the dialogue the characters are speaking. It's too distracting to keep jumping from their mouths to the subtitles and back again, and actually not good for the eyes either."

"You'll find in the long run."

"It gives me a splitting headache." My father glared at poor Hamilton as if challenging him to deny that he, too, suffered this optical hazard if the truth were told.

26

His brother-in-law's familiarity with French did not actually invalidate his strictures or qualify the point he was trying to make, since Hamilton also omnivorously attended Italian and Swedish movies, and even Japanese and Indian ones. All this entitled my father to an impatience in fact many-faceted. Because my uncle's international tastes in the cinema gained him an unearned kinship with intellectuals while putting my relatively more educated father at an undeserved disadvantage to a boob. As I listened to this futile exchange, I saw my father push up the sleeves of his pajamas as though, without rising out of bed, he were going to punch him in the nose for having returned so soon after his last visit.

"If the movies are ever to become an art form," was the nervous reply. Mumbling something about having a letter to write, my uncle left the sickroom for his own, giving my father a chance to let off a little more steam.

"He's never heard of the Oriental proverb about fish and guests after three days," he said. This attitude toward Uncle Hamilton continued more or less generally in the family until his later years when he began to play on people's sympathies by contracting a fatal disease. A number of the horses he bred had given handsome accounts of themselves on the race tracks, and one, a two-year-old named Glitterboy, had won a few fat purses including a Preakness. So old Hamilton was well fixed. "While people who really work, contribute something to society," my father said, no doubt alluding to his life as a sanitary engineer, "wind up with a big fat zero. How does he rate sitting this pretty?"

"By his sheer assiduity," I said. "Or maybe I should say his horses' assiduity." I laughed, but my father frowned again at the counterpane. There was no doubt the visitor's very presence grated on a man for whom tranquillity was of the essence. We agreed not to notify him any more of my father's coronaries, of which he had another, a year or so later.

"My God!" I said, grinning into the oxygen tent, "you must have a strong heart to stand all this."

That was what was needed, and not a lot of malarkey about how much better you look, and certainly not a lot of taxing relatives around. We held to our resolve not to telephone Saskatchewan this time, and luckily the emergency passed with no more misfortune than the need for another few months' rest.

My own spiritual health had its similar ups and downs, as embodied in my shifting relations with Father Enright. It was months after the last related confession that I again entered the church for the same purpose, running into him just as he was going on duty.

"Good morning, Sandwich," he said. "Slumming again, are we? I'm afraid I'm busy with poor lost souls."

"Wait," I said. "I've changed. I think you're going to like this. I've dishonored my father and mother, I've

28

cracked unseemly jokes, and I've even stolen a little money."

"Now we're getting somewhere," he said. "Come along then, and we'll hear you out." He led the way toward the confessional, inside which, collecting my thoughts a moment, and with neither of us pretending the fiction of anonymity, I became specific.

"I mean I haven't always been as patient with my parents as I should be, is what I mean, and some of my humor has been off-color. I'm becoming more and more guilty of lust."

"Splendid. This is the sort of thing we want to hear. Now, what about the stealing?"

He seemed impressed by the change in me. It was apparent in his tone, which was the tone of a person suddenly more hopeful about another, one who could believe, even, in the perfectibility of man. I exaggerated the theft, which had only been a two-bit piece from my mother's purse, and that promised me anyway, so it wasn't actually a theft, but it set him up no end, his pleasure that of a man of the cloth who finally sees a doubtful case beginning to get a grip on himself and to understand what the whole thing is all about.

I have said my aim has always been to give pleasure. Though we all have on occasion ulterior motives in making an impression, and though the best of us have axes to grind when least suspected, the sources of my

29

appeal are on the whole much as I have made out. And that appeal is genuine. You can't turn on charm that isn't there. You can't fake personal magnetism.

It was when my father died that my feelings toward the Church took a turn for the worse. My loyalty to him, and my identification with him, sharply reversed this impulse to please Father Enright. My father died very suddenly one evening the following summer when we had thought he was again convalescing. He was laid up in bed with an injury sustained a few weeks before, when, with the aid of a nurse, he had fallen downstairs and sprained a leg. He was sitting up in bed writing in a sort of journal he kept, in which from time to time over the years he had jotted down his thoughts and observations. I was sitting near the open window, working on my own collection, without much inspiration. My mother was out visiting a friend.

The day had been sultry, and a storm was brewing. Now it broke with a sudden and frightening violence. There were a few premonitory growls of thunder in the distance, and then there was a crash so deafening, accompanied by a flash so blinding, that we both nearly jumped out of our skin. My notebook fell to the floor while the pencil shot from my father's hand. If the house hadn't been struck, certainly something nearby had. It was one of those ear-splitting peals such as one hears only a few times in a lifetime, that rend the air in a way that gives one the sense of being inside an explosion.

"Jesus H. Christ," my father said, looking at me. We were both white as sheets. "Brother!" I exclaimed, and then we both began to laugh. I rose to shut a few windows, for the rain was now descending in rivers, and to look around as I did so. No trees in the front or back had been struck, though there were few enough to worry about in that neighborhood. Snapping on several wall switches indicated the lights to be out in one part of the house. That was all. Later investigation revealed a fuse to have been burned out in the basement. When I returned to the bedroom I found that my father was gone. The lightning could be said to have struck him indirectly, as it were.

When asked about the circumstances of his passing, I was naturally pressed for details about his last words. I freely related the ejaculation with which he had taken leave of this life, omitting the middle initial which struck me as irrelevant. "Thank God," my mother said, clasping her hands in gratitude, which I in turn could not help being grateful to see. "He made his peace at the end." I saw no point in correcting her interpretation of the facts, which it was not for me to say was right or wrong anyway, the line between profanity and prayer being as fine as it is. They are both alike species of invocation. You might say my mother's own "Thank God" was an exclamation on the order of my father's, and his as heartfelt an outcry as hers. So why split hairs? Everything torn from the breast must be one to Him who made the heart it houses.

Some two or three weeks later I ran into Father Enright in front of St. Anthony's. The sight of his billowing robes sent me into a fit of fancy of the sort to which I am often prey. When I cannot clown, I make other people clown for me — the more inappropriately the better.

Now as Father Enright approached, I imagined that he did so with a jazzy step, snapping his fingers and waving his head as he sang a chorus of "Mississippi Mud." "It's a treat to beat your feet on the Mississippi mud, it's a treat to beat your feet on the Mississippi mud," he sang in a crazy-man-crazy style. He was like someone really "sent." The hallucination vanished as he extended his hand and offered his sympathies. "I'm very sorry about your father," he said.

"That's quite all right."

Why did I say that? Was answering him as though I were acknowledging an apology, rather than an expression of condolence, a way of accusing him of something? Like enjoying a solace my father had declined? Like not having shown up at the funeral? There was no reason for him to have done so since my father wasn't a member of the Church, and besides, I remembered now, he had been on vacation at the time. Nevertheless I continued to harden my heart against Father Enright now, out of loyalty to my father and this wish to identify myself with him. I did so by telling him an entirely different story about my father's last moments.

Since the funeral I had adopted my father's obsession, or it had adopted me. I now racked my brains for the last *typical* remark I had heard him make. Something that would be fitting, say, to put on his tombstone. Not being certain in my mind about it, I tried to remember what I had last read in his journal, or, better yet, what I had read in it that struck me as most like him. I finally decided on the entry: "All this stuff about faith and reason. Faith is slippers and reason is shoes. I never asked to be comfortable." I now told Father Enright that that was my father's last statement.

"Are you quite sure?" he said. "I heard he made a declaration of belief. Some sort of pious utterance."

"No," I said. "I was with him at the time."

We talked of other things — the church carnival then in progress, my newspaper route, which I wanted to sell to a younger boy because I was getting too old to peddle papers. Father Enright made a few suggestions for possible purchasers. Then he said, "I haven't seen you in church lately, have I?"

"I've been to mass. Not to confession."

"Nothing to confess?"

"Oh, sure. I commit the usual sins. And I don't believe in the Virgin Birth."

"Five Hail Marys."

"Right."

His little yellow eyes had their customary glimmer. They lit up like flashlight bulbs. Otherwise his broad face was impassive. As we stood confronting one another in silence, I had him let fly with another chorus of "Mississippi Mud."

I said very suddenly, "I don't see what my mother goes to confession for. What does she have to confess? A woman like that."

"Ah? Why don't you ask her? Well, confessions are what I'm going in to hear now. So if you're not in a buying mood, I'll see you around, Sandwich."

He patted my arm and turned into the church. I watched him break into a dance halfway up the stairs. He twitched his arms and rocked his head like a really gone cat as he vanished through the door singing, "Hey, hey, Uncle Dud! It's a treat — feet — sipp mud, it's a treat — feet — sipp mud!"

I shook my head slowly in dismay and continued on my way.

three

I HAD a slightly older cousin named Benny Bonner, also on my mother's side, majoring in psychology at the University of Chicago when I was in high school, who wanted to psychoanalyze me. He liked to practice on his friends in preparation for a career as a psychiatrist, the way a student barber learns his trade on customers in a so-called barber college. "You interest me," Benny said. "I could learn a lot about the comic type, and you might get some valuable insights into yourself."

I saw no objection, and so it was agreed that I let him give me a psychic haircut, so to speak. He was on the serious side. In high school he had been active in extra-curricular affairs such as literary societies, discussion groups, debates. As captain of the debating team he had been dismayed by the meager public turnouts, and written a scathing editorial in the school paper, denouncing student apathy. It did no good, but that didn't stop his agitation. He organized a mass meeting to protest student apathy. Four people showed up.

I took the Stony Island Avenue bus to Benny's place near the campus, a fifth-floor walkup whose long and steep stairs I mounted with shortening breath. I collapsed in his arms when he opened the door, clutching at his necktie and gasping out a story about having become separated from the main party with which I had scaled all but the final peak, and imploring him for a nip of brandy. I staggered into the apartment and sank onto a couch.

Benny was a stocky fellow with hair like the grass on a putting green, except for the color of course, who thought everything you wore had to "match." With a plaid suit he would wear a plaid shirt and sometimes even a plaid tie and handkerchief, thus anticipating some of the later effects of Op art.

"Can I get you something to drink?" he asked.

"I don't know, can you? Last time I was here your arthritis was so bad you could hardly open a bottle, and now I see your locomotor ataxia is worse. Don't you know they can cure syphilis now, there's no need for a lifetime of regret just because some trollop gave you a package. Have you got paresis too? Let's hear you talk some more, to see how far your delusions have progressed, how much degeneration has set in."

Benny laughed, shaking his head as he went into the kitchen for a couple of beers. He was still smiling when he returned with two cans from which the tops had been sheared, and from these tankards we drank sociably a moment before getting down to the first session.

"You're the clown of the family," he said, frowning studiously. "Humor is mysterious. Where does it come from? Whence does it arise? What is this impulse to crack a joke about everything?"

I remembered there was a story about Benny that as a tyke in rompers he had asked his father, after a spanking needlessly vigorous, "Just what are you twying to pwove?" It was probably apocryphal, but instructive as apocryphal stories often are, and no exaggeration of his drive. He even spent vacations in preparation for his career, taking jobs as a counselor in special camps and as an orderly in nervous sanatariums.

"I have a hunch it's going to prove valuable to me to begin by asking patients point-blank what they're dissatisfied about. People's frustrations tell a lot about them. Has anything been troubling you lately, Joe?"

"Yes. I can't sleep."

"Why not?"

"I can hear the mattress ticking."

After half an hour of this Benny sprang to his feet and began to walk animatedly about the room.

"It's perfectly clear you're a compulsive type," he said. "A more luscious example couldn't be found of the absolute *need* to make a joke about everything. You can't *not* horse around."

"Why is that, Benny?"

I was suddenly famished, but thought it would be poor form to suggest going out for a bite until he had run his clippers once around the back, so to speak, and been given a chance to turn over a few preliminary notions by way of evaluating me.

He proceeded to launch a very concise and well-knit discourse on the element in human life, after all basic to it, that we were dealing with. Taking off from the fundamental definition of the compulsion as "a strong irrational impulse to complete a given act," he said the impulse was found in normal as well as neurotic behavior. All habit was in a sense compulsive. Religious observances certainly were.

"I'm convinced there's a definite parallel between neurosis and religion," he said. "When you ask a neurotic *why* he goes through these elaborate washing or counting routines, the only answer he can give you is that he has this vague but powerful dread that something will happen to him if he doesn't. Precisely what your believer feels when he neglects his beads and communion. He'll be punished. Both are survivals of primitive superstition. It's not for nothing we call the neurotic's compulsions rituals. And the ceremonies of religion are neurotic."

"What has all this got to do with horsing around?"

"What?"

38

"The antic sense. What we're talking about."

"I think there you have the same basic need to discharge anxiety by making a joke of it. What have we laughed about so far? Exhaustion, arthritis, locomotor ataxia, paresis, and insomnia. A joke is, like prayer and hand-washing, a device for resolving fear."

What unexpected fruits these sessions bore! I made my break with religion final as a result of them. True, I had long been on the verge of a rupture with Rome, but it was Benny who finally brought it about. Religion was mass neurosis as he — and of course Freud before him — had pointed out. I stopped going to church. My religious life was at an end.

But some changes began to appear in my secular one as a consequence. They crept in imperceptibly at first, gradually becoming unmistakable.

The first thing I began to notice was that, although I no longer went inside churches, I made an *elaborate pattern* of passing them by. I sometimes went for blocks out of my way, not to avoid them so much as simply to enact the defiance of circumventing them. This followed a rigidly prescribed routine, particularly in the case of my old church, St. Anthony's. I would pause on the sidewalk at one end of the entranceway, and then walk past it in seven long strides. No more, no less. A nameless apprehension would seize me if I didn't.

I lost no time in reporting this development to Benny

39

once there was no mistake about which way the wind was blowing.

"Very interesting," he said. "It's the way a man paces off a length of property frontage. That's a yard's stride. Three feet. It wouldn't have something to do with the Trinity, would it?"

"What about the seven steps?"

"The seven original churches of Asia. I'm just thinking out loud, of course. The numbers as such aren't important, and keep changing, as counting compulsives will tell you. The important thing is the *progress you're making*. The insight you're gaining into yourself. That's what's of value. Well, we're not going to stop now, I guess!"

Now that the seven churches had been mentioned, I had to learn the names from the Apocalypse, so that I could recite them in stride as I executed the sequences: "Ephesus, Smyrna, Pergamos, Thyatira, Sardis, Philadelphia and Laodicea." We all have compulsions in mild form of course — we must step on sidewalk cracks, or avoid them, or touch fence pickets — and frequently they will have numerical features. It is when these rituals infest the entire course of daily existence that that existence becomes insupportable. I found that when mailing a letter I could not leave the postbox until the lid had clattered exactly seven times after I let go — no more, no less. My shoes had to be spaced seven inches apart when I undressed for the night. Only after getting down on my knees in front of the closet and measuring the interval with a ruler to make sure could I think of going to bed, and then rest was by no means assured. All hope of sleep was driven off until I had visually touched the four corners of the ceiling three times, of each window, of each picture on the wall.

I'm not sure whether it was before or after learning that Jung had found the number four widespread in abnormal behavior that I began to incorporate it into mine on anything like the scale traditionally claimed for it — but I think after. It was certainly afterward that a whole rigmarole of eating grew out of it. A square cookie or slice of bread had first to be cropped at the corners and thus more or less be bitten into a circle before being consumed in the more conventional manner. I had to take the fourth seat at a lunch counter, in a bus. Teeth had to be brushed in multiples of four strokes, these repeated four times making sixteen, an arithmetical extension that spread to masticating, breathing, even shaking the glass of hot Ovaltine wistfully imbibed before retiring. Slighting these requirements does indeed bring a fear of dire consequences, a dread no less profound for being vague and undefined. This is the only explanation we compulsives can give you for persisting in our irrational and, as I say, taxing conduct.

Poured into these exhausting acts is evidently energy

we feel guilty at not having discharged where it belonged, which would account for the ablutionary turn
they often take. Washing my hands and face was bad
enough. Bathing was a ceremony that grew more grotesquely baroque each day. Eating utensils had to be
given a furtive but systematic rub with one's napkin
before they could be used without fear of contamination,
causing one's family or one's hostess to wonder what one
was doing in one's lap. This was not living. After a day of
it — climaxed as begun, with the hour-long stylized exertions in the tub — I would drop bone-tired into bed. I
would drag myself, hardly refreshed, out of it to face
another. I finally called Benny and told him the pass
things had come to.

"This is a neurotic result of discontinuing the practice
of religion," he said. "All that will appease your conscience is a set of procedures *as rigid as those abnegated.*
The compulsion *is* itself a ritual. You see?" And he
smiled at the simple sagacity of the parallel.

"But you told me religious observances were neurotic
compulsions! So I scrapped them. Now you tell me
neurotic compulsions are like religious rituals. You explain each with the other, till you've got me swallowing
my own tail. Where does this leave me? Where will it all
end?"

"With progressively more insight."

Insight continued to spread until I was one pooped

Joe. In the case of bathing, a numerical sequence hitherto sufficient for the entire body had now to be enacted on each limb, separately, and what held true for washing also did for drying. I got in and out of the tub seven times, or took seven consecutive showers as the case might be. I again telephoned Benny and told him that a stop simply had to be put to these debilitating rites if I wasn't to wind up at the foolish farm.

He said he might be able to see me the following evening. He was preparing for an important quiz, but he would fit me in if it was urgent.

I climbed the five flights of stairs in a bona fide version of the fatigue I had once humorously simulated, after a night of the insomnia about which we had also joked. Benny was in the doorway smoking a cigar. I flopped down into an armchair and said, "Can you recommend a good psychiatrist?"

He stood contemplating me, his face slanted away from the smoke of the cigar as he buttoned a loose shirtcuff. "I told you clowns are basically hostile," he said. "Hostile and anxiety-ridden."

Suspecting that Benny didn't quite realize what a kettle of carp this was, I now launched a long and detailed account of how matters stood to date, far more graphic and harrowing than any hitherto, that finally seemed to get through to him. He showed he was impressed with a characteristic mannerism. He raised his

43

eyebrows and puffed out his cheeks, which made him resemble one of those wind deities depicted as swelling the sails of ancient ships, in maps based on misconceptions of the earth.

He put out his cigar and strolled to a closet, where he took a cap from a peg. "Let's go for a walk," he said. "Clear our heads. And the exercise will do us good."

"I wish I'd never heard of compulsions," I said, trudging down the stairs behind him.

"You'd have come to them in time. Better to have the shakeup we were headed for when we're young, and have someone to help see us through it. Yours shows some conflict we've apparently got to dig deeper into."

"I think I've got a few shingles missing as it is."

"Easy does it."

Benny was a great believer in taking "breaks" — deliberately turning away from a problem in order to suspend the surface cerebrations that often as not interfere with the free creative flow of the subconscious. A policy certainly amply borne out by experience. Who has not strained in vain for the answer to a problem, only to have it float into his mind when he was thinking of it least? In any case I had no choice but to accede to his methods if I was going to avail myself of his counsel.

It was a warm spring night. By nature a nocturnal creature, Benny loved to prowl the south side between the University Midway and Lake Michigan, fetching up at last in some all-night beanery or chili parlor for a midnight snack.

I lagged a step behind him. Watching him swing his arms as he marched erectly on, inhaling great lungfuls of fresh air, I thought for some reason of the time when we were kids together in a neighborhood adjacent to this, farther up toward Jackson Park. His mother, my mother's sister, had given me a two-volume set of John Bunyan for my eighth birthday. I had no idea what to do with this tedious collection, until the idea struck me of using it for bookends. I wondered now whether I had ever told Benny of this rather malicious fancy. Perhaps not, as it might have wounded him. I put the two books together again after my aunt's death, as a sort of tribute to her, and also by way of repenting this bit of early sophistication. I experienced no actual sensation of guilt now, yet a feeling of sadness adhered to the memory, that resembled guilt as the mist resembles the rain, etc., and that now attached itself to Benny as I pattered in his wake. It had something to do with the back of his head, and with the tweed cap, which was of the kind more normally associated with drivers of sports cars than with peripatetic thinkers. It had a narrow band running around the back of it, ending in buttons.

I saw that we were heading toward the lake, Benny's lead increasing. He paused to give a coin to a panhandler, who then solicited me; I was so far behind

Benny the panhandler couldn't see we were together. I also made a small contribution.

A spring across the busy Outer Drive brought us to the water's edge. Here Benny looked in both directions, selecting at last the northerly route for us to strike out in along the beach. To our left were now the hum of traffic and the lights of fashionable residential hotels; on our right boomed the lake. Were we going to tramp clear to the Loop?

We came at last to a low range of rocks. Benny said the climb would do us good. Again I clambered along behind him as he led the way over jagged boulders on all fours. We must have looked like two boys playing Stump the Leader. We reached the summit, a broad flat rock, on which we stretched out side by side. We lay gazing up at the stars and listening to the splash and gurgle of breaking waves below.

"I'd like to make a life's study of the connection between neurosis and superstition," Benny said at last, breaking his long silence to express the thoughts apparently generated by our constitutional. "How religion, a refined form of superstition, fits somewhere in between. I'll bet statistics would show that unbelievers are more superstitious than believers (they walk around ladders more), belief being a superstition, or a set of superstitions, sufficient to take up that slack from primitive man. Mencken, one of your great agnostics, admitted to being terribly superstitious. Your experience now shows again the substitute that rushes into the vacuum when religion is discarded. The thing about a background such as ours is that we can discard it intellectually without shaking its grip on us emotionally. What nobody ever sheds completely is the principle of punishment. Put God out of business, we can do it just as well ourselves . . ."

I dozed off, no doubt missing comments of some cogency, but I was too bushed to listen. I became intermittently aware of his voice droning on without taking in what he said. Finally he shook me and said it was time to be getting back. We would return by a roundabout route which would take us past an owl joint that served bang-up hamburgers. Trudging farther and farther in his rear, I turned over in my mind the feasibility of going to bed with my clothes on, as a means of circumventing the stylized ordeal of disrobing.

The owl joint was one of those white-tile lunch counters favored by people in a certain segment of society winding up a night of festivities. It was early for such clientele now though — barely eleven o'clock. The only other person at the counter was a man in a railroad switchman's uniform who sat turning the pages of a newspaper over a steaming cup of coffee. We ordered our hamburgers and coffee.

I took out a small pocket ruler and measured the distance between my plate and coffee saucer, and between these and the edge of the counter. Benny was hungrily wolfing his sandwich, but he watched with interest as I made sure both of these intervals were the required seven inches before falling to myself. He nodded. "I'll lend you a book on compulsions," he said. "It's the definitive work on the subject."

"That ought to have a lot of pointers in it," I said.

Though I was now spending more time at rituals than when I had gone to church, a merest glance at the book indicated that I had hardly scratched the surface. The sheer fund of available eccentricities was staggering. By Christmas I was able to report to Benny that I now never went out the door of the house without stopping and backtracking several times before feeling I had done it right, and could continue on, each time wiping my feet obsessively on the mat.

"Probably related to the washing thing," he said. "That's often hygienic as well as moral. You have a fear of contaminating the house."

"But you don't understand. I do it when I leave the house too."

"You wipe your feet on the mat before stepping into the *street?*"

"You got it, Jack."

He puffed out his cheeks again, looking more than ever like a wind deity. His eyes dilated as he held his breath, presently let out in a long, thoughtful exhalation. "Ouch." Other than that I never heard a whimper. I never heard a whine. He took my troubles like a man.

"Joe," he then said, "how long is it since you've been to confession?"

"You want me to go back to the fold?"

"Not necessarily. I just want to play a hunch I've got."

We had been for another walk, this time through whirls of light snow, light as smoke, and were sitting in a chili parlor on Stony Island Avenue. He dropped several oyster crackers in his bowl and stirred the result.

"It's significant that your symptoms have reached this peak during the Christmas season, also the peak of joyous celebrations in the church you've forsaken."

"The analysis needed time to take hold."

"What?"

"Nothing. What's your hunch?"

"Go to confession again and see if it eases your tensions any."

"But you consider all that abracadabra."

"On a rational basis, yes. But the value of the confession for unburdening the individual is one the Church has always shrewdly known. We psychiatrists use it in our own way. We're engaging in it now. What harm could it do?"

"We'll see," I said, with an odd laugh.

I approached St. Anthony's hesitantly. I paused outside a moment to collect my thoughts. I felt nervous about the experiment I was undertaking, even apprehensive. I darted glances in both directions up the street to make sure I wasn't observed, then slowly approached the stone stairway up which I had not walked in months, and in years for purposes of going to confession.

I counted off seven steps, then seven more, using some spillover on the porch. I continued counting all the way through the doorway and into the church. I dipped my hand in the holy water and crossed myself in the traditional manner, but sensed instantly that once was not going to be enough. I repeated the act, then did so one more time before my nervous tension had in the least abated.

I slipped quickly through the shadows to where the confessionals were. I stood a moment, breathing heavily. My heart thumped as I scanned the interior stealthily from behind a pillar. There was no one kneeling at the altar, where only a bank of candles fluttered in the gloom. There didn't seem to be a soul about. Then from a confessional in which a new priest named Father Ryan was scheduled as on duty came a low murmur. An old woman wearing a black glove on top of her head presently emerged and, gathering her shawl about her, crept out. After a last moment of irresolution, I hurried into the booth, closed the door, and began whispering rapidly through the slot:

"I have committed adultery in my heart. Not once, but seven times."

"God will forgive you, my son. Not seven times, but seventy times seven."

Very interesting. Was the priest a neurotic too?

"You know what we're told," he continued. "There is more rejoicing over the one sheep that has returned to the fold than over the other ninety-nine."

"Oh, don't say that! No more figures please!"

The priest seemed somewhat taken aback by this exclamation, but I thought it best not to try to explain. He heard me out and gave me three Our Fathers.

Well, they were not enough. I went through the penance assigned once, sensing instantly that they would not do the trick. I ran through three more, adding a last prayer to round out the seven dictated by maniacal stress. Only then could I get to my feet and run out of the church without any danger of being seized from behind by the Devil.

I lost no time in reporting this development to the wind deity — who puffed out his cheeks with bulging eyes and exhaled a breath sufficient to drive any ship into harbor, or hopelessly out to sea.

"I don't like the looks of it," he said.

This seemed to me grounds for optimism, at least. Benny's record left one with so little stock in his opinion that it could be taken as safe proof of the opposite. But

51

though I had resolved to dispense with the services of this healer, I felt it no more than fair to agree when he said he ought to see me in action before he could intelligently evaluate me as of now.

At that late hour it was easy to find an empty church. The wind deity sat on the end of a pew and watched while I spent a quarter of an hour making passes in the air and genuflecting till my bones snapped and crackled like a bowl of breakfast cereal. From time to time he offered a comment, and he took some notes. At last we buttoned our overcoats again and strolled down the stairs into the late-January cold.

"You're a long way from the synthesis of conflicting elements that a really good adjustment on your part is going to require," Benny said. "The factors to be resolved are so complex. The socio-religio-ethical-neuro-logico — "

"I've really got to be going," I said. "I'm beat. I'll give you a ring later in the week."

"I've been thinking. Why don't we try hypnosis?"

"I don't want to sleep for a thousand years. Just eight hours."

The plan on which I secretly hit to get myself through this was, simply, to see what I would see. That old folk remedy on which we rely more than we realize. I would resume my religious practices, however riddled now with neurotic features, and see whether the compulsive colorations they had acquired would result in a subsidence of the neuroses themselves. To see whether the re-embraced sacred rituals would drive out the profane, to put it in a nutshell.

For a while it was touch-and-go. My point of view was now such a skimble-skamble that it was impossible to tell where faith left off and derangement began. The need to double and triple conventional devotionals continued, so that I was crossing myself thirteen to the dozen and genuflecting away at a rate that made it look more like a form of calisthenics. Then all of a sudden I began to see daylight. The severity of both sorts of compulsions abruptly diminished, more or less together, until the point was reached when neither "seriously interfered with daily life" — the textbook yardstick for determining whether lunacy exists. I am not now, nor have I ever been, nuts. I simply carry around my share of the neurotic baggage we all lug to the grave, after a shakedown compromise of the sort that makes the journey after all worth it for most of us. I continued with my religious observances for the emotional (and of course aesthetic) value in them, while recognizing them as rationally not defensible at all. This all works both ways. If pious practices are neurotic, neuroses can take on something of the dignity of ceremonial custom. There is nothing wrong with endowing that ritualistic immersion known as a bath with some sense of conscious procedure, provided only one bath is taken and not five or six, and time is left for other things. Such as tea, that charming communion also almost compulsively sacramentalized.

This is not to deny that most compulsive practices are of a low order, serving no purpose but the relief of elementary tension. They cannot be defended — neither can they be condemned. I stay in the shower the way other people stay in the tub. At public performances I always clap in units of seven, which can be repeated indefinitely depending on the length of the audience applause with which one's own must be integrated. The tempo can be speeded up or slowed down, as one senses what its duration is likely to be. There is no sense in winding up clapping alone just so the theater won't burn down or the roof of the concert hall cave in. Luckily these things all in the end become largely automatic, the complications arising when they involve social activities. My subjugation to the number three interferes somewhat with my dancing, since I tend to execute all steps in waltz time, even if it is a fox trot or a watusi being played. It all becomes second nature, at least when matters are running smoothly. It is in periods of stress that there is a flare-up, which continues until the crisis has subsided, when nervous patterns, too, again abate. Such intervals can also be accompanied by a like intensification of the religious — or if you will, superstitious —

side. It's true in my case, at any rate. The two together are like a pair of wings on which I sometimes beat my way through storms, sometimes glide serenely along under blue skies.

I let Benny think he had something to do with getting me out of the woods. What harm could it do? I did make him take back what he had said about clowns being inherently hostile. One night when we were having hamburgers and coffee at one of our owl joints I very good-naturedly insisted on paying the check despite the fact that he happened to owe me two dollars, which at that time was a lot of money to both of us. We were rising from our seats at the counter and reached for it simultaneously. A rather fierce scuffle ensued in which a sugar bowl was overturned and a cup and saucer sent crashing to the floor. We literally fought over the check. Benny had snatched it up, but now I grasped his wrist in one hand and with the other tried to pry his fingers open. We strained inconclusively for several seconds. Then with a sudden heave I flung him against the wall, to which I pinned him with a knee in his groin. The surprise, together with some pressure of my fingernails on the back of his hand, drawing blood, resulted in the release of the check, which fluttered to the floor. "You've been treating me," I panted as I stooped to pick it up, my lips twisted into a grin, "now I'm going to treat you."

four

THE shambles to which the apprentice haircuts led should not be construed as interfering in any way with our friendship, which bore other, far more important fruits than those having to do with my mental health. My association with the wind deity in that general period included a lot of womanizing in and around the campus neighborhood. It remained pretty much my orbit when I was of college age myself but working in an office because my father's death had suspended any thought of further education. That came back into the cards when the father of a girl I met, a stockbroker named MacNaughton, offered to put me through school when he saw that my interest in his daughter was firm.

He did so after the family had got a specially close look at me at a couple of dinners with them. I was chewing in multiples of twelve at the time, which made me strike MacNaughton as a young man of deliberation, a chap who "didn't rush into things or make hasty decisions." I thought them through thoroughly before making the next move. Another happy link in the chain of misunderstandings was the fact that my stopgap job was in the office of an investment house, which made MacNaughton assume I was interested in a career in finance. Since I wasn't interested in anything else more, I saw no reason to undeceive him, all things being relative.

My test scores and IQ put MacNaughton's own alma mater, Cornell, out of the question, but I didn't mind. I am not impressed by the Ivy League establishments. Of course they graduate the best — it's all they'll take, leaving to others the problem of educating the country. They will give you an education the way the banks will give you money — provided you can prove to their satisfaction that you don't need it. There was a good second-rate college in Wilton, a north shore suburb near the one to which the MacNaughtons moved while I was courting their daughter, and in which we ourselves eventually settled too.

Betty was called Naughty because of her last name, but her conduct might have earned it for her anyway. The first time I saw her, at a party into which the wind deity and I dropped one Saturday night, she was dancing on top of a table. She was doing the Charleston, not seriously, but more as a parody of the flaming youth of a bygone day. She wore a string of beads long enough to jump rope with, as in fact she did when egged on by a hot piano player and a knot of rollicking onlookers, and she would fling her arms into the air and push her hair upward in gestures of utter abandon. These writhing gyrations were all the more sensational because she was a plump girl — and more than merely plump. The implication of this takeoff was that she had herself acceded to a plane of wickedness, even profligacy, beside which that of another day was innocence itself.

I have said this was my first glimpse of her, but when we were introduced she claimed to remember me from high school. We finally worked it out that we had coincided at South Central for one term when she was in her junior year and I was a senior with a semester to go.

"I used to watch with awe while you walked down the hall with your clique at your heels," she said. "I remember some of your capers too, especially those with intellectual content. Like the time you sat down in the cafeteria that day your editorial on small portions appeared, and fell to with a jeweler's loupe screwed into your eye. Your walk came back to me just now when I saw you sashay in. I don't use the term disparagingly. It's the Jack Benny sashay. Graceful, even elegant, but with a kind of rueful self-doubt. It's the sort of stride I always think of when I read that line from *Richard Cory*. You remember it. 'He fluttered pulses when he said, Good morning, and he glittered when he walked.'"

"I must read him."

"Richard Cory is the character in the poem. It's *by* Edwin Arlington Robinson."

"I'm going to belt you one."

"Why?"

"No kid of ours is going to say when we're old and gray, 'Hey Pop, what did you do in the war between the sexes?' "

"Are you always this zany?"

"From day of deposit."

The hostess later said I was the life of the party as never before. I put in several phone calls to people we all knew, impersonating a disc jockey to notify them that they had won free trips to places they had just got back from. I delivered a mock lecture on changing morals, winding up, "And so if there's one thing I'd like to drive home tonight, ladies and gentlemen, it's Naughty MacNaughton."

I did, as it turned out. She had come alone, this having been a sort of open house, and she was weak from laughter when we climbed into her convertible about one o'clock. She asked me to drive while she sat drying her eyes and trying to pull herself together.

"Don't you take anything seriously?"

"Only medicine."

"These practical jokes. Isn't there an element of cruelty behind them?"

"It's the tale that dogs the wag."

"Don't."

Naughty's mouth, in hysterics, was like a burst pomegranate. Her mouth was like a portal flung wide, her teeth were like seeds spilling from split fruit, her breasts shook like ringing bells. She was still holding her sides, of which as I say there was plenty, when we got into her Hyde Park doorway. I offered to hold them for her while she dug in her bag for her key, slipping an arm under her coat. Some thoughts here inevitably entered my mind without necessarily tempering my excitement. She was clearly the category of girl at whose mother it would be fatal to look. A plump bride, a fat wife; there was no appeal from that stern truth. But no matter. She was in her Maytime, something molded by Rodin with a pastry gun. A good-night kiss was all she would permit now, in any case, yielding up the burst-pomegranate mouth with her mirth still quivering in her throat. I walked to my busline recalling a conversation I had overheard at the party, about the problem of finding some boy "fast" enough for Naughty. Somebody her speed.

Another date or two and then I took her to dinner at the Pump Room, where, speaking of investments, I blew half a week's wages. Whether out of deference to my purse or her figure, Naughty ordered sparingly. As I gazed about the famous restaurant I remembered my

mother telling me how a comedienne of her day, named
Trixie Friganza, grew so enormous in her later years that
the captain here, possibly the one who waited on us,
used to bring her two chairs to sit on, and that only half
in jest. My mother must have picked this information up
from the gossip columns or the movie magazines, because God knows she never set foot in places like this.
We were halfway through our dinner when the waiter, in
the immemorial manner of his kind, stopped by to ask
whether everything was all right.

I set down knife and fork and touched a napkin to my
lips.

"Anything but," I said. "I have chronic tonsilitis, an
allergy to eggs, and a neighbor who plays the glocken-
spiel."

"Yes, sir," he said, and wafted himself off.

Naughty's house afforded a fitting aftermath to such
an evening. Parquet glimmered in pools about the
Aubusson rugs, the light from silken lamps fell on deep
chairs and sofas upholstered in velvet and needlepoint,
while a softer illumination lay on unobtrusive landscapes
hanging in gilt frames between draperies of rich brocade.
When Naughty went off to get us something to drink I
wandered about admiring the objects in the room, avoiding glances into adjacent ones for fear of catching a
glimpse of her mother. I didn't want anything to cool
my ardor until it was too late. Marrying for money

deserves the obloquy in which it is held, but falling in love with somebody who has it is something else altogether.

We had been chatting and smoking for half an hour or more when I became restless and went around turning off lights.

"Horton will do that," Naughty said. When I had rejoined her on the sofa, she leaned back a bit, appraising me, and said, "You have a reputation for talking about the girls you go out with."

"Such as?"

"Harriet Sowerby. You said a date with her was like the Lutheran Hour."

"You wouldn't want that to get around about you, would you? It could ruin a girl's reputation."

Naughty said that I had an antic sense second to none she had ever run into before, which was at the same time sensitive and perceptive. "Your thrusts always go home."

"Is that what you want me to do? Well, I won't."

"The proverbial barrel of monkeys. You're so wonderful a person wants to fall down in fits and chew the carpets, to throw the windows wide and call down to strangers in the street what it's like to know you. I've told my parents about you, and they're dying to meet you. They're not home tonight."

Suddenly I broke down and said I had been under terrible strain and was in no condition for any more. I had been in an automobile accident that had left me with a German accent. The speech centers had apparently been affected. *"Ach, Himmel! Lieber Gott!"* I buried my head in her lap, nuzzling and whinnying as I burrowed into her plump thighs, up which I also ran an appealingly helpless hand.

She seized it passionately in both of hers and drew it up to her cheek, to which she held it for some moments while I continued whinnying and slobbering like a dumb devoted beast.

"It's not that I don't trust you, Joe. It's myself I don't trust — not the way you turn me on. I despise teases, that I'll never be. It's the other. That I wouldn't be able to stop something we'd both regret. There's too much at stake. I mean as far as I'm concerned. It's up to you to decide for yourself how you feel about it. As for me, it isn't that business about the boy stealing the bait and swimming away. That's too cynical. It's that I think the beauty of the relationship is worth safeguarding, don't you? I mean am I a fool for thinking sex to be all that important? That the Bride should be given as a supreme gift to her mate with all the closely cherished glory of the nuptial night? Who throws that away to seize the moment? 'Who sells eternity to get a toy?' as Shakespeare says in *The Rape of Lucrece*. I'm thinking of the future."

I was too, as my arm encircled her waist for another of

63

the kisses that were apparently to be the extent of my liberties. I had one of those visions to which comedians are prone, and in the grip of which they are helpless. I saw myself, years hence, planting a foot in the small of my wife's back in order to draw the strings of her corset tight enough for her to get into her dress and us to the opera. I shook my head as though physically flinging the image from my mind.

"What's the matter?" Naughty said.

"Dot Yehudi Menuhin," I said, puttering to a table with a humidor from which I took an expensive-looking cigar indeed. "We all know he likes to practice in his underwear. Well, now he wants to rehearse in it too — you know we're doing de Mendelssohn Concerto. So Koppelmeyer, mine concertmeister, says if Menuhin can play in his underwear, zo can he. Now the whole orchestra wants to play in long chons. Und how will I look up dere conducting in mine tailcoat? Hugo Sneederbunk will be ze laughingstock of ze musical world."

But I was wincing with shame as I struck a match and set fire to the cigar. I had my face in puffs of smoke as I paced these voluptuous rugs and knocked myself out to keep Naughty amused. Each such twinge of guilt for my churlish thoughts drew me to her the more closely. Thus does compassion forge chains far stronger than those of passion, and the spirit rather than the flesh lash people into pairs. Bait! I swam straight for the naked hook. I was caught. It was safe now to bring the mother on.

I smoked the cigar till I was nauseated and went home.

"Hugo Sneederbunk?" Naughty said on the phone. "Can you come to dinner on Saturday?"

"*Jawohl.* I be dere after de rehearsal. Und may God have mercy on dere souls."

I was still sorry about the incident of the corset, and reached the MacNaughton place determined to be nice and to make a good impression on one and all. When I was shown in by Horton, I knew instantly from Naughty's face that I was expected to perform.

"How nice to see me," I said, pretending to trip on the carpet across which I advanced with my hand out. "I go to London mit de whole orchestra tomorrow, you know. How good it will be to see again de Thames, to hear de booming of Pig Pen."

When she had composed her features, Naughty towed me across the room, saying, "Come meet Daddy."

She led me to where a man with black hair and a gray mustache sat in a deep chair with a Manila folder open in his lap. The mustache stirred as we approached, which led me to believe that I was going over big. But he was evidently smiling at something in his sleep, for Naughty had to shake him by the shoulder. The conclusion was that he had dropped off over his work.

"Daddy's a great forty-winks man. It's what keeps him going eighteen hours a day. Daddy, that Joe Sandwich is here."

Climbing to his feet, MacNaughton squeezed my hand as hard as he could, like a man testing his strength on one of those carnival machines equipped with a gauge for measuring the power in your grip. He studied my face intently, as though it might be such a meter registering the number of pounds of pressure he was ringing up.

"It's good to meet you," he said, baring a set of clenched teeth. He seemed to be displaying their perfection as much as smiling. It didn't surprise me to learn later that he was an admirer of Teddy Roosevelt, on whom he appeared to model much of his conduct, including the regenerating catnaps which are, of course, a trademark of the dynamic type. He stood erect and wore his hair in a crew cut, all of which gave him a very youthful appearance for a man of fifty, belied only by the gray mustache.

"Naughty tells me you've been in some kind of accident," he said.

"*Jawohl*, I —" I began, but some of his papers had fallen to the floor and I paused while he retrieved them, since it appeared I would need his full attention to get the routine across. He stooped to recover them, putting his pencil in his mouth in order to do so. At last matters were fairly well reorganized, and I resumed.

"*Jawohl.* I had a pad shageup in de Mercedes, und now talk like dis all de time," I said, gargling my words exaggeratedly. "Dose blows on de head can result in all zorts of traumas affecticating stuff like de memory und de locomotion und de caboose. Mit me it's de speech centers dot got permanently affecticated. *Ja.* I been going to doctors to get straightened around, but so far no luck. Maybe it takes anodder knock on de noodle to talk normal again, eh?"

MacNaughton exhibited his teeth once more, confronting me with them squarely, as though defying me to find a single cavity in them, or to display my own in competition if I so wished.

"How do you like a Mercedes?" he asked, returning to his chair. "Sit down." We all did. "We had one a few years back. You liked it all right, didn't you Naughty? I did too, but I found it a little cramped. Because of the steering wheel."

"Me too. If you got long legs dey feel a little stiff when you get out. My doctor calls dot condition de Mercedes Bends."

"How many miles do you get on a gallon?"

"Well, we couldn't compare de notes on de subject because I always burn olive oil in mine. It vouldn't go on nottink else."

I wanted to get out of this routine as soon as possible. I had of course never driven a Mercedes, and as for traumas, I was all this while really steeling myself for the mother. She would be down any minute. Meanwhile MacNaughton continued to exercise his business-executive knack for "drawing people out."

He glanced at the folder which he had laid aside and said, "It's curious the number of people in this world who are determined to make misfits of themselves. I was just going over an application from a young man who wants to be one of our account executives, as we call brokers. We have a training program for young people with aptitude. It's amazing what this one doesn't know, not just about stocks and bonds, but the economy in general. One of the questions in the questionnaire we have is, 'What is the gross national product?' No need to hit it on the button, but an aspiring broker ought to know roughly. He's nowhere near the mark."

"What is it?" Naughty asked.

"Well, let's see if Mr. Sandwich knows. Let's see if he's investment timber." MacNaughton looked at me and said, "Just off the top of your head, just taking a guess, what would you say the gross national product was?"

"Deodorants."

"Well, you're not even close. It's three hundred billion dollars, roughly. Just a whisker under that, actually. What are convertible debentures?"

"Removable bridges."

"Right." He looked over at Naughty with a jerk of his head in my direction. "A real card." He returned his scrutiny to me and said, "Seriously do you know what they are? We in finance always wonder how much the general public do know about something that really affects their daily lives as much as this in fact does."

I figured I had been horsing around long enough, even though I had been put on for the purpose, and that courtesy demanded I now give a sober reply. I had acquired a vague idea what the answer was from family discussions of my father's stock market problems. "I think they're bonds that can be converted into common stocks. There are also convertible preferreds."

"Correct," MacNaughton said with some gratified surprise. "And warrants. What are they?"

"Well, they're a sort of right to buy some kind of security at a later date, and at a fixed price."

"Pretty good for a chap your age."

My pleasure in the compliment was tarnished by a realization that my knowledge of money matters derived chiefly from family ineptitude in them, my father having had a long and well-aired history of investment failure, but I acknowledged it with a modesty MacNaughton must have been confident was false. I felt he was again quoting from the questionnaire designed for the selection of employees when he asked, "Do you have any hobbies?"

"Yes," I said. "I collect early American hurricanes."

"Mine's fishing. Deep sea fishing in particular, but I like trout fishing too. All kinds in fact. It's what I'm doing now I suppose," he said with a wink at his daughter.

I had no idea what he'd thought I'd said — "hurricane lamps" no doubt, a conceivable collector's taste. Maybe he just didn't listen, paradoxically a common failure of extrovert types supposedly interested in others, while people of ingrown and self-absorbed natures are often very attentive company.

"The last time I went fishing was with my father," I related. "We had new fiber glass poles, lots of lures, boots, fancy creels, the works. It was a small stream where a couple of barefoot boys were fishing with homemade poles cut from tree branches, and bent pins with worms on them. Well, we with all our expensive equipment caught more fish than those boys did."

MacNaughton looked at my head, as though reverting again to thoughts of the accident that had reputedly damaged my faculties. "You mean they with their homemade equipment caught more fish than you did with all your expensive gear."

"Yes, I suppose that's it." I could see he was a man in whose presence it was wisest not to tamper with clichés, or muddle established values. The flow of the conversation was in any event deflected by the arrival of the mother.

I have said that I had been bracing myself for this moment. One does not lightly face the prospect of seeing what one's wife is going to look like in fifteen or twenty years, even under normal circumstances. I had hoped to find Naughty taking after her father, directly I had seen him, but that hope was dashed. The stern alternative now hove into view behind me, announced by a ripple of greeting both musical and merry. I kept my eyes averted as long as I could, even as I rose. Then I took the full blast of reality.

Your first impression was that if a man sees a float in the New Year's Day Rose Bowl Parade that takes his fancy, and he has the means to indulge his whims, what is to prevent his buying it and having it shipped out? What is to prevent his even bringing it into the house if space permits, where it can bump softly along passageways and nose its florid way around the corners of doors? Then a closer look reveals the shimmering silks that had fostered this illusion to be a dress clothing a human form, with no legend encircling the waist reading "The Spirit of Citrus" or "Wolverine State" or "The Land of the Skyblue Water." What does remain of the hallucination is a face beaming with carnival gaiety. There is a *joie de vivre* in it one knows to be perpetual, subject to no fluctuations, a sense of radiant participation reflected in the rosy cheeks and sparkling eyes, blue as amethysts. There are dimples everywhere — in the knuckles of the hand extended to you, in the wrist, creased like a baby's, in the puckered elbow. The other hand is clenched at a bosom like a wave of ocean surf. Here is a woman who doesn't read the articles on slimming, but those entitled "Slenderness Isn't Everything" and "Let's Talk About Three-dimensional Charm." With a fresh spasm of anguish I thought of Trixie Friganza sitting on two chairs in the Pump Room, nearly reeling back into my own.

The initial shock wore off, but the stunned expression I kept through dinner (coupled with the compulsion to masticate in series) furthered MacNaughton's impression that I was a thoughtful sort, serious beneath a fun-loving exterior. Mrs. MacNaughton was certainly the most fun-loving, entertaining us with story after story. She was one of those people whose conversation runs almost exclusively to anecdote. She told us about her single prolonged attempt to reduce, or told me rather, the episode being familiar to the family. "I dieted faithfully, day after day, week after week," she related, "and at the end of six weeks I found that all I had lost was half a foot size." She shrieked with laughter.

I wondered had she a mother at the sight of whom MacNaughton had flinched in his day, and then whether Naughty divined what was running through my mind: she seemed to avoid my gaze. Twinges of compassion again followed swiftly on the heels of these reflections. Besides, such things cut both ways. Naughty had but to look at her father to see what I would be twenty years hence. And if I too had made my pile by then, I might very well have a mistress, a bit of fluff churning in gold pajamas in a Lake Shore apartment, where I kept her with very little financial strain indeed, and whom when flights of temperament required it I would take on business trips to New York, for a week's round of good restaurants and hit shows of the sort to which only the well-connected can obtain tickets. "A slender woman to take out, a plump one to go home to." Who said that? Some son of a bitch.

I had taken the worst of the shock, at any rate; we were over the hump. There are troubles from which the only relief is the reflection that they are hopeless.

After dinner MacNaughton with rather heavy craft contrived a few minutes alone with me, in the course of which the question of changing morals among the young was brought up. As speedily as he introduced it he narrowed it down to what went on under his own roof. There, he let me know in plain language, no nonsense would be tolerated. I supposed that having a madcap daughter made a father particularly concerned about the company she kept, and what she ran foul of in the way of local blades. His special curiosity about my point of view he justified on the ground that I was the first young

73

man Naughty had shown enough interest in to invite to dinner, and he had no alternative but to take me seriously himself.

Since it was obvious that I was going to have to bank my fires, I saw no reason for not taking credit for the chastity to which I was being condemned in any case. Therefore I strewed the conversation with assurances that nothing could be farther from my mind than the seduction in which I had been thwarted. "I would never abuse the hospitality of another man's house," I said. I was gagging on another of his expensive cigars at the moment, and the resultant tableau must have suggested a solid citizen of tomorrow indeed. Because Mac-Naughton promptly resumed the catechism aimed at nourishing hopes that here was a chap who might be taken not only into the family, but into the firm.

I continued to give proof of my passion in ways that Naughty loved best — by putting pickles in her purse, or a hardboiled egg, or a pair of pliers for her to discover in public and collapse in affectionate mirth as a result. Once she opened her bag to pay a cab fare and found a tube of anchovy paste inside. Another time a monkey wrench. She reported that on such occasions a wave of fondness would sweep over her the like of which she had never experienced before.

I once knew a man who had graduated from a college so obscure that in later life he could never remember the name of it himself. He would have to stop and think. This might now be the case with me had not Wilton also been the name of the town in which mine was located, and in which I eventually settled. Not to sell its economics department short, or my own interest in the subject either. Of course I knew which side my bread was buttered on, but I did show an aptitude for it that surprised me. We see me not only keeping up with my classroom work and cramming faithfully for tests but also devouring the weekly Market Letter for which the MacNaughton and Blair office put me on their mailing list. One of its features was a running Sample Portfolio of suggested securities, the value of which was totaled up from week to week, with the percentage of gain over the original hypothetical investment of a thousand dollars. I pitted against it a model portfolio of my own. By the time I graduated from college, the thousand imaginary dollars invested as a freshman had tripled in market value and yielded an average of two and a half per cent in dividends, while the MacNaughton and Blair portfolio had only doubled in value but yielded an annual four and a half per cent. The difference was between a choice of growth stocks in frisky new companies with low yield but equivalently lavish possibilities for capital gain, and a selection of prudent equities paying substantial dividends but offering little excitement in the way of price movement. Or between headstrong youth and conservative age.

The wedding was, in any case, a social event such as only seasoned members of the latter can afford, though threatened by a disaster I might have anticipated.

I was striding in full fig toward the Episcopal Church where the ceremony was to take place when I saw, approaching along the sidewalk, a figure dressed in farmer's clothes — overalls, blue denim shirt, and a broad-brimmed straw hat full of holes through which tufts of hair projected. A beard completed the conformity to the traditional caricature of the hayseed. He was carrying a shotgun and had his jaw set in an expression of rustic determination.

It was a moment before I could collect my senses. Then a sickening realization swept over me that this was one of the bunch from high school times, bent on the sort of prank for which we were famous, and that had marked our appearance at many a neighborhood wedding then, with myself often as not the mastermind.

"Well, here's the varmint hisself," the newcomer said with an excruciating twang as I confronted him on the sidewalk. "Know what's good for you you won't try any smart aleck stuff at the last minute. We have a way of dealing with slickers who don't do right by our daughters in these parts."

"Look, Hank," I said, recognizing Hank Walters behind the spinach. "A gag is a gag, but this is ridiculous.

You mustn't do this. You must go away immediately. It's *embarrassing*."

"Gag? Go away? Don't know's I get your drift, Bub," he said, his chin whiskers wagging as he looked around at the crowd of onlookers beginning to collect. "Just goin' to a weddin' I want to make sure comes off is all. Well, see you in church, as the sayin' goes." He turned and walked up the stairs, clutching the shotgun by the barrel.

Physically ill, I sprang along behind him, feeling I had been sucked into a nightmare. I wanted to strangle him then and there. But drawing abreast of him with as much composure as I could summon, I seized his arm in a fierce grip, steered him past a couple of horrified ushers and marched him down the foyer toward a door. I had no idea where it led, but I opened it and shoved Hank into a small anteroom into which dangled a rope hanging from the belfry, shot in after him and slammed the door behind me. Only surprise and a strength born of desperation enabled me to overpower him in this fashion. I pinned him against a wall and grasped him by the lapels.

"Now look, Hank. This isn't the south side of Chicago any more. It's the North Shore suburbs. A fashionable Episcopal Church where this sort of thing *simply won't go down*. If it gets a laugh it'll be only at you. You saw those ushers. They won't let you in, Hank. They'll call

77

the police first. I say this for your own good. I know what these people are like."

The upshot of it was a compromise. He would picket the church but not enter it, much less try to occupy a front pew during the ceremony. Secondly, I would circulate favorable reports of his effort, always continuing to do so in later life, like a good sport and with every implication of hilarious outcome. Thirdly, I promised to honor a tradition the old bunch had when one of their number got married. The bride would drive briefly through the neighborhood with the groom lashed to the front fender, like a deer to a returning hunter's car. She had bagged him was the idea. I had no intention of making good on any of these pledges, of course; they were simply a means of getting him out of the building while I bustled off to those quarters from which I was to emerge to claim my bride.

I didn't see Hank again. I looked neither to the right nor the left as we tripped through a squall of rice into our waiting limousine. Nor did I glance out the window as we shot away toward the country club where the reception was to be held, and where I soon threw myself into the role of life of my own party. "What happened to the girl I married?" I said, peering under tables with champagne glass in hand. My only relatives were my mother, my Uncle Hamilton, and my cousin Benny Bonner. "The thing that never ceases to amaze me,"

Uncle Hamilton said, strolling toward the table on which the gifts were displayed. There I found Naughty, and gazing at her across my champagne glass, I murmured, "I can't wait to get to the hotel."

"Joe, for heaven's sake," she said. "This is our wedding day."

I did it like Bert Lahr at the end of *Waiting for Godot*. Told why he can't do something, he nods and emits a long "Ah!" of understanding though his face is an uncomprehending blank. Naughty was not exactly pleased with my conduct. I had "given her the eye" during the ceremony, and said "Let's go up to my place," as we trotted out of the church, and now I was going around cock-a-hoop at my own marriage feast. I was behaving in a thoroughly randy fashion there.

It was midnight when we arrived in the bridal suite of the Loop hotel where we were to spend the night before flying to New York, there to set sail on a Mediterranean cruise. I sat upright in bed looking into the next room where Naughty was dancing, dancing. She waved a long silk scarf about in gestures of lyric abandon. Occasionally she would pause to sip from her champagne glass, or twist a grape from a cluster in a bowl of fruit, or to stand at the window with arms outflung, as though she wanted to embrace the entire city, the night, the world itself. "Come to bed, Naughty," I called from time to time. But she went on like an orgiast in this night that she wished would never end. She dreamed again, as she often had, of what married life would be like, imagining the house we would live in, the garden, even the pets we would have.

"We are married," I said. "This is it."

Her romantic ardor mounting to fever pitch, she began to recite poetry. She regaled me especially with Shakespeare, whom she knew by the yard. She asked whether I had any favorite passages from the sonnets or the plays.

"All I can seem to remember is the line about the two-backed beast," I said. "That beautiful image of two people coupling. Of the twain becoming, at last, one."

"How can you think of that at a time like this?"

I dropped back on the bed and drummed my brow, racking my brains for a reason. "The point you're trying to make," I said, and thought of Uncle Hamilton, unable to go on.

She was shy about our first night together, that was it. She needed a little relaxing, something to break the ice. I sprang out of bed, and from the complimentary bowl of fruit seized a banana which I held out to her like a microphone.

"Ah, here's a young lady maybe we can get over here for a word. Miss, would you tell us where you're from? Oh, Ishpeming, Michigan, eh? And what brings you to Chicago, the Windy City? Oh, you're here for the

World Series. And you say you went to Marshall Field to buy tickets and found it's a department store and not a baseball diamond at all? She says she thought Marshall Field was a baseball diamond, folks, isn't that rich? Well, you look tired from your trip, Miss. You need a good night's sleep. And so as a gift from our sponsor may we present you with this bed, all made up with Wamsutta sheets. And remember the motto of the manufacturer. 'We supply the bed. The rest is up to you.' "

"Don't you have any pajamas?" she asked with averted eyes.

"No. Why?"

"None at all?"

"No. I never wear them. I sleep in the raw."

"You mean you don't own a single pair of pajamas?"

"No. Why should I if I don't wear them?"

"You're a married man now, Joe. You have somebody else's sensibilities to consider. The least you could do on your honeymoon is dress for it. I see we've got some shopping to do tomorrow."

The marriage counselor was a dapper little man in his fifties. He had a round, very shiny face which gave him the appearance of "beaming" when he was doing no such thing at all, and which was topped with a tuft of sparse blond hair — or I should say hairs, since you could count them. They gave the impression somehow of not having been there originally at all, or belonging there.

They looked like straws that had been driven into a post by a tornado.

He had what seemed like an open manner but was more or less a device for gaining people's confidence. In no time he had wormed out of me that I was white, male and twenty-three. Naughty had had a couple of preliminary sessions with him. I had declined the private interview to which I was entitled, like a sort of equal-time right, on the ground that I could trust my wife to give an honest and intelligent account of matters. After a few minutes of general discussion, he made his point.

"It takes two people to make one frigid woman," he said, and they both glared at me.

"Well, making one is no cinch in any case," I said, and laughed like hell to show I didn't think much of the gag.

The counselor smiled and, lining his fingers up along the edge of the desk, said, "You have a comic slant on everything that I think is fine, and I'm glad for this chance to meet you, because it confirms the impression Mrs. Sandwich has given me of your home life. Her complaint is that you make a joke of everything."

"I'm an arch support."

"What?"

"Nothing. Go on."

"All this is very well, but we have to take into account the sensibilities of others. No relationship is possible without that. We have got to put ourself inside the other person's skin, in even the most superficial of daily affairs. How much more in that most intimate of bonds."

"Well, all right, I can tone it down. I'm willing to try that."

"She says you're given in particular to ribald humor, and a very gamy brand of that. I see what she means. You do come on strong, don't you?"

"What it boils down to," I said.

"What it boils down to is that Mrs. Sandwich is a bride. And a bride has certain delicacies. Bawdiness is fine — any sound marriage has it — but that should be all in good time. It should be worked up to slowly. The bride is still in the poetry stage of love. Things are expected to be Beautiful — with a capital B. You're starting too high, as they say in the theater. You can't ride roughshod over a maiden's sensibilities. You may think you're breaking the ice but you're only increasing her, well, call them inhibitions. Now, is there any other trouble between you, that I should know about to get the overall picture?"

"Nothing I know of," I said. "There's the usual old girl friend, but I've seen her lately, and that ghost has been laid."

"Have you ever thought of psychiatric help?"

"I've had that," I said, and told him about Benny.

Benny was just setting up shop in town, and needed a leg up. Every feather in his cap he could get. "It's Dr. Benjamin Bonner, and he's down here on Michigan Boulevard." I was careful not to say he was a cousin, or that he had nearly sent me round the bend, which was probably a technical quibble as these things went. As the counselor jotted down his name I made a mental note to call Benny about this and discuss it with him. It was important to get our stories straight.

When we left the building and began to walk down the street, Naughty took my arm. I knew she would. Behaving in the way I had, like a goon, confirmed the picture she had painted of me and vindicated her, whereas turning on the charm and all that would have put her in a bad light as a woman full of imaginary grievances and fancied slights — a Complaining Woman. It was clearly the moment to seize.

"I suppose I did get off on the wrong foot," I said. "I'm glad now you brought it all out in the open. No more goon stuff. I'll try to remember you're a lady."

"And I that you're a man."

We left it that way. Thus the fruit must be delicately gathered, not roughly plucked, apparently; the citadel won, not stormed. Tenderness carried the day, the night, till at last the lovers fainted into sleep.

He awakes to quicksilver on the sunlit wall, and in the mad languor of morning sees her blue eye watching him

from the pillow. The tentative, almost apologetic solici-
tations of his hand resume, and a sigh as her eyelids
flutter shut tells him she will accept proof of his love yet
again. When the sweet tumult is spent, they lie for a
time in silence, wreathed in one another's arms. Then
she draws the sheet up and smiles upon her risen lord,
who must go forth and dig some gold out of the city, to
lay at her feet at evening.

"Wonderful," I said, yawning as I drew on my robe.
"You told me you were Scottish, but I see you've got a
little chink in you."

She reached out of bed and flung a slipper at me as I
jumped into the bathroom.

I came out drying myself. "Sorry I have to leave you so
soon, Mazie, but I'm a busy tycoon in the hardware
game. I'm a screw and bolt man."

I had actually not regretted the honeymoon. In the
course of our Mediterranean cruise I had discovered that
I was the victim of something called Ménière's syndrome, a malfunction of the mechanism of the inner ear
which is responsible for equilibrium, and which can
convert the visible world into a load of spin-dry wash
without warning. Things become bolluxed up firmament-
wise, with attendant nausea. I had had childhood intimations of it — motion sickness, slight bouts of vertigo
on garden swings — but nothing serious, at least on dry
land, and at least so far. Aboard ship the ailment came

into its own. I was seasick most of the time, and it was only in the brief intervals in port that I even tried to make love, and then only with the faltering skill of the convalescent. A doctor in Naples diagnosed it for me, and gave me a new drug for it, something more effective than Dramamine, but not enough so. I spent rather a good deal of time alone in the stateroom while Naughty wandered about in search of fun. I would make occasional sorties to look for her, mounting companionways with both hands gripping the rail and holding my eyes shut except for brief periodic glimpses to memorize the next segment of deck or corridor to be traversed. "Come to bed, Naughty," I would bleat, but she would be in the recreation room or tavern giving her impersonation of going to the dogs. She would writhe erotically, pushing her hair upward with both hands in the classic delineation of an orgy. I would smile wanly from the doorway a moment, before picking my way back to the stateroom. "I'll be right down, honey," she would say, and the other passengers would laugh. They probably thought I was a drag on her, and wondered what she saw in a sick square who ventured on deck only to vomit. Wherever I went and it was possible, I tried to keep my eye focussed on the horizon, which everyone said was the way to maintain your balance and keep from jettisoning your cookies.

The condition kept me off Naughty's back, so to speak, for the duration of the honeymoon, but now back home on dry land, and with things straightened around, we made up for lost time. I was quite myself again, and she the old glutton for entertainment. To lend flavor to an intimacy soon familiar, I would pretend we weren't married, or that we were married but I had another wife, stashed away in a nut house so she wouldn't give us no trouble. Then I was a member of a vice syndicate bringing her north for a life of prostitution in one of the larger cities, who had fallen in love with his charge. I flung her uproariously onto the bed with the declaration that she was the juiciest piece I had ever spirited out of Buenos Aires, and that I wanted only to be near her, to be her ponce.

"Why can't I just be me?" she said, smiling from the bed, cueing me through these antics. "Why do I always have to be a whore or a burlesque dancer, or a Japanese girl you're bracing yourself to show your conservative parents? Why do we always have to be living in sin?"

"Catholic upbringing." I was toe-dancing around the room, wearing only an ascot and a pair of her earrings I had seen on the dresser and screwed on for hacks.

There's a percentage of us who set great store by the freedom to wander about the house in the altogether. It was how I usually came down to breakfast, unless wearing a cummerbund or a pair of her silk stockings, or a derby which I primly tipped good morning. Once I pulled on Naughty's girdle and waddled around in it till she was in hysterics. "It's to show who wears the pants in the family," I said, and she absolutely collapsed. We had a great deal of sport with gadgets. Often while occupied in the relish of her flesh I would mark her with rubber stamps, of which I had collected quite an assortment in stationery stores and from the office. "Fragile" was tenderly impressed on her breasts, "This Side Up" inked below that, and "Important" still farther down. Once I got hold of a set of government beef-grading stamps and labeled her "Prime" from head to foot.

After this first burst of sport and excitement, however, I began to notice a falling off of response to my little attentions. There was a flagging of interest, not abrupt or steep at first, but distinct. It was discernible. Once she actually reached for a bedside book in the course of a rather erotic sequence on which I had embarked, and began to read. I sensed that I must try harder. I share the universal fascination with spray cans, and will buy practically every one I see. I can't resist them. Once I came across one for spraying jelly on your toast, an aerosol bomb called Jamist, coming in a variety of flavors. I bought a can of strawberry, with which I persuaded her to let me lightly coat her bosoms before falling to. These given their due, your correspondent grazed avidly southward, till the suspense was unbearable — was he a creep as well as a card? I came up for air, and grinning apologetically over at her explained, "Love is an art. I thought you might notice my craft ebbing." She nodded, her eyes fixing me again over the crest of a book I was dismayed to note, and smiled to show that she understood, that life was rich and full, now, and humor part of it.

As our jaded senses called for ever stronger stimuli, ever sharper excitements, I intensified my exertions correspondingly. I waited outside the bathroom door for her to emerge from her bath, holding in my hand a bottle of soda pop, which I shook up with my thumb over the opening when she appeared, and trained a fine jet over her nude body, pursuing her fleeing form down the stairs and through the house in order to do so, defending these corrupt practices on the ground that nothing human was alien to me.

Failing by these and other ever more exotic devices to arrest her sagging spirits, I got out my collection of funny names and read aloud to her from it.

"Mr. and Mrs. Pushcommon," I began, after settling myself with a highball, "Cora Loudermilk, Chester Paste, Commander and Mrs. Chickensoon, Wilbur Leftsuckle, Lord and Lady Wobleigh, Prince Phumaphong Phooey, Maharajah Nkrumah Nah —"

She broke in to protest that the passage was familiar to her. I had read it before.

This struck me as rather odd I must say. For what other reason are we seized with the hunger to reread than that the passage in question has amused us before?

I derive endless pleasure from intoning over and over names that hold a special resonance for me. "Cora Loudermilk," "Modjeska Balkanblend" and "Mrs. Jellyquack" possess for me the bracing potency of fine phrases. They affect me the way "wine-dark sea" and "ghostly galleon" do people who turn to poetry for consolation and escape. They evoke a world of pleasure and delight, a sort of ideal world that lies beyond our mortal ken, yet haunts us with intimations of a possible perfection.

This demurrer at being read aloud to was not an isolated moment of impatience with what had formerly afforded boundless satisfaction. That would have been all right. The disturbing fact, as I have been trying to say, was that it was symptomatic of a decline in response all along the line. She wasn't amused when I telephoned her and in a disguised voice reported that I was a policeman calling to say that her husband had been arrested and booked on suspicion of stealing metatarsal pads from a chiropodist's. She was annoyed when she reached into her coat pocket in public and found a smoked herring in it.

The expression she continued to wear told me how much more acute than I had suspected was the need for comic relief. Combined with this factor was undoubtedly the natural need for ever stronger doses of a stimulant to which we have become addicted but to whose effects we are growing immune. So now I really knocked myself out to please her. I tied a tasseled bell cord on my dong and invited her to ring for service.

"Oh, for Christ's sake, get dressed will you!" she said. "We're due at the Shaws' in half an hour. And be sure to get all that ink off your — off yourself when you bathe. What if you had an accident and people in the hospital saw you stamped 'Overdue' on a place like that."

I did not remind her that the "precious gift of laughter," as she herself had put it, had been among the virtues for which she had found me irresistible in courtship days, or that because of it she had said, "Joe, you're one of those people who justify life." Far from it. I have always prided myself on having a fine sense of the needs of others, and because of this kind of built-in antenna to their stresses and requirements have always known where to draw the line. She was glum and out of sorts when we arrived at the Shaws' party for reasons I could do nothing about. She had had trouble getting into her dress, and was depressed over that. I was prepared to find the evening a total loss — forgetting those sudden, mercurial revivals of spirit of which women are also capable.

I looked over at one point midway the evening and out of a clear sky (that is, out of a decidedly cloudy one) saw her sitting in a corner enjoying herself no end with a guy named Al Franklin, whom we had just met, he and his wife being new to the neighborhood. Franklin had dropped her a pretty compliment on her hair, and that was only the beginning. He was one of those men with an inexhaustible repertory of stories. He had a million of them. He chain-told them, many in dialect. It's a gift I don't happen to have. But he did, and he made the most of it. He had the flushed expression of a man who knows he is making a hit. Naughty was in stitches every time I looked at her, once literally holding her sides as though they ached. She was having the time of her life, and why not? After all, she had met the life of the party.

five

L IFE at the office meanwhile offered difficulties ample to divert me from those proliferating at home.

I worked in the Wilton branch which MacNaughton headed, his partner, Blair, running the firm's Loop headquarters. My father-in-law did not spare me an arduous basic training as margin clerk and research drudge, nor the New York Stock Exchange and the National Association of Securities Dealers the stiff three-hour examination through which they put aspiring brokers. So that when I sat down at my desk, bright and early one Monday morning in May, it was with the feeling that I had earned the name I now bore, account executive. To find my satisfaction quickly dashed by a development suggesting I might have blundered into the wrong line of work. Watching the tape made me seasick.

This was my old Ménière's syndrome, first detected aboard ship. I had naturally had a little tape reading in the course of my apprenticeship, but in snatches of only a few minutes at a time, sometimes merely cursory glances as I paused on my way through the office. Nothing as concentrated and continuous as is required of a broker. A broker has to watch these hieroglyphics swimming from right to left across the illuminated screen *all day long.* His only respite is to shift his gaze periodically to the Dow-Jones news bulletins, which are vertical, streaming upward on a screen near the tape — or I should say tapes, since there is one for the New York Stock Exchange and another for the American. The desk I had been assigned was close up, compounding my troubles, since I'm farsighted and must, for example, sit in the far rear of a movie.

By noon I was quite nauseated. The head broker, Fido Harrison, noticed my distress and surmised its source. He may have seen me pull my wastebasket out from under my desk and set it in the aisle beside my chair, in readiness for an emergency too urgent for a bolt into the men's room. I admitted what the trouble was when he stopped by to inquire, and he said the thing to do was not to keep twitching your eye from quotation to quotation, and certainly never to follow the figures across the screen, but to focus at a fixed point, either the right edge of the screen where they make their entrance or the left where they vanish, and at the same time develop the attitude of *paying the whole thing no mind.* This was similar to the counsel given at sea, to keep your eye on the horizon and ignore the pitching and heaving beneath you.

The advice availed here no more than it had there, but I didn't tell Fido that. He didn't like to be told his business. He was a short man of forty whose nickname presumably derived from a terrierlike way of darting from desk to desk to ask how things were going, sorties punctuated by glances at the tape and frequent disappearances into the private offices of the corporation heads, for whom he acted as a sort of liaison with the cadre out front. Underlings usually rose when he stopped by, an etiquette that sneaking intuition told me was ill-advised, because of his short size. If there was any looking down to be done, Fido would prefer doing it himself. The question was academic in my case, since it was all I could do to sit up straight and raise my head enough to get his in focus. He was bald, with a remaining horseshoe of hair, like a wreath of victory that had slipped down in the tumult of the day. I would smile bravely as he went by, to say that I was getting the hang of it, though such was far from the case. By one o'clock I was glad to take my lunch hour, if only to hurry to the corner drugstore for some Dramamine, and to sit at the lunch counter and reconsider my position.

As I roosted there, trying to ignore the plate of chicken salad I had ordered to justify my doing so, a new element entered the picture. Objects known to be stationary were behaving like the tape figures from whose remorseless flux I had come out to gain an hour's respite. The waitress kept flowing from right to left while the counter swam steadily upward, like the Dow-Jones news bulletins. The former would vanish as though spirited away on a conveyor belt on which she was standing, only to be jerked mysteriously back again, and the latter rolling woozily toward the ceiling also to reappear in the same fashion. As though this were not enough, the entire mélange of hallucinations was reproduced in duplicate in the mirror behind the counter, amid a phantasmagoria of oranges and pastry. I was convinced I was cross-eyed when I picked my way, unnourished, into the street. Here the kinetic anarchy continued. The sidewalk rose up to meet my feet, causing the soles of my shoes to spank the pavement prematurely, or else receded, giving the illusion that I was walking around the town on stilts. I felt like a remittance man picking his way in the last stages of locomotor ataxia among the island ports to which he has been relegated by his family, about which I had once joked with old Benny.

Luckily I had almost no clients yet, but I had a few, and the phone did occasionally ring and I would have to give a quotation or a coherent account of the state of the market. Whenever possible I would simply sit with my eyes facing front but closed, my head in my hands, and imagine limericks going by on the Dow-Jones, or news bulletins reading, "POPE ABSOLVES JEWS OF RESPONSIBILITY FOR CRUCIFIXION BUT BLAMES SWEDES" or "CBS BUYS EPISCOPAL CHURCH. STOCK ZOOMS." When the bell rang at two thirty to sound the close of trading on the Stock Exchange, I was as groggy as a boxer who had been saved by it. Nor did the tape really stop when it did — it swept on as the highway does in the mind of the motorist after a long day's travel.

I lay on the living room couch with my eyes closed after dinner while Naughty soothed my brow with cold compresses and murmured assurances that I would have my sealegs soon. Daddy had told them once of another such case, that had come out all right in the end. She seemed to have recovered her humor. In fact she was smiling every time I opened my eyes, which I did at intervals, and once or twice she broke out in peals of helpless laughter.

When after a week I still didn't have my sealegs — or whatever the sedentary equivalent of that might be — I decided I must consult somebody. Benny. What harm could he do me in this instance since it wasn't really his field?

Or so I thought. He insisted Ménière's syndrome lay well within his province since there was a strong and growing body of opinion that it was largely psychological, at least in many of its victims. People subject to psychosomatic troubles or with a history of nervous maladjustment were more prone than others, he said, to the hyperstimulation causing (it was thought) the inner ear malfunction in question.

He asked me to describe my sensations in detail, and I did. "It's only a question of time," I said, "before I puke all over my desk. Or somebody else's desk."

The wind deity puffed out his cheeks in respect of the proportions of the case, or to indicate some enlargement of his grasp of the problem this time under review. He was wearing a striped blue suit and, in keeping with his Pelion-on-Ossa conception of dress, a striped shirt and striped tie with it. I closed my eyes every time he went by me as he paced his office, a small, pleasant room high above the old Boul Mich, agreeably decorated before it had fallen into his clutches.

"You never returned to the fold, did you, Joe?"

"Oh, Christ, do we have to open that can of tomatoes again?"

"I was just wondering if you hadn't some degree of faith justifying observances in themselves not important. What's the picture on that now, old man?"

"I go to the Episcopal Church to please Naughty, who goes to please her mother, who, I hope, makes God happy."

"You could resent all this, and the resentment manifest itself in the job you have thanks to them, and that

98

you have to keep to remain a family man on their terms."

"But I like these people. Mrs. MacNaughton is a fountain of good humor, who gets on great with my mother. She's the shape of things to come as far as Naughty's concerned, but that can't be helped. Besides, I don't like silhouette women. I like plump ones, and I don't mind fat ones if it comes to that. I don't want to go to bed with a plank."

"I don't think you should worry so much about her getting fat, Joe. These two-dimensional spooks are the vogue only in fashion magazines. In real life you wouldn't want them. What about MacNaughton?"

"He's marvelous. You know the American legend about the tycoon, the human dynamo, who deeps charging his batteries all day with catnaps? *MacNaughton is always asleep.*"

"I sense the portrait of a fool being painted here. I get that feeling, under the surface protestation of fondness. If that's what you feel, Joe, don't deny it. Don't keep the lid on. Let it out! Acknowledge it at least to yourself."

The conflicts with which I was being decimated did not stop here. Benny now aired a paradox that was double-pronged. I not only resented the MacNaughtons dragging me to the Episcopal Church because I was an atheist. I resented their taking me away from the Catholic Church because I was still a believer. We were all familiar with the boast of orthodox indoctrinators, about giving them a child till the age of seven.

The conviction that I was riding a carrousel persisted whether I closed my eyes or no. Circular argumentation may have been what we were once more irretrievably embarked on, but the exposition did nevertheless in part answer to that inner ambivalence we all share in some way, and that in my case had already manifested itself in behavior patterns inaugurated during Benny's first round of treatment.

He asked: "How's the counting coming?"

I gave a loud laugh without opening my eyes, as if to ask what he thought the chances were of eluding the suzerainty of numbers at a job which consisted in the intravenous assimilation of figures in fractions of quarters and eighths.

For there was a recrudescence of all that. The difficulty worsened with the need to watch specifically for fours and sevens — my old numerological nemeses — and the fact that this particular attention to market prices had no genuine bearing on the vigilance required on my customers' behalf heightened the guilt presumably responsible for the compulsion in the first place. Vicious circle indeed! In this condition I was more than susceptible to the digestive tensions notorious in occupations of this sort. It's no wonder investment people are prone to ulcers; the linings of their stomachs are eaten away by eighths of a point.

Under Benny's guidance I now had the full-fledged nervous breakdown we had somehow fallen short of the first time around. That it was in the cards was indicated by a cycle of behavior which included this compulsion to counsel my clients in terms of market gains and losses coming in fours and sevens; a return of washing rituals; and a revival of the calisthenics in churches. "What are you doing, slenderizing?" a priest lurking behind a pillar asked me. The chains of repetition seemed to me like those special, often penitential, devotions saints and holy men set themselves, such as prayers intoned while long stairways are mounted on one's knees. I reviewed my condition in a restaurant next door to the office, from where I could watch the tape much better through two panes of plate glass and a small intervening court than I could from my desk. I was stirring my coffee in an almost mystical fatigue when Fido Harrison joined me at my table.

"General Motors is up three quarters," I said, nodding at the tape through the window.

"How's the dizziness? You look like something the cat dragged in."

"That's all right. No, I'm O.K." Nevertheless, I slid the knot of his tie up till his eyes popped from their sockets, and I caught them in my hand and dropped them into my coffee cup, which I stirred briefly before gulping off the contents with a pleasant smile.

Luckily the market in these first weeks was in a state

of doldrums. There was no economic news of any interest. Neither institutional nor private investors were putting their money into anything. Turnover was on the average of a scant three or four million shares a day, and the tape, as a consequence, was mercifully slow. The hangers-on in the office fell asleep in the spectators' bleachers at the front. Trying to cheer my colleagues up during these unprofitable days helped me forget my own troubles.

With time on our hands, we spent a lot of it reviewing portfolios and then calling customers up to suggest switches as a way of drumming up business. One of the clients I had inherited from my retired predecessor was a woman named Mrs. de Shamble, a divorcée noted for her rather featherbrained taste in equities. "Well, I've finally weeded the dogs out of Mrs. de Shamble's portfolio," I would say, and hold up an empty folder. Then the whole office would roar with laughter.

One day she came in, and I must say I was rather surprised. Up to now I had only dealt with her over the telephone, and from her voice had mentally evoked a somewhat dowdy creature in lumpy tweeds. What I saw was a slim woman of about $35\frac{7}{8}$ in a black silk suit and a light blue froth of scarf at her throat. She weighed about 120, down $5\frac{1}{2}$ from last Friday's close. She had brown eyes and a clear white skin, but some inner corrosion was unmistakably expressed in her face. She was too well groomed for one o'clock in the afternoon. She said she had only a minute, being on her way to a meeting of some charitable organization, but she was still seated beside my desk an hour later, when I suggested a bite of lunch.

"I've lost eleven thousand dollars in two years," she said when we were settled at a table next door. I became a wind deity in the manner of my cousin Benny, puffing out my cheeks and bulging my eyes to show I was impressed. I sensed that my dizziness was gone. There was not a trace of it. In this manner can one stimulation drive out another. For the moment my head was cleared, even though in another sense it was spinning.

What Mrs. de Shamble and I had in common was: guilt. It didn't take much conversation to disclose that we shared a certain deep-seated, nagging remorse over our abandoned faith. Mrs. de Shamble's intellectual history was far more checkered than mine. I had merely left the Church. She had spent the years since her break with Rome wandering from one religious sect to another, searching for some emotional equivalent of what she had lost. Her life was a sort of spiritual vagabondage. Her present harbor was some kind of cult which stressed the principle of anonymous well-doing. The idea was that to receive credit for our benefactions vitiates them both for the recipient and the giver: the one is oppressed by a sense of obligation, the other tarnished by the egotistical satisfactions all too present in good works.

We became a little hysterical, as people can in moments of mutual self-revelation on short notice. I caught her hand, and my face flamed at the scent of perfume. She invited me to lunch at her house, which was nearby, and on that occasion told me something of her ordeals as a wife. Her husband had been an apparently unstable manufacturer of garden equipment who, in fits of temper, would slam the door without going out of the house. He would simply rise and walk over to it and open and shut it with deafening detonations many times over. He would keep it up until pictures shook on the walls and bric-a-brac danced on the shelves. This struck me as a curiously sinister way to behave.

After a good lunch and a bottle of wine we rose and embraced. I kissed her several times. She caressed me feverishly, opening my coat and then beginning to fumble with the buttons of my shirt. I shook my head and said, "No," and hurried back to the office.

We think we can escape guilt. I know better now! That remorseless auditor will seek us out wherever we go. Even as I stumbled out of Mrs. de Shamble's house the memory of her hurt face began to haunt me. All that night I saw her wounded expression. In addition to spurning the gift she had offered me — the gift of herself — I had abandoned her to the shame of censorship, no less keen because implied rather than stated. "It's not worth the taking, and you're a tramp for offering it to me," I had in effect said. Very subtly, I had compromised her. I had behaved, in fact, like a cad.

That was one thing. Another was the contrition experienced on one's wife's behalf. I had kissed another woman — that was all. For such a bauble I had betrayed the woman I was married to? Far, far better to have done so for something more equal to the jewel bartered away. One hears of a wife's saying, quite rightly, after a glimpse of the other woman, "You mean you'd leave me for *that?*" Such outrage would be equally valid if the "that" referred to the degree of pleasure rather than to the extent of the rival's charms. I felt all this acutely every time I looked at Naughty now. That bit of slap and tickle with Mrs. de Shamble became more tawdry by the hour. The only way to redeem us all would be to raise it from that shabby level to something more like adult romantic enterprise.

When Mrs. de Shamble's honor had been restored by being taken to bed, it was she who arose from it with the bitterest remorse. A characteristic need for expiation seized her — and here her present religious bent came into full play. The suggestion was made that we do some good work in a quarter, and under circumstances, for which no corrupting credit would accrue to us.

"Mrs. Ditwielder, who lives behind me there," she

said, wringing her hands as she paced her living room floor, "is in very bad shape. Her husband died and she has no money — she can't even buy oil for her furnace. She depends for heat on firewood, and we neighbors take turns chopping it for her. Fortunately she has a good woodlot. But she keeps running short. Why don't we go chop some for her?"

"She'd find out," I protested. "Then we'd get credit."

"She doesn't know you. So even if she saw you, it would be the same as not being seen. The neighbors just sort of slip in there and out again, like elves."

"What will you do?"

"I'll get the axe."

That was how I came to be sneaking through an intervening grove of maples, axe in hand, to the back of Mrs. Ditwielder's property. The forest rang with my blows as I felled a young tree and then set to work chopping it into lengths suitable for firewood, to pile on what I could see was a dwindling stack of cordwood nearer the house, a small cottage of white clapboard. I wondered what good logs that needed a year of seasoning would do her now, but that was not my problem. I had no time to ponder it now, at any rate. As my axe came down, in a mood of admitted primitive exhilaration, I heard a dog bark, and saw what looked like a fairly vicious German shepherd bounding toward me through the brush. I dropped the axe and streaked for Mrs. de Shamble's. She had been watching at the window and had the door open for me. I sprinted through it into the kitchen and sprawled across the waxed linoleum just as the dog sprang up the porch stairs. The door was clapped shut in the nick of time.

"The thing we could do is rake some leaves at the Y.M.C.A.," she proposed after a few moments' consultation. "They have a call out for work volunteers, you know. The place looks a mess, and they so need the money for other things."

"Why do we have to do anything at all?" I asked. "Aren't we sorry enough? I'm afraid that doing some good deed, whether for praise or not, will give us the illusion of having made up for our wrong, and make us stop punishing ourselves, which we shouldn't do. Let's keep our conscience on the job by all means."

"Mrs. Jack Gardner did Lenten penance by scrubbing the steps of Boston's Church of the Advent."

"That was New England, with the Puritan conscience. This is one of the American suburbs. We're supposed to be a little decadent here."

I tried to stall her awhile by detaining her with the casuistries of the subject in this fashion. A glance at my wristwatch indicated that I had fifteen minutes to get back to my office from my lunch hour. Dangling a leg from a knee, I leaned back on the couch and said, "What are some other penances? That people have done?"

"Who?"

"Anybody? Different individuals under stress."

There was no doubt that the description fit Mrs. de Shamble. I was now certain that I had got mixed up with a crazy woman, from whose clutches it behooved me to extricate myself at the earliest possible moment — which seemed to mean humoring her intellectual eccentricities until I could make my getaway. Otherwise there was no telling what she might do. She might even call me up at home, and then there would be hell to pay. So I mentally resigned myself to doing a spot of volunteer work for the Y while she discoursed again on the purgative value of unthanked philanthropy, quoting large sections from a pamphlet issued by the society to whose teachings she now adhered, as well as from a novel by the late Lloyd Douglas in which this theme of self-effacing generosity was also propounded. Glimpses here and there recalled the sport for which the dire payment was now being exacted: the open bedroom door, a bust of Mozart with a man's garter, mine, circling the brow, the buckle dangling down over the nose. A sobered Mrs. de Shamble noted my look and went over to remove the evidence of our revel as she talked. I thrust it into my pocket when she gave it to me. Why did one's clowning so swiftly pall on the women it had once delighted?

The ideal of anonymity was not strictly realized in the expiatory task on which I now embarked. As I was raking leaves in front of the Y and dumping them into a cart left out for the purpose, a car stopped and a woman got out. It was my wife.

"What in God's name are you doing here?" she asked.

"This is Cleanup Week. We're all asked to pitch in. You know that."

"What the devil is the matter with you? What are you raking leaves for on your lunch hour?"

I propped the rake against the cart and, holding my palms a foot or two apart, moved them in parallel tracks to indicate a swath of the lawn where I had been working. "You mean all in through here?"

She looked at me sharply a moment. "Is this your idea of a joke? Or do you think you should see someone?"

"Perhaps you're right," I said, grasping at deliverance on that note.

The sanatarium which Benny recommended was in Chicago. I took a train in from the suburbs. The conductor came down the aisle collecting tickets with a copy of *Vogue* under his arm. He had evidently snatched it up from a vacated seat on his rounds, and hadn't had time to stash it away wherever train personnel put periodicals they want to take home for themselves or to their wives. I sat next to a man who chewed tobacco. Every once in a while he laid his head back on the seat and looked at the ceiling, as though assessing a target at which he might at any moment let fly. Three seats down a man rose and shook his finger at a woman smoking a cigarette in a car not specified as a smoker. I hoped that when I came out I would be able to adjust to society better than I had been.

My room was a small but pleasant one on the second floor. I worked on my collection, read, and smoked a pipe a great deal, or I should say pipes. Most of us take a stab at them from time to time, giving up the habit but keeping the pipes, and I had accumulated several over the years, all of which I had on impulse thrown into my grip at the last minute. I now found it relaxing to amuse myself experimenting with the various characters the pipes suggested. I had a short, blunt briar which was for resisting change. Then a calabash with a curved stem, such as would be smoked by a man who can't see what the hullaballoo over Kafka is all about. "Hold on there," he would say, turning it around to point the wet stem at you, "when you say this Kafka catches the horror lurking in modern man, I want to know which modern man. You, me, or my good friend Tom Hathaway over there." It was the perfect thing for the sort of chap who makes you define your terms and no nonsense about it. The large, stout meerschaum with a covered bowl was for an even more substantial type — someone determined to put an end to skinny dipping in the area. This was the character I liked to assume at greatest length. "We're going to see to it that this town becomes a decent place for decent people to live in," I said, rapping the table as I drew on it, "but we're going to have to get a move on. It may already be too late, with the new element moving in at the rate it is. The place is going to the demnition bow-wows I tell you. We'd best get a committee up."

I was puffing away in this vein when the doctor came in. He seemed depressed. He sat sunk in a thick clump of chins, which gave him the downcast look of pigeons sitting on rooftops in cold weather. Dark circles under his eyes and a stooped carriage suggested marked fatigability of long standing. Perhaps not too much insight. I did my best to cheer him up.

"What goes up the chimney down and is red all over?" I said, but he shook his head gloomily. "You'll be here for months," he said. "I've got the story. Hanging all those things on your clapper and defacing your body like primitive man. What do you put your wife's girdle on for?"

"Show who wears the pants in the family." I explained that symbolism was big these days, but he again shook his head pessimistically. "It's not a good outlook," he said.

"Ah, come on," I said encouragingly. "Tying all that stuff on your dink may be cause for alarm, I'll grant you. But look on the bright side. We're winning the cold war, the economy has never been healthier, and it seems they've come up with something for the common cold. So buck up. Things aren't so bad, you know. Here's another." I gave him the following brainteaser which I had got from Fido Harrison at the office the week before.

Three men go into a hotel and ask for a room. The clerk charges them thirty dollars for it, taking a ten-dollar bill from each in payment. After they move in the clerk realizes he's overcharged them. The rate for the room is only twenty-five dollars. So he sends the bellboy up with five dollars to divide among them. On the way up, the bellboy decides to give them only three dollars and keep two himself. Thus with one dollar rebate for each man from his original ten, each has contributed nine dollars to the price of the room — making twenty-seven in all. The bellboy has two, making twenty-nine.

"What happened to the other dollar?" I said.

The doctor puzzled over it for a few minutes, running through the totals in a low murmur. "Don't tell me!" he said, rather jumpily. "I want to figure it out for myself."

He came back next morning looking haggard. He had sat gnawing his pencil till all hours, then fallen into a brief, fitful sleep with the problem still on his mind. I started to say something and he cut in again. "Don't tell me the answer! I want another day at it anyway."

The next morning he was at the cracking point.

"O.K.," he said, dropping into the chair. "I give up. What is the answer?"

"There isn't any," I said. "It isn't a trick or anything at all. The dollar can't be accounted for no matter how you look at it. Except to say that you can't add and subtract both — or maybe that you can't mix two problems. Because there are two. One about the thirty dollars and another, entirely separate one, about the five. You can account for each amount separately, but not both together. The fallacy is in trying to combine them. They have nothing to do with one another."

He smiled for the first time since I had seen him. The reassurance that he wasn't a dunce, that he hadn't failed a test of intelligence, made him positively beam. He was in the best of moods when he left the room.

His spirits continued to rise throughout the next day, and the next. You could see him blossom. Very possibly his mood was due for a cyclical recovery in the nature of things, but getting off the hook in regard to the brain-teaser was certainly a contributing factor. By the end of the week he was quite himself again, and I was allowed to go home.

When I got back to the office I saw a strange man sitting at my desk. I asked to see MacNaughton immediately, and was told he had wanted to see *me* as soon as *I* came in.

His secretary announced he was asleep. I paced outside in the hall till he woke up. The snoozes for which human dynamos who can catnap at will are celebrated

— Edison, Churchill, heroes of that stripe — reverse the classic concept of slumber as a negative, or passive, thing, in that they are literally willed intervals of ten to fifteen minutes from which the go-getters awake refreshed and ready to hit the ball again — reflections of the same drive that requires them. They are able to catch forty winks in easy chairs or even at their desks, as Napoleon could on horseback. I knew that MacNaughton wasn't sitting at his desk, or lying on it, as he never tired of recalling Edison had done between flashes of creative inspiration, much less dozing on horseback like Napoleon, but stretched out on a daybed he kept in one corner of his office. I envied him this gift. *I couldn't sleep at all.*

At last his secretary said he was free, and I was shown in. He was at his desk, and certainly wide awake. I noticed how dense his eyebrows were. They seemed part of a disguise, as though each night he removed them as he did his shoes, peeling them away like a wearied actor in a taxing role after another day in a game in which it paid to be beetle-browed.

"How are you feeling now, Joe?" he asked.

"Fine. The rest did me good, and I think I'm over the hump on that vertigo business. It was nice of you to visit me." He and Mrs. MacNaughton had been to see me a couple of times.

"Not at all. I just hope you're rested up now." Behaving as though nothing had happened, he cleared his

114

throat and said, "I think you're going to work out all right here, but there's often a problem of finding the right *niche* for a man in any organization. Brokering — or that aspect of brokering — may not be your speed. We've run some of your clients' portfolio figures through the Honeywell in your absence, and there's been a grand drop in capital value of eighteen per cent. In that same period the average for all our other brokers shows a net gain of four per cent, in a bear market. The only conclusion left to us is that you're something less than a whiz as an investment counselor."

"I don't think I can be held entirely responsible for that, sir," I protested. "A broker buys the stocks his clients tell him to, for the most part. He doesn't force them."

"In some cases yes, and against his better judgment. But he can persuade them wisely in most cases, and over the long haul. The fact remains that your customers are worth eighteen per cent less than they were before you took over."

He was reading some figures in a folder on his desk.

"I see you recommend an awful lot of Buck Rogers stocks. Space corporations and electronic breakthrough outfits and what not. These growth and glamour stocks are risky, you know. Very risky. Fly-by-night stuff with which MacNaughton and Blair can't afford to be associated."

"Most of them were in the model portfolio I kept

when I was in college, and that ran several percentage points ahead of yours, if you'll recall."

"College is one thing, real life another. And you know we're a conservative house, who emphasize quality equities and yield. Investment, not speculation. I see you got four people to buy Astro-Nucleonics at six something and it's down to two now, and paying no dividends. Mrs. Caslow is a widow, you know. She can't afford to put her money in all these 'sure things' on hot tips. She should be buying AT&T."

"It'll come back. They just got a fat new government contract on a gravity instrument."

MacNaughton removed the hornrimmed glasses through which he had been perusing the figures, and folded his hands on the desk as he regarded me across it.

"I'm going to give it to you straight from the shoulder. Do you know what they call the stocks Joe Sandwich recommends?"

"The little office joke about hat sizes you mean?" I was referring to the low-priced issues I tried to get my clients in on the ground floor on, for which the market quotations are reminiscent of hat sizes — 6⅞, 7¼, and so on.

"No, that's not what I mean. This is something they say behind your back, outside the office as well as in it. Your fame is spreading. I told you I was going to give it to you straight. The stocks Joe Sandwich recommends are known in the trade as laughing stocks."

I absorbed details of his office for later transmission into the portrait of an ass. Why, I wanted to ask him, were the books along the edge of the desk turned so that visitors could read their titles, rather than the one for whom the references were presumably intended? If he wanted one, did he spring from his swivel chair and pop around to run a finger along the spines? Or was he familiar enough with his treasures to recognize them from behind? And another puzzle while we were at it. As long as he was bent on impressing callers, the only explanation for the arrangement under review, why did he not set out selections more calculated to excite admiration than such hackneyed staples as Bartlett's *Familiar Quotations,* a dictionary or two, the *Thesaurus,* and a manual of investment terms? The daybed was in a corner, and on a stand beside it was another volume, from which you might supposedly snatch a thought before dropping off. Was it for this that Edison toiled between snoozes to produce the electric light bulb and the phonograph that was ancestral to the three dictaphones within handy reach here? Hah? Hah?

"I think the thing for you to do is transfer for a bit to the Research Department."

"But I've just been there," I said, protesting what was in effect a demotion. "In fact that's where I started."

"Not long enough. And this will be different, because it will be a long-range thing. You won't just be giving data a lick and a promise, the way you did for your orientation. You'll be studying it, and maybe writing out analyses for us to chew over at the top level. You already know the growth stocks. What you need is a solid underpinning in the more conservative equities." MacNaughton tilted back in his chair and smiled in a more avuncular fashion. "Five or ten years from now you could be writing the weekly Market Letter."

I took the things from my old desk to my new one in a back room known as the Library. Then I went out for a walk to compose myself, promptly catching sight of Mrs. Caslow, the widow to whom I had recommended the collapsed growth stock MacNaughton had alluded to. She was wearing a shawl and pulling along two little girls, equally shabbily dressed. I ducked into an alley till they were gone. I watched them vanish when it was safe to emerge, shaking my head sympathetically.

I kept running into my clients for several days in a row. The laws of probability include one providing for these unexplained "spikes" in a statistical graph, called the law of the recurrence of unlikely events, or something of the sort. We're all familiar with such flukes — not seeing somebody in your office building for years and then running into him several times in one day, letters crossing in the mail, and so on. This spate of coincidences included a second glimpse of the widow, Mrs. Caslow, and then a third. By that time I was padding through the streets in sneakers and smoked glasses, with a soft hat pulled over one eye, feeling sorrier for myself than ever. I don't understand the constant disparaging references to self-pity. The term keeps cropping up everywhere, like Mrs. Caslow herself, always with the same underlying assumption that it is to be deplored. Why? Certainly much can be said in its defense. Had it not been for a bit of well-timed self-commiseration now and again I wouldn't be here to defend it, and neither I suspect would some of its detractors be here to belittle it. A style of tight-lipped endurance would long ago have split me down the middle and sent me to the cleaner's for keeps, whereas an occasional bout of sheer maudlin wallowing in melancholy enables one to pull himself together, get back on his feet, and, as the grand old wall motto has it, "Keep on keepin' on!"

I learned early that mystic solitude in which we all walk (you too out there, you yacking extrovert) — can remember, in fact, the exact moment when the truth broke upon me like an apocalypse. It was the luminous hour of dusk, in the dead of winter. I had gone as a lad of six to play with a new boy in the neighborhood, at his house. He behaved so obnoxiously that his mother decided to punish him for his rudeness to a guest by depriving him of something he wanted most at that moment, which happened to be the guest. "You don't *deserve* such a nice playmate as Joseph," she said, and out I went. As I stood there in the cold, jiggling my feet on the blue snow, looking in at the brat playing with his toys and munching cookies in the warm, well-lighted parlor, what was there in all God's world to do but feel sorry for myself?

Benny once arranged a blind date for me and then at the last minute canceled himself out, leaving me to fend for myself with a girl I had never seen, who lived on a street I had never heard of, in a quarter of town I had never been. It was pouring rain, moreover, and in view of all this I decided to set out directly from the office where I was then working, at the job I'd had to take when my father died. Having neither hat nor umbrella, I made a dash for my second-hand Chevvy wearing a typewriter hood. The girl turned out to be a butterball in yellow wool, as round and about as high as the hassock on which she remained sitting while she read her own poetry aloud to me. She might as well have been standing on it, for it was declamatory poetry of social protest, in which the author expressed her scorn for tradition and her love for the working classes by rhyming "duet" with "suet." For lines intended to be inflammatory these had remarkable sedative properties, especially for a man who had been working hard all day. However, I managed to murmur a few words of praise, and then, in the manner of young blades of the day, I patted the couch on which I had by easy stages contrived to dispose myself at full-length, and said, "Lie down. I want to talk to you."

Instead we had to run out to Clearing, a remote western section of Chicago, and pick up some petitions. They were mimeographed manifestoes addressed to the Secretary of Labor by an organization to which the girl belonged, demanding action of some sort on a current industrial dispute. It was still raining cats and dogs, plus which we ran out of gas halfway to our destination. A quick reconnoiter in the rain revealed a filling station a quarter of a mile ahead, at the foot of a long slope fifty feet from the top of which we were stalled. If we could just push the car those fifty feet we could coast the rest of the way — or rather if I could, because someone had to steer.

I got behind the Chevvy in the pouring rain and shoved, again wearing the typewriter hood. From time to time I would lift it above my eyes to look through the back window and make faces at the girl, sitting snug and comfortable behind the wheel. I was, again, feeling sorry for myself, and why not? What has any self-respecting man recourse to under such circumstances but some honest, solid solicitude for himself? The girl had no humor, thus the laughs with which people can see themselves through under stress were out of the question here. Being the salt of the earth cut no ice — she was impervious to anyone else's qualities. Self-pity was all that remained. "You poor boy," I said aloud, soaked to the skin and grunting stertorously behind the inching Chevrolet as the rain drummed in torrents on my cowl. "If she really loved the working classes she'd give better proof of it on a night like this than read that half-baked stuff and then make you chase clear out to Clearing to get some petitions that are probably no better written from some sodding sod who probably hasn't done an honest day's work in his life either. Well, baby, we're going to lay some pipe when this is over," I panted, inaccurately as it turned out, through gritted teeth.

What was indicated was a real wallow in the nearest bar, when I could get away, followed by a good bit of Tchaikovsky at home. I played the last movement of the Sixth, the *adagio lamentoso*, over and over, accompanying the New York Philharmonic on my clarinet, walking around the room as I did so in long woolen underwear, which was how I had heard Yehudi Menuhin practiced the violin. The music is of course sheer mush, but I managed in its pauses to interpolate some even treaclier arpeggios of my own, sometimes augmenting my contribution by howling like a dog, sometimes standing before a pier glass as I played, or pausing to give myself a bittersweet smile of understanding and sympathy.

Mrs. Caslow was coming at me for the third and last time. She had her two little girls with her again, and they were clutching brown paper sacks that had the air of containing materials for all of them to twist into paper flowers, for sale to kind neighbors and people hurrying to the theater. I flattened myself into the nearest doorway, again gritting my teeth and cursing my luck. Had she seen me? Footsteps came nearer. Then Mrs. Caslow was facing me squarely from the sidewalk.

"Any more bright ideas, *Mis*ter Financial Expert?"

"The government contract fell through, as often happens with glamour stocks, but they're getting another," I said, stepping out of the doorway and removing my hat. "It'll come back, mark my words. All stocks fluctuate, you know."

"It's down to two and a quarter. From six and seven eighths."

"I'll buy it from you at what you paid," I offered wildly.

"No, thanks. We don't take charity."

"Then won't you join me in some lunch? They say that new Chinese restaurant across the street is excellent."

"Thank you again. The answer is still the same."

Now, the woman had no one to blame but herself, in the last analysis. A broker never forces anyone to buy anything. He supplies information and makes helpful suggestions. All investors are subject to the breaks of the game. Mrs. Caslow might have bought Astro-Nucleonics then at 2¼ (as I certainly would have advised!) and sold it six months later for 6⅞, and the story would have been the other way around. Nevertheless, I felt wretched. They were evidently in classic penury. I shook my head sympathetically as I made for the Chinese Gardens alone, there to drown my disappointments in several stiff drinks and some food. I polished off a pot of tea. While chewing a fortune cookie I detected an alien sensation, and, turning to look into the small wall mirror in the booth where I was sitting, stuck my tongue out and found adhering to it, sure enough, a small strip of paper on which appeared the assertion that I must be careful in money matters. Still gazing into the mirror, I shook my head and said to myself, "How do you stand it?"

Thus one bends in order that he does not break — the whole point I am trying to make in a nutshell. There is nothing "narcissistic" about it whatever, since our all being in the same boat is never lost sight of. One sees it through by frankly and freely embracing the total human farce of which he forms a modest part, a miniscule fragment in a hostile, or at any rate incomprehensible, Whole. Contemplating myself in the glass with a piece of paper hanging out of my mouth, or clarinetting away in long johns, I know that there is nothing quite like me in the universe at that moment, and that is a kind of comfort. Doing these things is a way of affirming myself, of upholding the dignity of man if you will, or at least a little of my end of it. I will never understand the Theory of Relativity, but I have an excellent picture of Einstein with his tongue hanging out a mile. He apparently put it out for the photographers — a request few would rate in this world, and fewer still feel secure enough to comply with. Anyone doing it in private is operating at the other end of the status spectrum. What do you do in front of your bathroom mirror? I'd give a pretty penny to know. I pause to contemplate myself when I'm shaving, because a man is at his best with his face covered with lather. Anyhow, the photograph is a newspaper clipping which I keep in a drawer and take out occasionally to look at, though not often, and not for very long at a time, since it is a little rich for my blood.

Self-pity, in conclusion, hurts nobody, offering, indeed, an interior mood all the more conducive to giving others their external due. I never beat my wife, or even ever speak a harsh word to her. I'm not boasting about this, because the explanation is obvious. A man busy nursing his own wounds has no time to inflict them on others. I didn't rush home to unload the news on my wife, after my session with her father. She was out anyway when I got there, which gave me time to get a better face on myself. I had a few drinks, of course, and then took a long hot bath, dispersing the pall of dread by getting in and out of the tub seven times. As I was drying myself I heard the front door open, and I went downstairs knotting the towel around my middle.

"We're going to have dinner out tonight," I said, "because guess what. I've been kicked upstairs."

six

THE NEWS that I was getting ahead in my line of work made Naughty's spirits bloom anew. I nearly said "boom," and I might very well have, because the good times immediately following were like a bull market at home. I find that there are worse metaphors for human existence in general than economic ones, since everything in it represents some kind of transaction, a profit-on-emotion-invested *quid pro quo*, and all of it is subject to cyclical fluctuations. I suppose I tend to see life in those terms rather than artistic or philosophical ones because finance is my field. In any event the domestic graph was up. We were getting to know one another. We were honest with one another. "They threw away the mold when they made you, Joe Sandwich," Naughty said. We saw life together in humorous terms, always vital to a solvent marriage. We laughed about our friends, our neighbors, and of course ourselves. Above all our cleaning woman, Mrs. Munkey. And it is ironic that this major source of mutual amusement on the home front was what put an abrupt and shattering end to the long bull market there.

Naughty was full of Mrs. Munkey when I came home from work one evening after her first day there. "I can't wait till you meet her. She's coming again Saturday, so you'll have a chance to. The only thing is, you've got to be careful what you say and do, because she's a terrible gossip, and as they say, a dog that'll bring a bone will take one away. So put something on, and let your speech be 'Yea, yea' and 'Nay, nay.' "

Mrs. Munkey had a toxic mouth all right. I sensed straight off that her tale-bearing satisfied some kind of sex obsession, which some people can apparently have without being in the least aware of it. She was appeasing that demon when she told a story, for example, about a man whose wife she "gave half a day a week."

"I won't mention no names," she said, "because you'd know right away who he is, high up in the wholesale grocery business. He has a" — Mrs. Munkey looked away and modestly lowered both her voice and her eyes — "nother woman." Then in one of her miraculously fluid transitions she began talking about a Mr. Spontini, who spanked other people's children. "Just like they was his own," she said. "He feels he's responsible for their safety when they're playing on his property, and that gives him the right to knock them about the ears and warm their sit-downs when they misbehave. Like going in the garage and showing each other their" — again the modest glance away — "front things."

Saturday became one of the two days Mrs. Munkey continued to "give" us, giving me also the chance to cultivate her over midmorning coffee in the kitchen. She was a rather short, hard-breathing woman, rectangular in shape and very muscular, whose need to dominate the conversation met no opposition from me. The klatsches were occasions for putting her on as far as I was concerned. "Did you know she carries a small can of some kind of acid in her bag?" I said to Naughty one day after a morning under Mrs. Munkey's spell. "In case she's attacked. It can blind a man. She says it's illegal but that isn't going to stop her."

Mrs. Munkey eventually urged some such protective device on Naughty, who would seem to need it more because she got into Chicago oftener, and even New York. The rise in sex crimes was a favorite theme of hers, and she regarded all males as potential offenders here, taking the Christian view of the act of evil as being unnecessary so long as the desire existed in the heart. As the years passed with no evidence of anyone's want to molest or even suggestively accost her, she became increasingly more harsh in her views of what "should be done with these people." Life imprisonment for any kind of morals charge becoming, at last, among the things she was "diametrically in favor of." Measures for self-defense became likewise more drastic, till finally she carried about with her a purse-size tear gas dispenser — a small atomizer, like a perfume atomizer if you will, with which she was prepared to spray and render instantly harmless anyone approaching with intent to have forcible carnal knowledge of her. She gave Naughty pointers on how to cope with more run-of-the-mill offenders to be encountered on a modest everyday scale, such as strangers who take advantage of the proximity and pressure in crowded elevators and buses. "Bring your heel down *hard* on his toes," she said. "*Stab* him with it so it really hurts. Bring your knee up into his groin — *mmph!* — like this, as hard as you can, and an elbow into the pit of his stomach . . ."

Like many people with a morbid turn of mind, Mrs. Munkey read widely in manuals and other scientific works aimed at sexual health, and her grasp of the terms was often understandably inaccurate. At one of our klatsches she seemed to be delivering a long harangue about "all this auto-eroticism."

"All this what?" I said.

"Necking in cars. They're up to it at the age of fourteen, and at eight o'clock in the morning on the high school parking lot, I can tell you."

Naughty said that my face was more than straight. Chin in hand, I leaned across the table and gazed at Mrs.

Munkey with an almost adoring expression. "You've got a fine man there, Mrs. Sandwich," she said later. "Thank God for him. Democratic, always ready to give the other fellow a chance. He don't have much to say, but give me the quiet ones. They run deep."

My sobriety fostered the hope that I might some Sunday go with her to hear a Chicago evangelist whose tabernacle she had joined. Like many impossible people, Mrs. Munkey had a "spiritual" side, even a dash of mysticism. She was at one with the All. It was her relations with everything else that were out of whack.

One Saturday morning we slept late, Mrs. Munkey not being expected. She had asked for the day off in order to fly to Cleveland and visit her sick sister. I welcomed the leisure, looking forward to a morning of amorous dalliance. But Naughty eluded my overtures, then seemed guilty about having done so, and as she had on occasion before, felt constrained to broach the subject of her "limitations." That always made me uneasy, and as usual I averted the threat of serious discussion with another mock scene.

"Oh, my God!" I said, beating my head as I plunged through the door and into the hall. "Oh, what an empty thing a marriage can be, what a travesty on what was meant! Here I am, married to a woman in name only. I'm married to — a spinster!"

I froze at the top of the stairs. Mrs. Munkey stood in

the vestibule below, quietly taking off her coat. I had opened the back door to get the cream from the porch and that was the way she always entered, in a neighborly way, without knocking.

I got into a bathrobe and went down.

"Why, Mrs. Munkey," I said. "I thought you were in Cleveland."

"My sister's much better. We decided to postpone the trip until Christmas."

I stood paralyzed. She seemed to take a long time to hang her coat up in the front closet. I spent the interval staring dumbly at her broad back. When she turned around I went into the bedroom again.

Naughty was sitting on the bed. She was beating it with both fists and repeating softly, "Son of a *bitch*. Son of a *bitch!*"

"Why?"

"*Why?*" She turned around to make sure I had closed the door. Then she went on in a tone somewhat louder than the hysterical whisper in which she had been carrying on, but still subdued. "*Why?* You've just as good as broadcast it all over town that I'm frigid. You might as well have hired a sound truck and driven through the streets announcing it. What she knows everyone knows in a week. I *told* you we had to be careful." She paced the floor beating her head in earnest as I had jocularly a moment before. "Oh! This is a nightmare!"

"But how the hell was I to know she was in the house? And she must realize I was clowning."

"Why? How could she? She's never seen you do it before. You never do anything but put her on because she's such a find. She has no idea what you're like at — Christ, I nearly said at home." Naughty pummeled her head some more with both fists. Then she pulled herself together with an effort. She turned and faced me. "She doesn't know what a card you are, but she's going to find out. And now. This instant she's going to start learning what a scream you are. You're going down there in the kitchen where she's working and you're going to clown. And you're going to clown, and you're going to clown, and you're going to *clown*. Until she can see that what she overheard must have been a joke."

"God, this *is* a nightmare."

"Yes, isn't it."

I pointed down the stairs. "You mean I . . ."

"Yes. That's right. You're going down there and amuse Mrs. Munkey. Good luck."

I put on a suit and went reluctantly down. I walked around into the dining room, where I stood irresolutely listening to Mrs. Munkey in the kitchen. She seemed to be cleaning the oven, as far as I could judge from the sounds and a peek through a crack in the door. At last I got hold of myself and walked in — as far as the doorway.

133

She was cleaning the oven with a wad of steel wool and some kind of scouring agent. Her head was inside it. For a second I thought of shoving her into it and closing the door and roasting her dead, like the wicked witch in the fairy tale. I watched her for some minutes. She was very muscular indeed, with shoulders as powerful as they were broad, and her exertions had uncommon vigor to them.

Presently she pulled her head out and stepped over to the sink. Well, we may as well get this show on the road I told myself, and went in.

I walked with a limp, holding a hand on one ham. "Picked up a sliver," I said. "I'm a great committeeman, you know. I sit on lots of boards."

Mrs. Munkey nodded. "It's important to do something for your community. After all you live in it, and you might as well go to some effort to see to it that it's a decent place." She ran a pan of water and carried it to the oven, setting it on the open door.

I made an aimless circle of the room, and fetched up at the window. I stood looking out of it with my hands in my pockets.

"Driveway's got to be resurfaced," I said. "The Middleton Paving Company turns out to be notorious for using inferior asphalt, so I think I'll get Sullivan to do it this time. He sings in the church choir, and they say he has perfect pitch."

"The snowplow is what's death on driveways. And on the edges of the lawn too, because the gravel is all bulldozed to the sides and into the grass. The thing to do is have the gravel paved into the surface, if you want gravel as many people do, for the rustic effect. That way it isn't hardtop, but it isn't loose either. Oil penetration I think they call that kind of surface."

What *was* this? Had I blundered out of the lower-case absurd that was my native and proper element and into the notorious upper-case, which was not? There was nothing to do in any event but grit my teeth and plow ahead. Perhaps if I switched into another key, something more the sort of thing Mrs. Munkey had overheard, and as the result of which we were now threshing helplessly in her net. To say she had overheard it was giving her the benefit of the doubt; more probably she had been eavesdropping.

"Look at those people standing in line down in the street there," I said. "They've been waiting all night in the rain for the standing room for my concert to go on sale. Makes a person feel humble. The doctor says he won't answer for the consequences if I go on with this tuberculosis. Well, I'm not going to let those people down. There'll be blood on the keys tonight — *but I'm going on!*"

Mrs. Munkey rubbed her nose with the wrist of the hand in which she was holding the wad of steel wool. I

135

slumped against the wall and thought, "Such stand-
ards." I began a comic ramble about where I had met my
wife. "I was reading a paper at a scientific convention in
New York. It was the lobby of the Waldorf, and the
paper I was reading was the *Times*." I could hear
Naughty on the stairs, listening. She knew I wasn't going
over at all, and that I needed help. She now tripped
lightly into the kitchen, her smile a hideous effigy of the
Merry Marital Mixups on television.

"Still horsing around? Such a nut. You never know
what he's going to say next. When he's serious. Oh, good
morning, Mrs. Munkey."

"Good morning."

I shuffled out, muttering to myself. "The Waldstein
Sonata is trying to tell me something I know I'll only
understand as I'm playing it for the last time . . . I
can't worry about those people out there though. If
they've got wet feet why don't they wear pumps? And
what's the matter with their hose . . ."

Naughty laughed and said, "Nut," above which I
could hear Mrs. Munkey, "Got this oven about clean.
Shall I start polishing the silver now?"

The episode now took the following turn, as I was
able to grasp it by hovering about the periphery. I never
witnessed anything directly, and neither woman ever saw
me, but I remained in flitting touch with every development by what I could hear from adjoining rooms and

piece together by logical inference. It must have happened roughly in this order.

Naughty went into the living room to dig out some of the silver from a sideboard there, and after delivering it to the kitchen where Mrs. Munkey had her polishing paraphernalia set out, she came back to the living room, where she sat on a couch and briefly hammered it with her fists. Then she rose and drank directly from a bottle of sherry in the cellarette. After that she wandered about watering plants, remaining within earshot so Mrs. Munkey could hear her whistle to herself, and occasionally refilling the watering can at the kitchen tap. Once I peered in from another door and saw Mrs. Munkey, a buffing cloth in hand, her arm going like a piston rod. Naughty kept taking generous swallows from the sherry bottle, and when she felt she had enough Dutch courage in her to tackle the adversary, which was soon, for she has a very light head, she paused in the doorway to size her up — much as I had done a short while before. Mrs. Munkey, say, had just shot her fat arms characteristically into the air to readjust her thick tortoiseshell hairpins.

"Of course lots of women *do* have that trouble, one hears," Naughty said. "That Mr. Sandwich was joking about."

Mrs. Munkey said, "Sometimes it's physical, sometimes it's mental. And sometimes —" From the top of the stairs up which I had noisily galloped to advertise my departure I could not catch the rest of the remark. Cautiously I crept down into the dining room again.

"No, Mother Nature's not perfect. Far from it," Mrs. Munkey expatiated, as she brewed and poured coffee. "She turns out women not built for the job they were born for, and that's the God's truth. When I was carrying Woodie I had trouble, which could be expected because he was such a big boy, but I had the same identical thing with little Fern, and her only four and a half pounds — and me a big woman." The names of Mrs. Munkey's children always made her sound as though she gave birth to vegetable matter. The rattling of cups and saucers obliterated a good deal of what immediately followed, and it was not till the women had settled themselves at the kitchen table, which was near the door just beyond which I now lurked, that my comprehension of the talk was revived. It was a fairly intimate one, thanks in no small measure to the liquor Naughty had imprudently taken aboard, which had the effect of lowering her defenses rather than stiffening her courage, and I could imagine Mrs. Munkey taking advantage of this to foster a sense of sorority calculated to make the other twice the victim she already was, modulating her voice in a manner inviting all those who were weary and heavy laden to come unto her, and she would give them rest.

"Is it that the desire isn't there, dear? Cream and sugar?"

"Just the saccharine tablets please. You mean with this friend of mine I'm trying to tell you about? I shouldn't be talking about her, but you don't know her, and she's thinking of going to a psychiatrist anyway."

"There you have to be careful. Some psychiatrists are good and some aren't, but they all have one fault."

"What's that?"

"They pry into your personal affairs. Does this woman we're talking about have any other troubles, that show up in this and might cause it? Like is she alone a lot because her husband is, say, out every night on committee work or something? On local boards? There are what they call committee widows, you know, just like golf widows and office widows."

"I think her husband is out a lot," Naughty said, thinking she was fabricating while I silently pounded my head against the wall.

She was now quite under the influence of the wine, or so I suspected. Otherwise she would not have been so completely sucked into this sisters-under-the-skin camaraderie with Mrs. Munkey, whose earthy, common-sense manner she was even adopting, as though they were washerwomen chatting by the riverside on matters of immemorial human substance.

Mrs. Munkey took a loud gulp of her coffee and moved the discussion onto more intimate ground.

"If it's the desire as such, and only that, there are of course things to take for it. Herbs and so on, they say." Here she enumerated a number of aphrodisiacs, most of them, indeed, bearing long accreditation in folklore — honey, peanuts, asparagus. "And, of course, oysters."

I could sense Naughty looking at her blankly. "They're for virility."

"That's what I say. And now days they also got pills. Such a woman might consult her physician about them. Of course there's one other . . ."

Mrs. Munkey must have cast a glance toward the stairs up which I had supposedly gone. I stood still as a mouse in the dining room.

"You can go at the problem from the other direction. The man."

"You mean . . . ?"

Surely a single sharp, taut-mouthed nod from Mrs. Munkey here. "I done it to Munkey once," she said in a near whisper. "It's easy to put in their food. They can't taste it, and it does tone them down. I can vouch for that. You get some peace, especially if you're carrying. You're not carrying, are you? No. Well, you can get it at any drugstore and it's perfectly simple. They use it in all institutions."

Of which marriage is one, I thought as I stumbled

toward a side door, hoping to rush out of it before I could grasp her meaning.

I walked a good mile down the road to where there was a wayside coffee stand. I had my wallet in the coat I was wearing, and I sat at the counter over a cup of coffee. By that time I had more or less pulled myself together, and I telephoned home. I thought it was time I got in another lick or two from my own direction.

"This is Captain Muldoon," I said in a suitable brogue when Naughty answered. "Would you be after bein' Mrs. Sandwich now? Ah, well, this is news you won't be likin'. We've got your husband down here at headquarters on a charge of car theft. If you'd as lief he stayed here and cooled off we quite understand, but if it's back you'll be wantin' the spalpeen we'll have to trouble you for five hundred dollars bail, and that in cash."

"For God's sake, Joe, we're having a serious conversation," she said. *"Please."*

Not sure I had heard properly, I rang the house again and as soon as the phone was picked up there I said, "This is Reverend Steerall, pastor of the Church of the Unwarranted Assumption, and it seems your husband has gotten himself into trouble with the law again. This is worse than the metatarsal pads. He says he's not responsible because he's a nervous wreck. He says you have a cleaning woman from such a good family she rides her broom sidesaddle."

"That's quite all right," Mrs. Munkey's voice said, this time.

When I got back home I stole around to the back where, under cover of some shrubbery, I raised my head stealthily and peered into the kitchen window. They were still at it. Mrs. Munkey was doing the talking, very vigorously and yet very earnestly, gesturing as she leaned forward across the table to make a point. Naughty nodded meekly as the tears rolled calmly down her cheeks. It was hard to think she was entirely unhappy. I could hear but not distinguish what was being said, except for an occasional isolated word that told me nothing, such as "him" or "whenever." Bent over, I slipped out of the foliage and came around to the front door. I entered breezily.

"Hello, hello! What a relief to get out of the clink. When they booked me they said, 'Anything you say will be held against you.' So I said, 'Sophia Loren.' But nothing ever came of it and here I am."

They regarded me levelly over their cups, simultaneously lifted. There was resentment in their sisterly gaze, even accusation. I gave a weak, apologetic smile and went upstairs. I closed the bedroom door behind me and stretched out on the bed, where, my head propped on a folded pillow, I stared out the window.

142

It must have been another half-hour before I heard Naughty's voice calling out some occupational allusion to Mrs. Munkey as she mounted the stairs.

She came into the bedroom, closing the door behind her. She walked to the window. There she turned to face me with her arms folded.

"Have a nice chat?" I said.

"Everything is a joke to you, isn't it? But everything. Correct me if I'm mistaken — if I misrepresent you. I mean I want to get this straight — about you — and as they say, us. I want to understand the man I'm living with."

She was neither angry nor visibly agitated. Her manner was steely, her voice level.

"I want to make sure I understand the character of the man I'm married to. My husband. Would you say that's a fair estimate, statement, or whatever you want to call it — portrait maybe — of you? That you regard mankind as a joke and life a farce?"

Involuntarily I glanced toward the rack where I kept my pipes. For a moment I almost wished I had the calabash from behind which you made people define their terms. But the absurdity of so thinking, of having such a thing cross your mind at such a critical moment in your life, so proved the truth of the accusation that in a flash of self-comprehension my protests crumbled and I honestly had to agree.

"Yes, I guess that's fair enough," I answered. "I guess I'll have to buy that. Life is a joke." I added, finger upraised, "But that doesn't mean it isn't worth living, or that the dignity of man is in any way —"

"Do you think it's a philosophy of life that'll see you through this, well, this vale of laughs as you obviously consider it?"

"Well, we'll just have to see," I said, not so much to continue the discussion as to break it off. I rose and began to dig clothes out of the closet to take to the cleaners. "Let's do some shopping and try to forget this. We'll have lunch at Maurice's, and I'll buy you a good steak and some of that draft Löwenbräu."

"What if something happened to you? Some kind of disappointment or something. What will you do then?"

"We'll just have to see," I repeated. "What stuff do you have to go to the cleaners?"

The era of good feeling was over, the cycle we had just been through at any rate. There would be others, but this one had drawn to a close. Naughty was impossible to amuse no matter what I did, so I wisely refrained from trying, though natural spirits cannot be wholly repressed. It wasn't for a good month that I saw her really laugh again, and that was when I nearly emasculated myself on the bedroom bureau.

It was a waist-high chest of drawers standing against one window. You had to lean across it to raise the sash.

144

Once I tried to do that on a hot summer night just after stepping out of the shower. The top drawer of the chest was partly open, just enough for the family jewels to slip through, for I was of course naked. At the same time, as I bent forward to raise the window the pressure of my upper legs pushed the drawer shut. A howl of pain brought Naughty running, to find me holding myself with both hands as I hopped about the room. It was a while before she could quiet me down, and a good deal longer before she could recover a straight face. Of course nothing would do but that she let me take measures to make certain everything was all right.

They were not successful. Her recurring flutters of mirth proved too great an obstacle to lovemaking, and nothing came of my attempts. Which naturally brought on fresh spasms of apprehension. It was all a very vicious circle indeed, and as she slept peacefully beside me that night, I lay stark awake till morning, the issue in doubt, nursing my horror.

seven

A S a result of these upheavals Naughty and I arrived
at another of those accommodations that are a special
product of human chaos, another exchange of those
compromises and concessions without which no union
can survive. I agreed to renounce the view that life is a
farce, hardly congenial to one born to perpetuate it, in
return for which Naughty tried to correct her own de-
ficiencies as a mate. She ate oysters for her virility,
undertook a series of exercises designed to correct in-
hibition — one of which consisted in lying down on the
floor and enacting the pantomime of riding a bicycle
upside down — and pored over a succession of marital
guidebooks, often far into the night. "Come to bed,
Naughty," I would plead from upstairs, but she was
obsessed with sex, just what happened in physical conjunction, how it worked, and so on, sometimes not
retiring until she met Uncle Hamilton blinking his way
up from the Late Late Show. For that bland irritant of

long ago turned up in his eternal role as guest, this time in my house. His reappearance came about in the following manner.

Naughty and I were due at an open house buffet supper some friends named Ethel and Robin Weems were giving to celebrate their tenth anniversary. It was a Thursday, and I had to work late helping put the Market Letter to bed — the niche MacNaughton had rightly prophesied I might yet fill. Clients I had served in my broker days still frequently called, insisting on seeing me, but they were barred from the back room in which, surrounded by an accumulating mulch of analytical material, I lucubrated my weekly Letters and my individual stock opinions. The Letters were often conscientious rehashes of other investment-house advisories drafted by people better able than I to sustain the continual excitement of truths like, "The line's participation in a generally upward economy as reflected in an 11.4% increase in piggyback freight . . ." I was fascinated by the computer we used for these precision calculations, and would sometimes feed into it data on human relations supposedly not subject to such arithmetical finesse. I once fed it some loosely gathered statistics bearing on the sexual relations and then asked it the question, "Are women more trouble than they're worth, and how much?" The answer came out, "Yes — 11%." I let Naughty volunteer some calibrated aggravations of her own, by way of rebuttal, on the basis of which the machine said men are 14% more trouble than they're worth. I combined these figures into a master question asking whether life was worth living, and it refused to answer, like the television network Vote Projection Indicators on election nights when it is still too early to tell. One is always pleased to see machinery behaving coyly.

The only one who ever came into my "library" was Fido Harrison, the friend of my nauseous period, and now my immediate superior, delegated by MacNaughton to keep a sharp eye specifically on my individual stock opinions, which were supposed to be scrupulous representations of what had been decided at the regular midweek office conference. We tended to nibble on one another with long teeth. We became sort of distant intimates, if I may so describe the mutual wariness with which Fido and I went through the pavane of collaboration. He scrutinized my copy every Thursday afternoon, preparatory to my drafting the final version mimeographed and mailed out Friday, for weekend consumption by clients. I was supposed to poke my head into the big room at hourly intervals or so, to keep abreast of the market I was analyzing, but there was still too much danger of the customers in the bleachers there including some erstwhile recipient of my counsel. I would scuttle out to lunch with my face averted, and even then sometimes found myself being pursued up an alley by a small investor, if not always a widow, wanting a word with me. Sometimes when I knew there was somebody out there to be avoided I would slip out through a window in the men's room onto a small court leading to a convenient side street. I was once chased all the way home by a retired gentleman whose life savings had apparently been spindled, stapled and mutilated in an electronic-component issue I had recommended. As I hurried home through the winter dusk to a supper of lettuce leaves and grapefruit sections, I thought I would like to be in another line of work even though I had found a tolerable niche in this one.

On the afternoon of the Thursday in question, I was writing a letter of application for a job as a salesman when Fido Harrison walked in, his leather heels clicking in Prussian fashion on the floorboards. I kept a bottle in my desk from which we usually poured a nip into paper cups at about this hour. Sipping his, he circled my typewriter to try to get a look at what was in it. To divert him I handed him a stock opinion I had just composed:

INTER-AMERICAN BANANA CORPORATION. This recently revamped import firm has streamlined its entire executive structure, resulting in qualified men for key posts. In July the marketing division will initiate an advanced booking program aimed at minimizing distress sales of excess and rotten fruit. Other triumphs will be introduction of new banana species which are resistant to plant disease and windstorm, and diversification into promising new fields such as freeze-dried foods. Dividend: 0.02%. OPINION: Recommended for sophisticated portfolios able to absorb risk speculations for long-term capital appreciation.

"We decided at the board meeting *not* to recommend it," Fido said, laying the paper back on my desk.

"We did?"

"Yes, don't you remember? Mr. MacNaughton said it was too much a risk even to write up as a risk stock, and Blair generally agrees on those next-to-nil yields."

Oh, darkies, how my heart grows weary! In my Market Letter I was saying that "despite the recent plunge of 15 points in the Dow-Jones Industrial Average, it has not penetrated the December reaction low of 557.45, regarded as the danger signal. It hovers a whisker above that, and our forecast is that it will hold, that there will be a rally sparked by the return of the institutional funds to the trading scene, and that the present bull market will then resume its long upward climb."

"That's interesting," Fido said, laying that down too. "Because the December reaction low was penetrated twenty minutes ago."

"No kidding."

"There's a selloff going on right now that's good for a nosedive of at least another twenty points, and another fifteen-billion-dollar paper loss. The bull market is over. This is a pool of blood."

"Well, then, let me just . . ." I said, picking up a pencil to make a few last-minute changes in the analysis.

It was close to nine o'clock when I arrived, unbathed, unshaven, and out of sorts at the Weemses' open house. Robin and Ethel were old-house snobs. This was a hundred-and-seventy-year-old farmhouse with the original beams and floors, and, of course, the original Formica kitchen-tops, electric broiler and steel-wool insulation, to say nothing of an intercom system that must also have given the original occupants many hours of pleasure and convenience. News of the War of 1812 must have been exchanged over it, threats of Indian raids communicated swiftly from room to room by means of it.

The Weemses were in the thick of a war themselves, the sex revolution. Robin was on leave from the Wilton College faculty in order to conduct, with Ethel, some researches on the physiology of sex. They took up where Kinsey left off. Together they measured the somatic changes — respiratory, circulatory, epidermal — characteristic of the erotic experience, with the laboratory instruments necessary to record these phenomena affixed to the participating subjects. To find volunteers willing, to say nothing of able, to lock successfully in amatory combat with all this investigatory gear lashed to their members would seem a feat in itself, but there was evidently no lack of them. They were said in some cases to be recruited from the Weemses' circle of acquaintances, and speculation was rife who they might be. Robin had already to his credit one of the manuals in which Naughty was engrossed, and it had been chiefly her interest in the subject that had been responsible for the progress of our friendship with the Weemses. I had paged through it myself, and it seemed good of its sort, suggested by such chapter headings as: "Taboo and Fetish," "Precoital Play," "The Afterglow," and the like. It was hard to imagine Robin and Ethel themselves engaged in the rollicking act on which they were authorities, but then the physical conjunction of any two people, not including oneself, is always inherently grotesque. Robin was a thin pale man who was always nervously pinching his lips together between his thumb and forefinger, as though in fear of saying something not corroborated by scientific evidence. Ethel was much the sturdier, but without sex appeal, though that is of course no gauge of erotic capacity. That a woman isn't appetizing doesn't mean she isn't hungry. Her brand was certainly all over Robin. His flannel shirts and hairy neckties echoed the forthright fabrics with which she herself dressed, and with which she decorated the house. The same "earthy" tastes characterized the table fare: red meat and nuts, home-baked bread, fruits and cheeses. Asked once what he had had for dinner at the Weemses', a local wit had replied, "Provisions." For all her militant tastes and positive temperament, there was a streak of something vaguely irresolute and mixed-up about Ethel. As I trudged up the porch stairs, dragging my briefcase, I hoped I would not be arbitrarily handed a glass of red wine for a cocktail, along with a slab of that certain robust cheese to which the Weemses were partial, and that I called a prehistoric munster.

The house was jammed. I shot a look around the living room to make certain Naughty was present and happy. She was. She interrupted a dance she was doing for a group of onlookers to come kiss me and say she had two surprises for me. One was that she was going to work for Ethel and Robin as a volunteer, tabulating and collating profile studies of the entwined subjects, and performing other chores of a secretarial nature. I was delighted because of the pleasure she herself took in the prospect of doing something worthwhile. The second surprise she would let me discover for myself. She plucked an old-fashioned from a passing tray for me and, taking me by the elbow with a charming gesture of turning me loose, said, "Look around."

Sipping, I took in the crowd of standing guests. The room was a caldron of conversation, in which a word caught here or there, at best a phrase, was like a bubble bursting on the surface, its identity instantly lost in the general din. My eye was drawn, as it inevitably was here, to an enormous tapestry dominating one end of the living room. The scene was one of medieval warfare, perhaps the Battle of Hastings. The visual bedlam depicted merged with the auditory one set up by the guests, as though the babble assailing one's ears were the indistinguishable cries of the armored hordes locked in mortal combat. From these, from the clashing spears and plunging steeds, a small figure seemed to detach itself, anachronistically clutching a cocktail glass, wearing oatmeal tweeds illusorily woven into the arras, to shift its weight a moment and execute a gesture before being again swallowed up in the confusion of military tumult. Memory offered a teasing clue to one person I knew who could so completely vanish into any environment, certainly be integrated with a tapestry against which he leant. At that moment the figure managed a slightly more successful extrication of itself from the fabric and came forward, hand extended. I recognized Uncle Hamilton.

"I figured it was high time I," he said, wringing my hand.

"It's good to see you, Uncle Ham," I said, greeting him with one of the rare contractions of his name in order to conceal my vexation at the very sight of him. My mother was now dead, and apart from the still unmarried Benny I was the only relative he had left, so the danger of being stuck with him as a house guest was a clear and present one.

I fired a look over my shoulder in Naughty's direction. She was still dancing for the circle of which she was center. She wet a finger and touched it to her hip, like one testing a hot iron. She had phoned Ethel, on my uncle's turning up that afternoon with no warning, to make sure it was O.K. to bring him along. There was no doubt of that once the extent of his means had been established, for financial support for learned projects is hard to come by. College support was only temporary, except for the equipment its science laboratory had supplied, and one of Naughty's duties would eventually be to throw into high gear the drive on private philan-thropists and special foundations. My uncle had written us a letter some weeks before vaguely "promising" to show up without supplying any specific facts about the time and nature of his arrival. It was his way just to "get in the car and mosey on down," as though there were some conceivable element of relaxation in never know-ing when he might turn up.

"I didn't want you to go to any," he said, smiling into his glass.

Today I was too busy admiring his hair to listen to what he was talking about, or I should say I was too busy worrying about my own. It very much looked as though I was going to lose it, and with it the hope that I might in this regard have taken after my mother's side of the family, with their luxuriant and long-lasting mops. Uncle

Hamilton's was gray now, as gray as his handlebar mustache, but it was still all there. It lay in thick undulations from his brow to the back of his neck, and even up around his ears — small wrinkled ears associated in childhood with the dried apricots he fished from his pockets as a treat, for he was passionately devoted to dehydrated fruit. He nibbled it in the movies and before the television set, an instrument that now enables people like him to live their lives over again in the form of old films. I gazed in envy at his thatch as he talked about that, muttering something about an actress of a few decades back who was said to have settled in this part of the country. He even looked about in hopes of finding her here. Neither of us was paying any attention to the other now. I was as abstracted as he, thinking about my thinning hair and a possibly related affliction, itching scalp.

I often awoke to find I had been scratching myself furiously in my sleep, in the same way that hay fever victims (of which I am also one) will awaken to find themselves rubbing their inflamed eyes. The combined prurience, during the pollen season, can be quite something. But I am not worried about scratching my eyes out, only my hair. In those days I wore a tweed cap to bed, and later also a pair of mittens, as precautionary measures. Neither a barber I first consulted nor a doctor could do me any good. They both told me it was a nervous condition, brought on by tension or worry, or some emotional conflict capable of being reflected in psychosomatic disturbance. Was anything worrying me? Nothing — except losing my hair, which was falling out by the pound. Another vicious circle, since in that case the fear of losing it caused the itch that made me claw half of it away in the frenzies in which I came to, it being no exaggeration to call them that. I would hold up sad combfuls for Naughty to see, casting her looks of such mute despair that she would have to leave the room with averted face, for another of those fits of hysterical laughter that we are told to equate with sympathetic tears. I could restrain myself when I was awake but not when I was unconscious; hence the motoring cap (later a beret) intended as a protection against this involuntary reflex. It was far from foolproof as it usually came off at some stage of the night — as was sometimes the case with the mittens, or perhaps garden gloves, with which I consigned myself to the sandman. It lay overturned on my pillow beside my snoring head once when, toward dawn, I opened my eyes to find Naughty gazing at me, the bed rocking with her laughter. My mittened hands were folded on my breast in the accepted mortuary pose. I naturally cut my nails to the quick.

That Uncle Hamilton had no one to leave his money to any more than his hair was swiftly borne in on the Weemses, who, once he had come firmly into focus as a man to be tapped for moola, spent the rest of the evening buttering him up in a way everyone knew to be brazen but him. He was still with us after three days, three weeks. We gave him the single downstairs bedroom, potentially a maid's room, which he was tickled to death to have because of its proximity to the television set, to which he remained glued till the small hours watching old movies. He slept till noon and then often as not strolled down to Main Street for a matinee. So that he was not really underfoot in the worst sense of that term. And there remained the hope that he might yet justify his existence by contributing to the research project into which Naughty now passionately flung herself.

The enterprise had linked up with a national organization called Sanity, Inc., a federation of projects aimed at promoting sexual adjustment. Applications for grants from foundations being entangled in the customary red tape, there remained for the moment only public solicitation, and I became a Block Captain for the fall fundraising drive. Pressed for information about the nature of the cause by people whose doorbells I rang, I would speak ambiguously about mental health, hoping it would be confused with Mental Health as an established collecting organization sufficiently for the occupants of the house to kick in a few bucks. Ten houses netted me only two dollars and a half — two one-dollar gifts and one fifty-cent piece, reluctantly thrust through the door by an irascible woman with red hair. The next door was opened after a very long delay by a man I could hear clumping down the stairs as he called out something rather disgruntled to someone else. He was in a bathrobe, under which bare feet were visible, and his hair was rumpled.

"What's this outfit trying to do?" he asked in a gruff voice.

"We demand a full sex life for everybody," I said.

"You get me out of the sack to tell me that?" he said, and slammed the door.

After one or two other wretched attempts, I stuffed my worker's kit with bills from my own wallet and turned it in. Out of loyalty to Naughty, however, I didn't want to give up, and so I asked to be switched to Special Gifts, that part of the drive, delegated to blue-ribbon workers, devoted to hitting prospects with real money — like the knucklehead under my own roof. Friends active in the Red Cross and the Symphony Orchestra let us raid their files for prospects in this category. I was assigned five, and given a "prospect card" for each.

One was a man named Beasley, who was said to have amassed millions in the grain market. Telephone attempts to make an appointment being fruitless, I set out to beard him one evening in his home without one. He lived in baronial splendor in a mansion lost in acreage encircled by a high cheval-de-frise. A double gate was closed but not locked, so I pushed it open and started on foot up the drive, swinging my arms doughtily to generate courage. A full moon lighted my way. It took me five minutes to reach the house, which was dark except for a scattered light or two burning in its remote depths. I walked up the stone stairs to the porch and rang the bell.

At first nothing happened. Then a series of responses in a low key began to gather inside, almost inaudible at first but building steadily in intensity, as though under the hand of a skilled theatrical director. A light went on in the vestibule, but no one appeared at the door. Instead an upper window slid open and a voice said, "Who is it? Who's there?"

It came from so far up that I had to leave the porch and walk twenty paces back into the drive to see where it did. It had been an elderly voice, of a sex not yet entirely clear. Nor was the light in the window bright enough to tell from that distance whether the head thrust out of it, like a cuckoo out of a clock, was that of a man or a woman. A tasseled nightcap seemed to crown it.

"Who are you?" It was a man.

"Who I am makes no difference," I yelled modestly upward between cupped hands. "Sanity, Incorporated —"

"Just a minute!"

The figure receded without wholly vanishing. It could be dimly discerned in the background, gesticulating and calling to others in the house. There was a round of muffled exchanges within that took possibly three or four minutes. From the tone they seemed like rapid urgent consultations among disturbed inhabitants as to what course of action to pursue in face of the doorbell's having been rung at that hour, perhaps nine thirty. The opened window was at the top of a circular tower to the left of the main entrance. The tower, a silolike protuberance possibly symbolizing the owner's interest in wheat futures, had two other windows in it, set so as to suggest a spiral staircase running from top to bottom. Suddenly they all three sprang alight, and there were faces at all of them. It was, indeed, like three-level stage dramaturgy.

"What do you want?" someone called down.

"Money!"

Now the entire premises blazed with light, including landscape illumination in the full glare of which I myself suddenly stood. Floodlights on every hand poured radiance on me. The front door at last opened and a large dog streaked across the porch. Simultaneously a loud crunch on the gravel driveway signaled the arrival of a police car, into the back of which I gratefully scrambled with the dog snapping at my heels.

Praise for the speed with which cruising squad cars

reached the scenes of threatened robberies was the first order of business, eulogies in which I wholeheartedly joined the jumble of agitated residents gathering on the drive, all rather elderly, and motley in the sense that one or two wore nightgowns.

I was on my way to the station house for booking before I thought of the prospect cards with which to prove I was soliciting funds, not stealing them. The cops drew to the curb to examine these after I had located them in one of my pockets. Together with other identification they managed to establish my innocence, and the cops opened the door of the car to let me go, with the warning not to let anything of this sort happen again.

I almost wished the dog had managed to sink his teeth into my shins. A bloody nephew would have driven home to the obtuse Hamilton how desperate the plight of Sanity, Inc., really was. But the story I unfolded, together with my general state and what Naughty was able to contribute, did have enough propaganda value to make him finally sit up and take some notice.

"We're a local chapter of the national organization," Naughty hammered home to him, refusing to let him return to his television set until he had heard her out, and speaking slowly and with great passion. "Anything we raise we can earmark for the research project we're working on. I of course work for nothing, as a volunteer, but the project itself needs money. To keep going for a year we need ten thousand dollars."

"Ten thousand," he said, nodding slowly, and apparently unfazed by the sum. "I'll send you a check as soon as I."

It was clear from this and some subsequent mutterings that he meant as soon as he got back home. But when would that be? The problem of getting rid of him became doubly urgent. We racked our brains for devices to hasten that day. We hinted of other guests soon to arrive, of trips we ourselves contemplated, even going so far as to suggest that we might wish to visit him in Canada, a proposition not feasible until we had seen the last of him here. But nothing could dislodge him — until the obvious hit us like a ton of bricks.

He wanted to meet this retired actress, Laura Pribble, settled in a nearby house where she was rumored to spend the lonely nights watching reruns of *her* old movies — watching herself, that is, as a young girl. She had been washed up by the time I began attending movies, so I had no idea whom my uncle was talking about.

"I never look at television, Unc, so I know nothing about these old pictures people are always talking about," I said. "But was Laura Pribble a star?"

"Oh, no, more of a featured player, with a certain wry sad-funny something all her own. You'd rank her with —" Here he mentioned some actress of the moment I wasn't familiar with either. I promised I would scrounge around and dig up somebody who knew her.

The trail led to a friend connected with a local orphanage that happened to be Miss Pribble's pet charity. There was to be a benefit chamber music concert in the town library, followed by a reception and tea at which Miss Pribble would pour. I bought three tickets at twenty-five smackers apiece and took Unc.

It was raining cats and dogs, but the downpour made a pleasant sound on the rooftop as the fiddlers sawed away at Mozart. I sat with bowed head like a transported music lover, but actually drafting a suite of my own to be called *The Four Seasons*, of which the movement entitled "Summer," frankly autobiographical, would be a polonaise depicting the ravages of hay fever, in the course of which the musicians would be required to take snuff for the sake of verisimilitude. Other movements would be subtitled "A Broken Spring" and "A Nasty Fall." I was trying to work winter into the opus when the concert came to an end and we rose and filtered through a narrow doorway into a lounge where Laura Pribble, indeed, sat pouring tea. It was Mrs. de Shamble.

Stark, staring mad, I inched forward between my wife and my uncle toward the head of the great table laid out with gleaming silver and platters of cakes and cookies. I was glad to find this Jezebel manqué doing penance at

164

last in some cause of enduring social worth, though I had an uneasy suspicion that I would rake leaves at the local orphanage yet before being permitted to close my eyes in death.

"She was adopted herself, you see," a gaunt elderly woman was whispering to Uncle Hamilton behind me. "A foster child."

"That's very often the reason in back of things like."

So that was how it was. Anybody could pick her up now because nobody had as a child. That it, cats? I looked around for people I knew, but there were none. My wife vanished with her cup and I stood next. It was only at that moment I realized I could perfectly well have introduced Mrs. de Shamble as a former client of mine, but now it was unnecessary.

"Tea or coffee?"

"Coffee, please."

"Cream or sugar?"

"No, just black."

"Well. How are you?"

"Fine. And you?"

"Just fine. It was good of you to come."

"It's a good cause. May I present my uncle, Mr. Bonner of Canada. He's a great fan of yours. A great movie buff, but a particularly ardent devotee of yours."

"Well," she said, putting out her hand as I moved aside. "Any uncle of yours is an uncle of mine."

She was "on," smiling the smile and darting the

glances that, I could see now, must have been the raw materials of her brief vogue. The conscious manipulation of expression would suddenly lapse and she would draw back into herself. This hovering threat of preoccupation is characteristic of egotistical natures, and I remembered it from my brief encounter with her, at the same time realizing how it might make for the style of "wistful" comedy for which she was apparently remembered. The frazzled vanity to which I had fallen momentary victim was impossible to hide beneath the guise of modesty with which she pretended to hear out my uncle's torrent of praise. She lowered her eyes to the table and made some adjustments among the cups and silver, but she was eating it up. Never articulate the best of times, Uncle Hamilton was now reduced to an incoherent pulp. He simpered like a schoolboy at his first dance as he jabbered compliments in splintered English. They were still tumbling forth when, rather cravenly, I left, mumbling some excuse in his tradition. I strode toward my wife, laughing as I stirred my coffee, black though it was.

"Well, this is rich! She's a customer of ours and nobody at the office knew who she was behind the married name she goes by. She's Mrs. de Shamble. Or they never told me. So she can't have all that following," I said, dropping my voice to a discreet whisper.

"I suppose you'd say she's special," Naughty said,

nodding. We adopted that exaggerated show of interest in one another's remarks that couples often affect in public conversation. I returned her smile with that polite, keeping-the-conversational-ball-rolling expression that always makes me howl when I see other married people up to it.

"She's like a Stutz Bearcat would be to a car buff, say. She probably uses her private name so it'll get around that she wants to be left alone. No better way to keep in the public eye. Look at this turnout."

"We must try to catch one of her movies."

"Soon as we can call our lives our own again. She was apparently an urchin type back then, but still she does look young for — what? Pushing forty would you say?"

"She's not on the sunny side of that any longer. She's had her face lifted. You can tell. Here comes Unc."

He shuffled up and took his place between us. A deep flush suffused his face, which even seemed to alter the color of his mustache. The teacup trembled on its saucer as he looked at the floor, pinching his nose. He shook his head, not believing his luck.

"Never in my wildest. That'll certainly give me something to. And we must all make most generous."

"Of course," I said. "It's another good cause, of so many the world is full of. We can all support them far, far better than we do. Especially those of us with means."

The evening was a success in its immediate objective at least. We had no more than begun to drive away in the drumming rain, after the most fleeting goodbyes to the besieged Mrs. de Shamble, than Unc began to mumble about going home. A happy stay had been triumphantly topped with a plum of which he had never dreamed, and he was content to return to his own beloved pasturage and his own fireside, there to let these events settle into place among his cherished memories.

It was two days later that we saw his back, and two weeks more when we heard from him by mail. It was a long, grateful bread-and-butter letter, from which, as Naughty unfolded it, fluttered a check for ten dollars for Sanity, Inc. There were hints that he had also made a substantial contribution to "your splendid orphanage."

"Well, don't be discouraged," I told her. "I've only just begun to raise money. Because do you know what? I'm going to hit Mrs. de Shamble."

eight

A MONTH LATER I had still not made good on these brave words I'm afraid. I was torn, as we say, among a variety of loyalties in the mental debate now raging with myself over whether actually to try nailing Mrs. de Shamble for Sanity, Inc.

First was my loyalty to Naughty, who had thrown herself into a research project aimed, after all, at sexual fulfillment in marriage — a cause as worthy, in its way, as the fruits of illegitimate unions. But fidelity to her also forbade further exposure to the locally booming Mrs. de Shamble (though this motive was hard to disentangle from the cowardice that made me shrink from such a reunion in any case). Loyalty to Uncle Hamilton called for some attempt to ascertain whether he had really given more to Mrs. de Shamble's charity than to ours, a suspicion that certainly had him in our bad books now. He deserved to have his name cleared if there were no basis for it. Lastly, there was loyalty to myself, calling for every effort to keep myself out of her nefarious clutches, as old Unc would have said in the large locutions of his day (in which tradition I must be counted, I supposed, an immitigable blatherskite).

I stalled by telling myself that she might not be in the monetary echelon involved — the Special Gifts category to which I had graduated. Of course I had access to her portfolio, now handled by a young man named Baker. It took only the most cursory glance to see that it had enormously increased in value since the days when I had overseen it. She was worth at least two hundred and fifty thou in stocks and bonds alone. Who knew what other sources of wealth or income she had? Land, rents from Hollywood properties, savings accounts. Yes, she belonged in Special Gifts. I reluctantly made out a prospect card for her and put it away in my desk.

The next several days were spent in a resumption of my debate, now more harrowing than ever. My stewing came to an abrupt end when Naughty greeted me at the door one evening with some welcome news. Robin Weems had telephoned to say that the university had voted to appropriate the ten thousand dollars necessary for at least one more year of the project. It was while we were drinking to this windfall that Naughty announced another. The equipment used for the research was kept in special university quarters where the experiments were conducted, but she had permission to have it in the house for a period of two weeks, an interval when Mrs.

Munkey would be away on vacation and thus not have her curiosity aroused by all the machinery ranged round the bed. Thus we could contribute to the data being compiled for interpretation by scholars a profile study of our own cohabitation.

"I hope you don't mind?" she said.

"Of course not."

"This is so much more private than the university lab. Not that there are any attendants or anything there. The machinery records everything and computers tabulate it. It's all automatic except for the human element. But this way, in the home, it'll be under normal conditions."

"I'm rarin' to go."

I found the experience stimulating rather than otherwise. Except that dressing for bed took ten times what undressing for it had. There were basically four pieces of equipment involved in these studies.

First was a small portable console containing appliances of an electrocardiographic type, plus a recorder capable of converting the graph-paper chart into a series of high-pitched beeps which could be stored in a memory bank for later interpretation by a computer. They were like electronic mating cries that were the end-product of conjunction, rather than its cause or preliminary, besides being conveniently emitted for one by another labor-saving device. The reading itself could be more or less thought of as a cardiogram taken *en extase*, with the latter feature affording larger diagnostic use in the event of a diaphragmatic infarction or other form of heart attack, in turn of unsuspected value to hospitals suffering from a shortage of patients. Leading from the machine were four wires ending in electrodes, which the principals lashed to their arms and legs.

Next was an instrument for recording alterations in blood pressure, for which each wrapped a band around his left arm, like that used with the ordinary sphygmomanometer. A broader version went around our chests, for registering respiratory changes in intercourse which were the province of still a third contrivance, of which the basic feature was a bellows set in motion by the flip of a switch. Already half mummified, and breathing heavily from the exertions entailed in winding ourselves in these cerements, we tackled the fourth and last device, a relatively simple one designed to record epithelial changes. The palm of one hand was coated with kaolin paste, and with it one grasped a fifth electrode. Now we were ready.

Abandoning oneself to erotic pleasure is sometimes difficult without encumbrances. I felt like someone about to swim the English Channel, then dive back into it in order to demonstrate feats of survival underwater, and finally to be bundled into a space capsule for transmission into orbit. There were Naughty's normal inhibi-

tions, such as we were in part trying to compile construc-
tive data on, and they were hardly ameliorated because
we were in a sense more fully clothed than usual. To be
ravished in a thicket of tubing, to the accompaniment of
throbbing machinery, quivering needles and digital beeps
offers hazards enough to a person of normal sensitivity. It
was obvious that even more precoital play than advised by
Robin Weems in his marriage manual was necessary
(assuming one could find what he was looking for), and
preliminary relaxing before even that could be under-
taken. I had anticipated this by taking the remains of a
bottle of dinner wine upstairs, and as I approached the
bed, tripping over strands of rubber vinework, I felt like
some computer-age Dionysus, enacting a rite propelling
us onward into a future in which the machines would do
the actual screwing for us, and consciousness be refined
into some kind of abstract numerical bliss, through
which we would float eternally as through a heaven of
pure equation. Pi in the sky, don't you know. Meanwhile
we must make do with the gross organs and exuded dews
we wished to supersede.

"So you're the new personnel manager," I said, ogling
her. "I trust you have a little opening for me."

To shock without offending had been from the first
the keynote of my re-education of Naughty. We were
breaking the ice. This would turn out to be a fine revel

yet, our very trappings and caparisons part of the lark, provided we were not electrocuted in the process. "Now I would like to introduce an upright member, one of long standing, who is a firm candidate for congress," I said, and pitched forward on top of her.

The bed was like a platter of noodles. It was a tangle of wires and cables such as marks a power failure after a violent windstorm. And a power failure threatened here as I saw Naughty languidly reach out to flip a few switches, closing her eyes after this gesture of imperial indolence. The hum of machinery commenced. Mercury rose in tubes, needles fluttered. There was a muffled clatter like that of a teletype machine, making me suspect we might be going out on the A.P. wire, if not on some closed circuit television. The bellows began to breathe beside me, like a disconnected lung. These remained the only action in the room.

"I'm tired," I said. "I've been taking my pleasure in snatches."

"Maybe if you recited some poetry."

I am one of those men who think poets should write like Tennyson and Browning, though close examination will reveal that we don't read Tennyson and Browning either. It's all very discouraging. However, I had just composed a love sonnet, which I now murmured into her ear, brushing aside a lock of hair and some cables to do so:

> A *husband named Duncan MacPhyfe*
> *Had to keep reassuring his wife;*
> *At the peak of his throes*
> *He would always cry, "Rose,*
> *I'm having the time of my life!"*

The machinery began to throb with an account of impotent hilarity. The very bed shook beneath us. The band for respiratory elevations encircling my chest became tumescent, threatening to strangle me like a boa constrictor. I was going to look good on the records. This in itself encouraged me. "Something seems to be caught around my — ah, there, it's loose," I said, and after a little beating around the bush, so to speak, I managed to find what I was looking for, and sank gratefully into it.

The telephone rang. I was expecting an important call from a man named Farber, a valuable source of information to me on special situation stocks. There was one in particular on which I had to have the data tonight, for a report due next morning, which he had promised to get to me without fail.

"Excuse me, darling," I said, taking it on the bedside extension, without dismounting her, as it seemed to me that would have been crude. I knew that everything was useful as to the data being collected here: that records of "interruptions" were also desired wherever obtainable, to chart relative susceptibilities to distractions while approaching *la mort douce,* as the French call sexual rapture.

"Hello?"

"This is Miss Lynd, Mr. Farber's secretary?" said a throaty feminine voice I knew very well, and whose possessor I had often tried to visualize from the sound of it. I had always found it extremely seductive over the telephone.

"Yes," I said, my pulse quickening. Out of the tail of my eye I could see the cardiovascular needle scribbling away furiously on the graph paper, while on my other side the artificial lung began to luff.

"He's at home with a cold, trying to catch up on some stuff, and I'm working late at the office. He just remembered he wanted to get these figures to you, and called me to get them out. They're the figures on Consolidated Potash?"

"Oh, yes. Could you hold the wire a minute while I get a pencil and paper?"

"Certainly."

I wedged the phone against my shoulder, in the manner of busy executives everywhere, while I fished for these objects on the nightstand with my free hand.

"O.K. Shoot. Now, do you have the pre-tax earnings for the year?" I asked, my voice hoarse with passion.

"Yes. Nine million five hundred and thirty-seven thousand dollars, or a dollar twenty-two cents a share. Of that, sixty-five cents a share was paid out in dividends, of which seventy per cent is taxable while thirty per cent constitutes a return of capital and is not subject to federal income tax as ordinary dividend income."

I jotted these figures down as best I could under existing hazards, not the least of which was, as I say, a voice so intimate and suggestive as to leave by no means certain that the interruption would not have to await an interruption of its own. The lung was panting ominously. It was touch and go. I found it really quite difficult to control myself. At last it was clear that the tide of excitements could not be stemmed, and I said, "Hold the phone," again and quickly dropped it.

The preordained paroxysms gathered, in the course of which I seemed to feel Naughty, too, fluttering like a hare in my arms. As soon as I could I picked up the phone again and said, "Sorry to keep you waiting. I think I have all the dope now except the earnings estimate for next year."

"A dollar sixty-two a share. Were you running upstairs?"

"Yes. Well, thank you very much. And thank Mr. Farber too, and tell him I hope his cold is better. Goodbye."

We were a long time coming down out of the clouds, and Naughty was a longer time collecting and collating her data after that. I had my own homework to do, namely the report on the stock issue, so that we were separately occupied most of the rest of the evening.

When I had finished typing out a rough draft I went back upstairs, to find Naughty stretched out in the bathtub. She lay back with her eyes closed, letting the washcloth float away from her. When she opened her eyes it was to gaze at the wall ahead and say with the voice of sinister calm: "You're awful."

"Wanna bet?" I answered good-naturedly.

"A woman hates to wake up and find she's married to a moron."

"I have my limitations."

"No you don't. That's just the thing. I remember how you looked at me that time we got married. You *ogled* me. Gave me the *eye* as I came down the aisle. Think of it. And I noticed you at Pixie Dinkle's wedding the other day. *You don't kiss a bride on the mouth*. You kiss her on the cheek. When you stand in line at a wedding you always look like a bum in a soup kitchen. And telling somebody to hold the phone while you —" She shook her head, as though words failed her.

"That data was as important to me as what we were collecting was to you. We're both in research. It's our bread and butter."

"You have no pride. You're an absolute and utter buffoon."

"You knew what I was when you married me."

"You might have spared me the proof."

All this blew over as quickly as it came up, of course.

A spell of bad weather. A lowering sky that will clear, the ebb of a tide that will again flow. Meanwhile human life goes on as it always has, and simply for what it is: a zoo in a jungle. I got out my clarinet and played it a good deal, usually when I was home alone and could join the best orchestras, via either phonograph or radio, caterwauling away to my heart's content in the manner that always wormed me of the thoughts that precipitated such melancholy binges — such as the notion that this life is a zoo in a jungle. What a terrible thing to have to believe!

A child was born of the profile study, that was the main thing. It was all that mattered. Yes, it was clear some fresh construction must be put on the desire for shellfish and the many other foods for which lusts were now expressed at all hours, and for which one happily dressed to forage in the middle of the night. "I'm going to have a child," she brought out one evening.

"Oh, Naughty, what'll we do?" I pretended I had her pregnant. Knocked up! In one unholy hell of a jam. "I'll have to quit school, it'll kill my mother," I said, stumbling blindly across the room. "We'll have to get married," and buried my face in my hands.

She laughed as she watched me from the chair in which she sat hugging her drawn-up legs, her cheek resting on her knees. "Will the scandal kill her?" she said, egging me on. She liked to feed me straight lines when she was really in the mood for horsing around. I was tickled to death for my part, and during this period knocked myself out to keep an expectant mother amused, in a manner that also let the romantic in me pour out of every crevice. "Think I'm going to take the rap for this? Me, who always played the field?" I circled the room with a fag hanging from my lip, telling her I was strictly a rolling stone, that I had changed my mind about being the fall guy for anything she happened to have in the oven. No broad was going to slip a halter around my neck that easy. "How they'd laugh at the poolroom to see old Joe wheeling a perambulator down the street because some cookie put the finger on him. How they'd laugh, it could be any one of them's kid."

We sometimes got a little tight together after dinner, and I would steer her toward the bedroom to give proof of my love yet again. I carved our initials on her ripening tummy, that is painted them on with the stopper from the iodine bottle. I pasted pretty little decals on her bosom bells, put a flower in her crotch. "Defile me," she would say. "Woman is clay longing to become mire. Victor Hugo." Her capacity for ribaldry was complete now, that was the thing. She had grown. Her gusto more than made up for those depressed and unresponsive spells earlier on. She would lie rolling her head from side to side in utter abandon. "Down from the waist we are all centaurs. Shakespeare."

The question of names came up, and we spent the usual happy hours mulling over them together — one of the pleasures of expectant parents. I said that for a boy I had always liked Hamilton, to which she cottoned too because there was some precedent for it in her family as well as mine. Margaret was our choice for a girl.

One night a few days after these things were settled, I again awoke to find myself being steadily stared at. Naughty was sitting on my bed in her nightgown, her brown hair in its plump nocturnal braid. Her hands were folded in her lap. I had again the uneasy sensation that it was her expression that had awakened me, this time an expression of the most intense scrutiny.

"You really would have gone through with it, wouldn't you?" she said.

"What?"

"Ham Sandwich. That's what he would have become. I only tumbled to it just now. I couldn't sleep, and I imagined myself calling to him, in the yard, in the nursery. But you knew all along, and you could have, would have, gone through with it. It was probably even why you suggested it. I can't even in my heart put that past you. You would have done that to your own flesh and blood. You'd better get up. This is serious."

I threw the covers back and got into my robe. She had risen and was pacing the floor in bare feet, wringing her hands.

"I'd have put a stop to it in time, I'm sure," I said.

"You're *sure!* You mean you're not sure? That's what the term means. That there's an element of doubt. He'd sell his own grandmother for a gag, they always said. Now it turns out he'd sell his own child. Is there no end to your depravity? I can't call it sickness. That excuses too many things. You know the difference between right and wrong. I would like to know, quite simply. Are you absolutely and completely hopeless?"

"This isn't fair. It might be a girl, you know."

"So you're only fifty per cent hopeless. Is that it? And for God's sake take off that ridiculous cap! *Let* your hair fall out. It might make you *look* a little more mature at least, and give you something to live up to."

I removed the motoring cap and also my gloves, with a glance into the mirror, as though to remind myself, "This, too, will pass." I laid the cap, overturned, on the bureau, and dropped the gloves into it, like a caller leaving his duds in the hall.

"I just wanted to see how long before you tumbled. A sort of game I was playing. I would have called it off in time. I have every confidence in that," I said, my voice thick with fear.

"You have every confidence in that?" She stood with arms akimbo, her feet planted apart, appraising me.

"Yes. Strong as the temptation would be, to a man of my temperament. I would have resisted it."

"When?"

"In the nick of time."

"When is that? The week before the christening? The night before? On our actual way to church, out of sheer horror of the consequences? Not having the guts to go through with it at the last minute?"

"Oh, I'd have the guts to go through with it all right."

"Good! That makes me feel better. That cheers me enormously about you, makes us all proud of you."

She continued evaluating me, while I gazed upward at the ceiling in an honest attempt to analyze the factors we were dealing with here, factors of some subtlety and complexity when it came to that. She herself seemed to be trying to salvage the maximum in dignity from the pieces we were trying to pick up and put together again, as so often before.

"Would something like conscience have intervened at the last moment, do you suppose, and made you do the sensible thing? The *decent* thing?"

"I should imagine so. Some essential decency, or probity. Call it what you will. It's hard for me to think I would let a thing like that ride indefinitely. Or just drift until it was too late."

"But we'll never know. Is that it? Well, *tell* me. Speak up. I'm groping for some reassurance about the man I married, and I'm also trying to help you retain some vestige of self-respect, assuming you're in the market for it. You don't seem to know yourself what you were up to, or what you had in mind exactly."

"Yes, I do. I had a deadline."

"What was it?"

"Three months," I said, arbitrarily picking a number not, in fact, settled on with any degree of certainty at all.

"Three months from when? From the time we decided on the name, or before the child was born? Or when I was three months gone?"

"Three months before he would be born. Or she, as I must keep reminding you."

"Meanwhile you could secretly amuse yourself thinking of the Ham Sandwich in my stomach. Not carrying it under my heart, as we sentimentally think, but in Mummy's tummy. Here!" And she vehemently smacked her middle with a palm.

"That's not true. Absolutely not true at all. And I wouldn't have gone down to the wire with it, as I keep telling you. What kind of person do you think I am?"

"That's what we're trying to find out, isn't it? That's what I wonder, and," she added, dropping her voice, "must apparently go on wondering to the end of my days, judging from your own muddleheaded confusion about exactly what you were up to in all this nonsense. I will never know whether you would have resisted the temptation, which, as you say, must have been overpowering to a man of your mental — makeup. I'm not angry, Joe, just sad. And a little hurt." She now stood gazing at me with such an air of wounded innocence, and so close to me, close enough to smell, that my senses swam and I wanted to reach out my hand as a sort of piece feeler, laying it upon her ripening breast as I drew her closer to me with the other arm. "I'll never know the man I'm married to. Is that it? We don't know whom we live with. We are permitted to guess, but we will never know."

We still hadn't decided on a name by the time the child was born, which happened rather suddenly.

I had mown an ejaculation into the high grass in the back yard, and was contemplating it a moment before expunging it with the power cutter, on the Sunday of the week Naughty was to enter the hospital to have the baby by induced labor. I had on canvas garden gloves, which I had first taken the precaution of stepping on to mash any spiders lurking in the fingers, and the surgical mask I always wear when I cut the lawn to sift out the pollen, dust and bugs thrashed from the grass by the mower, which can be unbearable to a hay fever sufferer. I had cut a few swaths, leaving the expletive untouched for the moment, when I became aware of Naughty gesticulating from an upper window. When I walked over and squinted inquiringly upward she said, "I think they're starting."

"What are?"

"The pains."

I hurriedly deleted the ribaldry, plowing a scribble through it with the mower, and, throwing off the surgical mask like a catcher going after a high one, and discarding the gloves in the garage, galloped through the kitchen door into the house.

"Dr. Mockridge said Wednesday. He said he was going to induce labor," I said, hurling a suitcase onto the bed. Claims that he would do so always made him sound like a strike negotiator able to persuade union czars to agree to terms against which they had been hitherto adamant. "That even the last of the week should be plenty of time."

"Well, it isn't. Or I don't think so," Naughty said. "Anyway I don't want to take any chances."

"Now, where are these pains? Can you tell exactly where they seem to be?"

"Oh, for Christ's sake! Let's get packed and out of here."

"Don't worry, baby, I'll have you at the hospital in ten minutes, and in ten more lying in bed wondering what the rush was all about."

Which was exactly what happened. By the time Naughty was settled in her room there wasn't a twinge to be felt. The pains had stopped. Nevertheless a nurse came in at regular intervals to thrust a hand under the bedclothes and look thoughtfully at the ceiling while she rummaged about. I had tried to telephone the doctor by this time, of course, but so far had succeeded only in getting the answering service. I now called again, with no better results. He hadn't checked in yet, but the voice at the other end was confident he would do so within the hour, to learn of this possible emergency.

Naughty was nervous and restless. She wanted distraction. She wanted me to talk to her, read to her, tell stories, anything, just to keep her mind diverted. I read a few anecdotes from a magazine I found in the floor lounge. Then, to keep her amused and relaxed, I reeled off some of the new additions to my collection. "Jasper and Suzanna Quonkle, Pearl Handel, Nan Tucket, Nina Knight, O. U. Mann, Mr. and Mrs. von Luciano, Carlos DiPloma, Lily Lipsake, Orville Banguish, Kunigunde Zweititz . . ."

Naughty began to laugh. Soon she was holding her sides. In the midst of this the nurse appeared with some medication, and she smiled as she went about her ministrations.

"Mrs. Yerball," I continued, "Mr. and Mrs. Bunsnatcher, Lester Poorcock, W. W. Tummy, Fracas W. Sostenuto, Mother Abelwhack, Lord and Lady Pishcredit . . ." By now the nurse was holding her sides and Naughty her stomach. "I think I may be going to . . ." she said, her face suddenly twisting into a grimace as she laughed. "Maybe you'd better take a look."

187

"All rightie, nightie," the nurse said, pulling the garment up, and feeling about with her hand again. "Just a minute," she said, and flew out of the room.

She returned instantly with another nurse, followed so closely by an orderly trundling a stretcher that he seemed to have bulldozed the two of them into the room before him. Naughty was loaded onto the stretcher and pushed into the corridor and down it with all speed. I trotted alongside, holding her hand as I continued reassuringly, "Jimmy and Peaches McEpstein, the Tubby O'Tannenbaums, Jim and Sissy Gowash, Little Amy Freesample, Dr. Whychop, Dr. Slumbago, Dr. Demensha . . ."

The two nurses ran at the front, holding Naughty's legs tightly together, each firmly grasping an ankle. "Try to hold back," one of them said. I remembered hearing that an obstetrician cannot collect his fee if he is not present at the delivery. "Everything will be all right in a minute." I could feel Naughty's grip tighten on my hand. "Just keep that up."

"Mrs. Yespickle, Mrs. Poopskate, Dr. Boxygen —"

"Not you — her! Do you want to kill her? Just keep squeezing his hand like that in both of yours, dear," she told Naughty, "whenever there's a twinge."

Simultaneously I was wrenched away by the other nurse and the orderly, for we had reached the delivery room from which I was to be barred. My wife's hand and mine were now pried forcibly apart, like the hands of vaudeville comedians in those routines in which their fingers appear to be inextricably glued despite all the exertions of the principals to free themselves, while in the distance I could see masked figures running to and fro, like chimerical gardeners. "Mrs. Eggslump," I whispered as I was flung back against a wall, or rather had knocked out of me with my wind in a final, involuntary exhalation of the words that had been on my tongue when I was overpowered. Just then the first nurse took another look under the covers and shot a glance at the second. The entire melee vanished through flapping doors as I stood feeling a bump on the back of my head and gasping for air, but not until I had imagined in that split second that I had caught a glimpse of a very red manchild grinning up at me from between erupting thighs.

nine

I HAD by now learned something disturbing about MacNaughton's plans for his money. The approach of a grandchild made him feel he owed me a complete and candid clarification on this point, so that I knew exactly where I stood and should not be deluding myself with false hopes and expectations about my own future.

He was going to leave everything to Mrs. MacNaughton, after whom it would be settled in trust on their coming grandchild or grandchildren (it was to be hoped there would be more). The handwriting on the wall was clear for me. I would be bypassed. It would be imprudent to let me get my hands on moneys of any quantity, was the implication. My investment history left no doubt on that score. Financial theory was my field, not its practice.

Stung to action by this blow, I had in the last months of Naughty's pregnancy embarked on what was at once the boldest and most sophisticated of my market ploys.

I had something slightly under seven thousand dollars in stocks, bonds and surplus cash. In other words, nothing. Adjusted for proportionate growth to age sixty-five, still nothing. Therefore nothing could be lost by shooting craps with it. Not that what I did was exactly that. I sold something short, a perfectly commonplace trading maneuver, though I had never attempted it before. It is only for the nimblest traders. A short position simply reverses the normal order of buying and selling. You sell a stock at a price from which you are confident it will decline, and buy it later at the lower quotation, borrowing it meanwhile to make good your delivery, and banking the profits. I had had my eye on an aerospace issue known as Planetronics, a Buck Rogers stock grossly overpriced after a sensational run-up based on government contracts for a solid fuel component. It was selling at forty times earnings, with no dividends, and I had it on inside authority, from Farber, that an unfavorable earnings report was in the offing. It seemed bound to plummet from its current historic high of 22. I sold seven hundred shares of it at that price and sat back to wait for it to sink. I had ninety days in which to buy. Most astute observers were bearish about the market in general then, including myself.

I now had a couch in my office, an old one I had snatched from disposal as two workmen were dragging it out to the alley. It had a few gashes and was severely herniated inside, but still comfortable for all of that. The increasing overtime I put in on the Market Letter justified it. I was taking a leaf from MacNaughton's book. Naps such as revitalized my father-in-law, however, remained elusive in my case. I supposed I would never become a tycoon so long as I was troubled with insomnia at the office. I lay stretched out on the couch one afternoon trying to count sheep when Fido Harrison walked in.

"Let Rome in Tiber melt?" he said, with his taut little smile.

"*You* let Rome in Tiber melt. I'm taking a breather. They're supposed to be good for you. Increase your efficiency. Anything up?"

"The market is."

"No kidding. How much?"

"Twelve points already at one o'clock, and no sign of any profit-taking. Looks like the skyrocket one or two of the bulls have been predicting. Aren't you in for something bass ackwards?"

"Oh, nothing much," I answered as nonchalantly as possible.

He had come for our nip, but I got rid of him as soon as I could after the paper-cup ceremony. I got a quotation on Planetronics from the Teleregister on my desk. It was up three points. I went into the bathroom. I could usually tell how the market was going from the condition of my tongue. I stuck it out at the mirror. It looked as though it had been torn from a soiled oxford. I called Farber's office to find out what had ever happened to this unfavorable earnings report he had promised, but all I got was the sultry secretary whose voice always inspired dreams of total ruin, saying he was out of town for some days. As a source of information on special situation stocks Farber was leaving more and more to be desired.

The issue went up two more points the next day, and another point and a quarter the next. A trader selling short must by law declare he is doing so, like a pool player calling his shot, and deposit with his broker an amount sufficient to guarantee the transaction, which is the market value of the stock (or the portion of it permitted by prevailing margin requirements). If the stock increases in value during the period of his short position he must ante up equivalently on his deposit. I got a bank loan on some of my other securities in order to swing the deal. Each time more margin was called for I had to make another loan, until all my equities including life insurance were tied up in a bind between the bank and my deteriorating short position. When my kindly neighborhood banker beat his spoon on the high chair for more porridge, Planetronics had just been awarded a government contract which sent it up several more points, making it impossible for me to extricate myself from the vise. In the end my seven-hundred-share flyer cost me about my total nest egg. It was plain I would never get rich, or even make that modest killing, by my own wits. I finished what was left in the whiskey bottle and went home to lay the facts at my wife's feet.

She was extraordinarily sympathetic, perhaps in part because she had just finished nursing her still unchristened firstborn to sleep, that one on whose birth I had collaborated by convulsing his mother into labor, and therefore felt in a mellow mood toward everyone, especially his provider.

"I suppose you thought you were doing a sharp thing," she said when I had poured us drinks. She sighed and added, "Well, if we're ever going to have anything, it looks as though we'll have to inherit it."

"Check. Well, there's only one way we'll do that. I told you what Uncle Ham said on the phone when he called the other night."

"Run through it again. What exactly did he say?"

"That a bachelor gets lonely at his time of life, and misses not having anyone to pass his name on to. He was very emotional about it. He said he'd *give anything* to be able to pass his name on to a grand-nephew."

"You're sure there was no doubt about what he meant?"

"Absolutely none. I even had the feeling he was trying to bribe me. Name the kid after me and you'll get my money when I go — he might as well have said it in so many words. Which gets us back to where we came in. And you know what? It's how I keep thinking of the kid every time I look at him. I can't help it. He's going to be a comic and it'll suit him."

"He certainly looks like you."

"He doesn't look like Herbert or David or Mark, God knows," I said, dismissing all the other names we'd had under consideration. "He simply looks like —"

"There's a comedian named Slim Pickens," Naughty said, quickly picking up her glass and drinking.

"And a very distinguished New England professor called Dr. Timothy Hay. We may be making something out of nothing to begin with. What's so terrible about not having a million dollars?"

"Nothing when you're young, but old age is ghastly enough *with* money."

"Or what's so bad about an unusual name? I mean what's the sweat, really? Most names are ridiculous when you stop to think about them, or were before we got used to them. Cotton, silk, linen, clay have all been put to use, and so have rye, bourbon and brandy. We know two sherries and a beer, and some of these are first names. Who wants a name like Learned Hand for God's sake, except one of the greatest jurists of all time? And how do we know he'll get his nickname from his first name anyway? He might get it from his last name, like you."

"And be called Sandy you mean. Or be Tony, after the last part of his first name. Rick Bradley's name is Frederick, you know."

"So then let's stop this agonizing and simply give the kid the name that seems right, without all these other extraneous considerations."

A tremor seemed to go through my Naughty as she sat bent forward with her hands between her knees, rubbing her palms slowly together, staring at the floor. "Wouldn't Unc leave it to us anyway? He doesn't have any other relatives but Benny."

"There's no telling what a quirky character like that will do. I mean what's to prevent his taking it into his head to leave every nickel of it to some society for the preservation of old movies, or found a benevolent organization for old horses. No, you can't bank on anything with Unc unless you do just what he does — lay your cards on the table."

She straightened slowly till she was sitting erect in the chair. "All right," she said, "I'm game. Call him and tell him the good news."

My uncle was if possible even more emotional than the last time. He quite broke up with gratitude, fragmenting his syntax more drastically than ever. "Needless to say I'll," he said, and had to pause to get hold of himself.

"What?" I said. "What's that you say? Operator, can

196

you give us a better connection? Now then, what was that you were saying, Uncle Ham? Something about needless to say. Something that goes without saying. Was it about some arrangement you were going to make or other?"

He cleared his throat very loudly and said in blubbering tones, "Needless to say you'll all go straight into my."

That was good enough for me. I told him no date had been set for the christening, but that we would notify him well in advance in case he should like to come down for it. He assured me there was no doubt of that.

Telling the MacNaughtons was a different story. It was again at their dinner table, round which we had not sat together since the announcement about the testamentary arrangements omitting myself. So in a sense there was a kind of justice in this blow for Mac-Naughton, as effect to cause. He had sown the wind and was reaping the whirlwind. He sat turning the choice over in his mind, and it was some time before the full force of its implication struck him. He set his dessert spoon down and said very slowly, "Ham Sandwich."

"That's right," I said, looking him square in the eye.

He was fit to be tied. He argued, remonstrated, importuned, and finally berated us, at last going so far as to threaten reprisals of a legal nature, about which he was not prepared to be specific save for dark hints that the machinery would be thrown into motion in the morning. Not only would he get his attorneys on the phone (the same that had overseen my removal as an heir and assign forever, no doubt); he would contact friends high in denominational circles, the Episcopalian equivalent of the Pope, who would bring influence to bear to see to it that the Church refused to christen a child any such name.

"The present rector's name is Satchell," I reminded him quietly, "so he's hardly in a position to tell me to pack mine."

At the height of this demoralizing squabble, the like of which we had never been through before, Mrs. Mac-Naughton left the table with her hands in the air, on the verge of hysteria. This so upset Naughty that she followed in her train. They fell on matching sofas in the living room, one on either side of the fireplace, and lay there carrying on. MacNaughton clung to the mantel with both hands, his head bowed on the backs of them. His knees seemed to buckle under him in an access of despair. At last he pulled himself together, as by a supreme effort. He straightened, and, turning slowly and deliberately to face me, he said: "All right. I'll change my will. I'll put you into it. I'll see that you're personally named heir to a substantial sum. If you want money that badly. I'll even deed some over to you now."

After that there was nothing for me to do but sail out of the house in righteous indignation, closely followed by

Naughty. Nothing will so stiffen a man's pride as the implication that he can be bought off.

It was a while before the effects of this shattering episode were sufficiently forgotten for us to even contemplate scheduling the christening. A cooling off period was certainly indicated. The interval was marked by a flow of presents from Canada that could only be called overwhelming. Of course it would be months before the recipient would be in a position even to realize their existence, let alone old enough to have any use for them; because the absurdity of some of the selections could only be proof of how Unc doted on his far-off namesake. Blankets and nightgowns and stuffed animals and possibly even rattles and other expensive crib toys made sense; but a hobby horse was grotesquely premature, as was a model airplane that came by parcel post one Saturday morning, with a note reading, "He can't fly it yet but his old man can, so amuse him with it until I can get down there and fly it myself."

It was a plane with a one-cylinder engine, burning real fuel, of the sort you often see people flying on tethers in open fields, apparently quite happily. It turns out they call for considerable mechanical aptitude, and it's not because I'm any Leonardo da Vinci, high on a peak in Darien, that I was eager to try my hand at getting this one aloft, but because of what I encountered in the set of directions. It was a very interesting coincidence:

If you have no previous experience, you must accustom yourself to turning around counterclockwise until you can turn twenty times or so without becoming excessively dizzy. This is necessary whether you start flying with this ship, the B-87 Helldiver, or our more simple trainer model. Turn three or four times the first time. Repeat after half an hour. Next day try six turns. Repeat after half an hour. And so on. In a week or less you should be ready to fly.

To a man who can scarcely orbit a smorgasbord table without losing his balance, not to mention his appetite, this is a crusher. I was about to throw up my hands when I paused. Many things that seem of the devil at first blush turn out to be providential. Could this be the corrective discipline I was looking for, suddenly put in my path in the form of an instruction leaflet for a toy? Might a set of exercises prescribed by a manufacturer as preparation for an aeronautical hobby be the very thing to straighten out someone suffering from Ménière's syndrome?

Obviously they would have to be practiced in secret.

I picked a spot behind the garage where I would not be observed, closed my eyes, took a deep breath, and began. I rotated slowly, making a half turn first, then a full. I took a rest, and after a few minutes decided to try for two. I was very gratified to note I could manage two, but my exhilaration was short-lived. When I opened my eyes again, it was to find myself heading straight into a lilac bush. The next time, I blundered into a wheel-

barrow, thinking I was headed in another direction altogether, such was my disorientation. I decided to quit for
the day and try again the next. I returned to the house,
marveling, as I often do, at the spins executed by ballet
dancers as a complete matter of course.

It struck me that there was really no need to be
practicing my rotations in the yard just because I would
be flying the plane there, or hoped to. So I did them in
the living room, the bedroom, even at the office, whenever I was alone and happened to have a spare moment.
One Saturday morning, my wife entered the dining room
in time to see me march into the side of a china cabinet,
bruising my nose and flattening a cigar butt I happened
to have clenched in my teeth.

"Why don't you give this thing up?" she said. "You
know it's no use."

I rushed downstairs to the recreation room where the
plane was, snatched it up, rushed outside into the back
yard, started it up and let it go. I had read the instructions through several times by now, and, despite a certain obscurantism on the part of the manufacturer, had
absorbed a few things about the care necessary in takeoff,
both in terms of the plane and the guidelines attached to
it (to the left wing, to command this counterclockwise
circle), but I forgot all that now in my frenzy and let the
infernal thing rip. I can't say it went out of control
because it never was under control, nor did I pause to try

to get it so. I was aware of Naughty watching from the living room window — or Twindow as the manufacturer of that calls the arrangement of two panes slightly spaced to provide insulation — holding Ham Sandwich up to the glass. I gave them a wave. The caution to make sure takeoff was downwind (in contrast to that of a real plane) was probably accidentally observed, for the Helldiver rose with a rush. It shot off to the right until all the slack was out of the guidelines, at which point it snapped violently back, like a bolting animal on a leash, made several crazy gyrations as a crosswind caught it, and then, after describing one more erratic loop, came straight at me.

I dropped the guidelines and ran for the house, beginning to gag a little. My feet became entangled in the strings, which was probably what saved my life, because I tripped and fell as the plane shot by where my head had just been. It went over with its insane whine, then must have got caught in a sudden updraft, for it rose with a jerk, leveled off, and made at full speed for the Twindow. I only saw my wife and son duck as a unit before disappearing from view.

I heard but did not see the crash, being bent on saving my own hide. I had recovered my footing, and now scuttled around a corner of the house. As a haven of refuge, however, this nook of the property left nearly as much to be desired as the open peril I had just fled.

There was a short, abrupt declivity in the lawn there, and as I started across it my foot met a patch of residual winter ice, along which I shot precipitately, and with that slightly delirious sense of having to accelerate momentum on a slippery surface to keep upright. I rushed down the slope, arms out, swooped full-tilt across a narrow gravel walk, and wound up espaliered against the side of the garage. And it was there at long last, after all these years of doubt and uncertainty, that I managed, quietly, to throw up.

Well, it was just such a calamity as the manufacturers envisioned for tyros foolhardy enough to try the Hell-diver without sufficient basic training, and my hat was off to them. With the lengths of surgical gauze turbaning my brow for some days, I couldn't wear it anyway.

Nor could the christening be held till I looked like something other than a piratical villain, by which time Uncle Hamilton had arrived on the scene and already been with us for almost two weeks. He played with his nephew every day and every evening until it was time to put him to bed, then set out for one or another of the local movie houses. Sometimes he would drive into Chicago for a revival or a new picture that interested him. One relief was that he never troubled us for dinner. He always left early and dined out for some reason.

The christening went through at St. Luke's despite MacNaughton's threats to pull the necessary ecclesiastical strings to have the ceremony stopped, even get me excommunicated. He was himself by now a doting grandfather. As we walked down the church stairs afterward, carrying our grinning bundle, Naughty whispered to me, "My God, what have we done!"

"Steady on," I said. "Don't make him cry. He looks thirsty, as though he could do with a little of that champagne too. Champagne, Ham? Little of the old bubbly?"

We wheeled him into the living room of the house for the christening party. Corks popped for an hour or more. At last my uncle, grown quite mellow under the combined effects of a family occasion of which he was a featured player and the wine poured to celebrate it, cleared his throat and said, "I want to make a little announcement."

Silence was quickly established. I shot Naughty a look, as much as to say I hoped he would be discreet and not embarrass us with a lot of maudlin outpourings, such as he was capable of under extreme emotion.

"I didn't plan to say this now, but now I feel like it. When you get to my time of life you either. Or you can do the. But I am not choosing the course of retreat, rather that of. Joe and Naughty, my beloved nephew and niece, know the many friends I've made here through them. Some of them are here, but not all. Through the course of my repeated visits here, most welcome to me, my friendship with one in particular has ripened into something a little more than that. Though I've kept it a secret, they must have suspected where I have been spending the evenings I didn't stay in with them and. I have been spending them with Miss Laura Pribble, known to some of you as Mrs. de Shamble. To be absolutely frank about it, I realize I haven't many more years left — they have dwindled down to a precious few — but those the good Lord sees fit to give me, she has seen fit to share with me. Yes, she has promised to honor me by becoming my wife."

Luckily there was lots more champagne left, and we quickly drank to that.

ten

I STRETCHED OUT on my office couch for a short breather. From the front came the tinkle of secretaries brewing tea. Through the window overhead could be caught a glimpse of blue sky and a few chimneys, from which plumes of smoke were torn by gusts of early autumn wind.

I closed my eyes, but private ruminations proved even more distracting than external scenes. The problem of insomnia at the office was evidently one I would never solve. The revitalizing snoozes into which dynamos could catapult themselves at will, once the object of ridicule, were now a source of admiration. I had been considering a mild barbiturate, or at least Miltown. In my fist I clutched a small transistor radio, the dial of which I rotated slowly under my thumb in search of some good music, but both of the stations on which I depended for this form of relaxation were playing Bach. All those monotonous variations both bored and exasperated me. I shut the radio off but kept it in my hand as a grenade with which to demolish anyone coming through that door from the front office.

The two-thirty bell had just rung, signalizing the close of the market, and the men and women over sixty-five who comprised the chief tape watchers were shuffling out of their bleacher seats and going home, their financial positions relatively unchanged. The Dow-Jones Average closed unaltered as it had for two weeks, despite twelve and fourteen million share turnovers day after day. Clerks and secretaries stayed overtime to keep up with the paper work. Today was Thursday, and I would work late to get my Market Letter out. My view was that the market was churning at the top, preparatory to either an assault on new highs or a corrective drop, unless some other construction altogether must be put on matters. Time would tell that story, as it does all stories. Naughty would be getting ready to take the baby to her parents' for dinner there, in keeping with what was now a regular Thursday occurrence. Perhaps Miss Wigglesworth, the new secretary now bending provocatively over the tea table, would have dinner with me?

Footsteps approached, the familiar Honor Guard click of Fido Harrison's leather heels on the hard floor. He was coming for his ceremonial nip. Drawing the pin with my teeth, I hurled the grenade, blowing him to bits.

"Knitting up the raveled sleeve of care?"

"*You* knit it up. I'm trying to catch forty winks."

He proceeded to my desk, where he sat in the swivel chair and pulled out the drawer committed to use as a cellarette. "Why don't you give it up? You're not the type," he said, pouring whiskey into two paper cups. Our unspoken pact — my silence about his drinking in return for his about my being an unemployable — grew more binding with the years. That did not rule out reminders of one another's besetting flaws, however, so there was a good deal of mutual ribbing, in Fido's case often sadistic.

"How did you make out on your checkup?" I asked as he handed me my cup. I took a sip and set it on the windowsill. "Did you pass your Wassermann this time or flunk it again? And what about your liver? Did the X ray show a scoop of *pâté maison* where that should have been?"

"Everything's O.K.," he said, returning to the swivel chair. He glanced at the sheet of paper in my typewriter, but I had screwed it down to where nothing I had written was visible, as always, and, as always, I relished his frustration.

Fido drank and leaned back, one hand caressing the horseshoe of hair encircling the back of his head.

"Well so. And how's your uncle? You said he went through the Mayo Clinic recently. Everything's all right I hope?" he added with a twinkle in his eye.

"Yes, everything's all right."

"Good. They're definitely going to live in Canada? That's set?"

"Definitely."

I refrained from telling everything I knew. I had learned something I hadn't the heart to repeat.

Mrs. de Shamble had enjoyed looking at her old movies in part because she knew they were widely enjoyed by others. The young people in the east, indeed the mod set everywhere, apparently made a point of catching them on television. This sense of being revived, of once more belonging, was a source of profound gratification to her, as it would be to a middle-aged woman, all alone, at midnight, in an empty cottage. Then the house of cards had collapsed. A magazine article had fallen into her hands, from which she learned why the in-crowd never missed her. She was camp — and unintentional camp at that. She never got over it. It broke her heart. She refused to see anybody but my uncle, without which redeeming relic she would have turned her face to the wall. She did not even want to see his relatives. She insisted they be married in private, and leave for Canada on the instant.

My hands laced under my head, I sighed and stared up at the ceiling.

"I believe I'm due for my checkup next month." These were biannual physical examinations required by the firm of all employees. "Good health is important, but it's no cure-all."

Fido sipped again and set his cup on the desk. "When did you first realize you were a clown?" he asked.

"When I laughed at my aunt's funeral. No. It was when I cried at my mother's wedding. Tragedy and comedy are basically the same, did you know that, Fido? Like love and hate. All the authorities say so. They have a common root. Do you know what that is?"

Fido shook his bald head, yawning. Ten years farther into his prime than I, he showed its ravages that much more. But I would soon be abreast of him, as a look at the back of my head through two mirrors, one held in my hand, attested.

"Don't you want to know what it is?"

"What?"

"The common denominator in tragedy and comedy."

"Oh, I guess. What is it?"

"Desperation. Or so Benny Bonner says."

Fido nodded, twisting his head again to see what was in my typewriter. "By the way, you keep talking about defensive stocks as though you think it means the same as defense stocks," he said. "There's no connection whatever. Defensive stocks is what we call issues that are not subject to cyclical fluctuations. Hence they are good defenses against downturns that might affect the market or business in general. Defense stocks are stocks in the field of military defense equipment. You've got the two confused and that's why entire paragraphs of your copy make no sense whatever."

"Yeah. Well, anyway," I continued, "what I was going to say was, Shelley regarded *King Lear* as a comedy. So did Yeats. He said *Lear* was gay. Coleridge said *Hamlet* verges on the ludicrous. Did you realize all that, Fido?"

Fido shook his head, pouring himself another small one.

"It's all *la vie*. You know — life. Now I'll give you a couple of dual-choice questions, or examples, and you tell me whether they're sad or funny. A man got killed on the Thruway the other day in an accident he got into trying to fasten his safety belt. Is that sad or funny?"

"Ask him. He knows as well as I do."

"An excellent answer, Fido. *You don't know*. It shows you're an intellectual, basically. When Benny was in high school he organized that mass meeting to protest student apathy, and four people showed up. Sad or funny?"

Fido grunted something in recognition of the question's being rhetorical, and yawned again. He closed his mouth with a snap, like a dog's on a fly, his eyes tearing.

"Did you know the yawn is considered an orgasm by some authorities?" I said. "Like the sneeze?"

"Jesus Christ. Are we going to sit here and go into things in depth again? Or not?"

"That's classified as an orgasm too. Naughty has been collating some tests on the subject. They've got a lot of money from that new foundation and they're using it to study phenomena that parallel the erotic. Any sensation that is irreversible is an orgasm. The whole thing is to help show the interconnection between things hitherto thought dissimilar or even opposite. Like tragedy and comedy. I don't know whether you quite got that point, Fido. About desperation being the common denominator? Do you?"

"I never gave it any thought."

"Well, a man with his secretary in trouble is funny, if he shoots her it's tragic, but he is scarcely less desperate in the one case than in the other."

A ripple of laughter from the front offices plunged us both into gloom. The voice was unmistakably that of Miss Wigglesworth, clearly visualized as bending over the tea table. The altar at which she officiated was improvised out of a folding table set beside one of the water coolers. Soon we would go out to join them in that more openly celebrated pause in the day's occupation, but we could see her vividly enough now.

"You don't have to get them in trouble to be desperate," Fido breathed.

"No. Have you noticed the elastic band just faintly discernible under that silk dress she's got on today? You know what it's the waistband of, don't you, Fido."

"That way lies madness. You'll never get your spoon in that pudding. So stop eating your heart out."

"Oh, my God. Just faintly discernible." I began to eat my necktie. "Think of the trouble this one's going to have getting the boys to keep their hands to themselves. Paws in the day's occupation."

"Personnel says there's one starting Monday that's really the end."

"The Market Letter said we'd be testing new bottoms."

Fido rose, wadding his empty paper cup and pitching it into the wastebasket.

"Do you suppose you'll ever grow up?" he asked.

"That's not for me to say, Fido. And what good will it do me if I do? Why do you ask?"

"I've got twenty more years here. Twenty years of talking to you. This togetherness. Bleeding Christ."

"There'll be no want of subjects, Fido. That I promise you."

"Well, speaking of eating, I'm staying down to get caught up too. So do you want we should have dinner together? Or not?"

"Swell. Let's make it around six thirty or seven, seven thirty or eight, eight thirty or nine. That sort of thing. We'll be in touch."

Fido went out, shaking his head and murmuring to himself again the name of the Nazarene.

We went to a fish house, the one at which my dear Naughty had eaten oysters for her virility. How long ago it all seemed now, yet how recent. Yes, the days drag while the years fly. There was a new headwaiter, a fresh, rather discouragingly supple young man with a fine sense of his calling. Well, I had worn out half a dozen of his kind here, and would outlast him. He wove with rather too much style up to our table, midway our dinner, to ask the immemorial question: "Is everything all right?"

"Certainly not," I said. "We came as young men to these parts and have lived to see coastal waters destroyed as nesting grounds for migratory birds due to industrial pollution resulting from governmental irresponsibility on both state and local levels. Perfidy and frustration are everywhere. Concerned with overweight, we order shell-fish because it's low in calories, only to learn that it is loaded with cholesterol. Concerned about cholesterol, we partake of the most innocuous combination imaginable — tea and toast — to be now told that they are both carcinogenic. I'd like to speak to the manager, please."

"I'm the manager."

"Ah, moonlighting. In that case you'll hear from my lawyers in the morning."

"Yes, sir. And who are they, sir?"

"Sturm and Drang."

We had both ordered lobster, and when the waitress tied a bib around Fido's neck he looked so like a melancholy child that I had to keep reminding myself what a dreadful gossip he was to keep compassion from ruining my dinner.

As for religion, I never practice it formally any more (except for ritualistically avoiding a church now and then), though I'm a Christian at heart, and though agreeing with most that the universe does reflect some kind of divine intelligence. Mirror my God to thee, yuck, yuck. Once in a while I drop into a church again to kneel at the altar for a word of prayer, though this is often a single supplicatory gasp as much accusation as anything else, such as "Give us a break, will Ya!" I am sometimes tempted to enter the confessional again and pour out a full account of my merits under pressure, my fundamental decency and tolerance and plain unadulterated *niceness* in the face of what seems to me trying and even appalling odds. There is on this earth something called human worth, I believe? For this there must be some eternal, or universal, counterpart of which it is a manifestation, and which authenticates it, as the gold in Fort Knox certifies as valuable those tinkling coins and frayed scraps of paper with which we do business, somehow . . . somehow . . . I often think the human nature of which each of us is a variant to be like those sorry bills: tattered; soiled; ephemeral; and grievously subject to inflation, but somehow miraculously good for obtaining food and raiment, and sometimes even castles on the Rhine. Perhaps one day I shall again slip into an "arbor," though the chances of drawing a priest as perceptive as Father Enright are slim. Whatever happened to him? Gone to his reward probably, though not certainly, for he was only in early middle age during those tender years of mine.

So I am like all of us, reluctant thinkers, emotionally resisting truths toward which we are intellectually borne; still dreaming of islands though the mainland has been lost; swept remorselessly out to sea while we spread our arms to the beautiful shore.

Back at the office, I worked a good deal later than Fido, perhaps because of the known distraction of Miss Wigglesworth out front there, catching up on the paper work dumped on her desk by the margin clerks and account executives. When I had the Market Letter finished, I went into the men's room to wash my face and slide up the knot in my tie. It was nearly ten o'clock. Miss Wigglesworth must be presumed to have eaten also. What about asking her out for a brandy? Or to lunch on the morrow?

I gazed squarely into the mirror over the washstand, and, after a moment's reflection, decided against it. If you look back you turn into a pillar of salt. If you look ahead you turn into a pillar of society. So what the hell. I would put on my hat and coat and go home, where I would have a brandy and some coffee with my wife, and perhaps later toy with a little Ham.

II
Wally Hines

one

THE first time I met Gloria Bunshaft I thought her nothing to write home about, an opinion that several years of marriage to her have done little to modify. It was at a college tea at which a portrait of the late Dean Wicker was unveiled. "It's very lifelike," she said to me. "Which is more than he ever was," I answered. She turned on her heel and walked away.

Women are of course notorious for taking everything personally, but there is usually some clue as to what offends them, so that one can decide what to reply, or whether to, since one's rejoinder may be something to which further exception is taken, and so on. Then the whole thing becomes hopelessly self-perpetuating, like sneezing into a handkerchief to which one is allergic. A man might establish a ceiling on the obscurity with which he is prepared to cope from a woman, something like the present administration's guidelines for avoiding another ruinous wage-price spiral. Parallels from the world of economics are not as farfetched as on first blush they might seem, since life is a continual transaction, and we are dealing here with the two great pressure groups of our time: men and women. It must be obvious on the face of it that women cause half the trouble in this world.

I could say that Miss Bunshaft struck me as a dumb blonde, her raven tresses to the contrary notwithstanding, a mere technical quibble, but I hope I am not so malicious as to have thoughts like that crossing my mind. Still, there it is. She had just read the New Testament and loved it. And so on. The impression of imbecility arose in part from her somewhat girlish diction, always charming in its way of course — "million dollars" became, on those rosy lips, "miwyun dowers" — and by her habit of putting "um" in front of everything. "I was born in um Cleveland," she would say, as though even so rudimentary a fact as that had to be momentarily groped for, and then mentally confirmed before stated.

Well, she was in any case not dumb from the neck down, as I observed watching her talk to somebody across the room, the library of the home of the present president of Wilton College where the unveiling occurred. I am supposed to be a critic, and so — I liked parts of her very much. She seems a high price to pay for a headache named Joe Sandwich, but that is getting ahead of the story. It lies up ahead in our collective future, then not so much as faintly guessed. She had graduated from Wilton a couple of years before, and now worked in the alumni office. I was a psychology instructor pushing thirty. So that when I call myself a critic I mean in the larger sense, as a student of the passing scene.

Old Protheroe, the artist, shuffled over for a compliment, holding onto his coat lapels for dear life.

"It's very lifelike," I said. He shuffled off again with his beagle eyes downcast, like a puppy that has been scolded for some lapse of behavior. Such horror of the facsimile has latter-day art bred into us that even blatant practitioners of it cringe in fear of being tarred with the stick. He wanted me to say the oil had values transcending the subject it would outlive. Well, I had no intention of doing so. We would all one day be regaled by Sandwich's imitation of Protheroe's "plantation shuffle." "Where you all want dis ole Caucasian to put dese bags?" he would say, and then Gloria would roar. All that was in the cards.

But that was an exasperation I would have to earn, and so the road leading to it, yet to be traversed, must be described.

Free of the White Anglo-Saxon Protestant darkey, who lived alone above a store and was said to eat his supper straight out of cans, and finding Miss Bunshaft also unoccupied, I stepped swiftly over to her side.

"I know that um representation is out of fashion these

days," she said when asked why she had huffed off, "but if you can't have it in portrait painting where can you? Not that I wouldn't defend it in general, as far as that goes. I don't know why everyone is always knocking um verisimilitude. The abstract expressionists pooh-pooh art that copies nature. Well, they're worse. They copy each other." In one of those flashes of insight by which we divine truths we have not been told, I knew she had a mother who said, "believe you me," and would herself one day reach that pass.

"That's not what I meant," says I. "I wasn't pooh-poohing verisimilitude or anything of that sort at all. I can't for the life of me see why you took it that way."

"It wasn't the remark as such. I suppose I was thinking of what you stand for on campus. The intellectual approach to everything. I was never in any of your classes, but you're known for that. You're brilliant, penetrating — You don't mind this criticism?"

"Not in the least. Fire away."

"You have minds like steel traps, men of your um ilk, you can analyze everything down to a gnat's eyebrow, but there's something missing."

"Heart."

She set her teacup down on a table and stalked out of the house.

Through two open doorways I saw her descend the winding stairway to the entrance hall. I hesitated for a split second, remembering that I had been hearing such strictures all my life. My cortical sheath was a quarter-inch thicker than everyone else's, and perhaps I should mend my ways. So lacking in flamboyance was I that even my entrails did not meander this way and that, like other people's, but lay neatly coiled inside me, like a firehose. Now was my chance to change all that — perhaps my last. To become a real person. My fate trembled in the balance. I watched her sink from view, like a swimmer drowning in the scenes-from-Williamsburg wallpaper covering the walls, then set my own cup aside and flew down the stairs after her.

Thus began my pursuit of Gloria Bunshaft.

What adventures she promised! I liked them with spirit in spite of myself, and she would be an adversary in a million. Passionate in daily life, reasonable in divorce. That is important these days. I have had several married friends, and I know divorce can be hell with the wrong woman.

It was a good block before I overtook her, and then nearly another before I managed to coax her into a tavern. There over a drink she explained in greater detail her objection to "men of my ilk."

It was not the predominance of intellect over emotion as much as the want of emotion itself, especially the feeling that makes attachment to another person possible. We *were* islands to ourselves, us guys. My being unmarried at my age made me suspect here. "How can I put it?" She paused a moment, groping for a parallel, and at length indicated the shirt I was wearing. It was bleeding Madras, a fabric to which men like myself were significantly enough addicted, for the term meant that the material "bled" when it came in contact with other garments, and must therefore be washed separately. A glance at the collar would reveal precisely such an instruction. That was our isolation and our shame: in the rough-and-tumble of the general human laundry, we tended to run.

"That's an interesting comparison," I said, "but a trifle cerebral for me."

She drank off her beer and stalked out of the tavern.

She later said I exaggerated this particular exit, insisting that having finished her drink she was ready to leave anyway, having another engagement, and that only the very um narcissistic sensitivity against which she had been inveighing had made me think her miffed by another of my "dry rejoinders." All this over the telephone when, my curiosity not to be repressed, I asked to see her again, suggesting dinner the next evening. She said she had another engagement. It all sounded military enough — these endless engagements of hers. We made it for the following Sunday.

"It would never work," she said, staring thoughtfully into space.

"We would be at one another's throats in a year, give or take a month," I said. Without my reading glasses I could see the blood vessel throbbing in her throat.

So I sensed a mounting excitement here, a kind of onrushing, nervous rapport such as can be generated between two people when utter agreement is felt on some score. We talked far into the night. It developed that her mother was a Lucy Stoner, refusing to become a subclassification of the male by taking his name in marriage, and insisting on retaining her own in line with the teachings of that aggressively feminist sect. To this day Gloria's father must introduce his wife as Miss Cockenoe — a name anti-aphrodisiac to the point of mysticism.

"I sympathize with that point of view," I said. "I believe in two people having their own um individu-ality." Her speech habits were deucedly infectious, and I for my part could imagine us murmuring these ums into downy, drawn-up covers far, far into the night. "That's one thing that's sacred. Individuality."

"There you have your bleeding Madras point of view again," she said. "Individuality is not number one with me, nor with God either. The Pair is. Communion. The Pair is the supreme reality."

"So if you want to communicate, keep talking. But if you want to commune, baby, shut up," I thought to myself thought I.

We were up at her place. I sat in a chair in the center of the room while she circled me steadily, airing her views. I had the feeling I was being picketed. Sometimes I would twist around to keep her in view over my shoulder, half expecting to see her shouldering a placard next time she hove into sight. "That's the danger we're in, the danger of playing it safe," she said, in a phrase obviously cribbed from somewhere. It sounded like one of Dr. Bonniwell's chapel sermons. "The only risk worth taking is the risk of personal commitment."

She paused directly in front of me, and for a charming moment stood with her hands behind her back, like a child who has recited commendably. How could my heart not go out to her? There are times when, sick of the rack of thought, weary of considerations as the poet puts it, a man would like to shut off the machinery of his mind and hurl himself into the arms of a dumb blonde, with hair of whatever denomination. When a man finds himself praying, "Send me a dumb broad." She is an archetype, almost a folk goddess, like the earth mother herself, perennially appealing to something in our deepest nature because she fulfills an irresistible need. I could have dropped to my knees and embraced her then, like a drowning man clinging to a spar. I nearly did so, but she began to picket me again.

I can't report an unqualified ecstasy at the prospect of marriage, but I did experience in the days that followed an incessant, tingling hum of excitement, nervous, chaotic, like the inebriating jumble of an orchestra tuning up, often so much more exhilarating than the selections that they will play. Since I intended to take a wife, I thought it no more than fair to communicate my decision to the one most likely to be affected by it: my mother.

two

MOTHER now lived in the tiny cottage on the outskirts of town to which she had been reduced when Father died some years before. We'd had a large, rambling house that Mother filled to overflowing with vacation mementoes, to say nothing of the grounds. The souvenir lamps and pillows and sugar bowls, the cabinets crammed with rocks and shells and other resort curios from nearly every state in the union, had their counterpart in the birdbaths and silver balls and iron animals disposed upon the grass. Our place had been finally indistinguishable from the wayside stands at which Mother had accumulated the gimcrackery that cluttered it, and so was this one. Father was a rather platitudinous man who said "Great Scott" and could get things for you at enormous discounts.

Now Mother was not going anywhere; she'd been. She picked her way about with the aid of a stout cane, which she flourished militantly when not propping herself with it, so that she resembled those formidable beldames of the motion pictures who are depicted as forever summoning their lawyers in order to change their wills. Thickset and red-faced, she had both the build and the color for cutting people off without a penny. All that was lacking for the role was money.

It was warm the day I called with my news, and she insisted we sit outside. As she picked her way toward the garden chairs beside the front porch, she poured out a customary torrent of complaint. Her eyesight was failing. She found herself swatting raisins on the kitchen table, thinking they were flies, and bringing her stick down on spiders that turned out to be scurrying tufts of lint. Her hearing was going, and she suffered from head noises. She imagined she heard drums beating. "And now there's this rotten article in *Life* attacking marriage."

I was not very attentive, mulling over as I was the matter uppermost in my mind, namely my current academic project.

As a psychology teacher I have become interested in that most tantalizing of all human phenomena, the wellsprings of laughter. Most theories of humor that have cut any ice have been propounded by philosophers, who must in turn range widely throughout literature on their explanatory forays, which means that I have developed a triangular distribution of interest, good for the mind but not for the career in this day of specialization.

I may very well publish and perish both. I was at the moment trying to sweat out a synthesis of the Aristotelean, Bergsonian and Freudian hypotheses of laughter, by applying them simultaneously to one of the great episodes in English comedy. You remember the classic scene in *She Stoops to Conquer* in which Marlow and Hastings enter Hardcastle's home thinking it to be a public inn, and proceed to order him about. It is one of the funniest mistaken-identity sequences in literature, the result of a practical joke played by Tony Lumpkin on his stepfather. No single theory has yet managed to explain all varieties of mirth. Nine tenths of what we laugh at answers to Bergson, another nine tenths to Freud, still another to Kant or Plato, and so on, leaving always that elusive tenth that makes each definition like a woman trying to pack more into a girdle than it will legitimately hold. I do not mind admitting that my dream of glory is to fashion a girdle into which it can all be tucked.

We were no more than settled in the garden chairs that each spring I hauled out of Mother's cellar for her, and each autumn put away again, than she sent me back into the house for the magazine with the article that had got her goat. It wasn't *Life* at all but some other periodical, and the title of the piece was "Marriage on the Rocks." It consisted of little more than captioned scenes from a clutch of recent Broadway plays about sexual unions, the parties to which were depicted as belting and flaying one another as though everyone were Gunga Din. One housewife had both eyes blackened while another lay on a bed with a bloody nose, her blouse torn away. A current smash (a good name for it) was entitled *A Bit of a Bitch,* and dealt with a woman who rather enjoyed getting the knuckles of people's fingers into a nutcracker and squeezing it shut. In the only actual lovemaking going on, the man's head was bandaged. The general conclusion, implied or stated, was that the home must go.

"Imagine anybody saying a thing like that," my mother said. "Of course it's not perfect. What human institution is? But it's the cornerstone of any civilization, and if it goes, everything goes. People should simply not go to see plays like that."

"There's no danger that they will," I said. "They can't get tickets."

"Where would the people who write such stuff be themselves if they hadn't had fathers and mothers to raise them in homes they now denounce? I wonder if they ever think of that. What alternatives do they offer? Live in sin? Wallow in the mire? The beasts of the field mate with more pattern and dignity than that. Even wolves are monogamous. Of course the home must stay. Of course get married."

This seemed as good a time as any to break the news that I intended to do precisely that. Therefore after a murmur of agreement with her general position, and a brief pause, I said, "Mother, that brings me to something of my own I have to announce. I'm going to get married."

"Married!" She looked at me with startled eyes, clutching her breast. "You must be mad. You're not serious, Wally."

"Never more."

"But you're all I've . . . You must be out of your mind."

I think I sensed what she meant. She feared being left alone in the world, an anxiety not only groundless but totally illogical in the circumstances. I no longer lived with her, I had my own digs now, and wherever else I moved to it would be just as close by. I tried to tell her all this, without much success. She had turned pale, and now slumped down in her chair. Her eyes fluttered shut, and then Mother began to slaver.

Frightened half out of my wits, I galloped toward the house to phone a doctor. As I reached the porch I heard her call over, in the "loud, clear" voice with which we are continually told people make their last utterances, "Get me some brandy."

I rushed into the kitchen where I knew she kept it, and out again, uncorking the bottle as I flew. She seemed to have pulled herself together somewhat, for she took the bottle from me and tilted it to her mouth. She was still slavering a little. I planted myself squarely in front of her as she drank, for the cottage was on a fairly busy street and I wanted to shield Mother from passersby, a notoriously morbid class.

Having taken several sips, coughing and spluttering like an engine once more starting up, she gave me the bottle back. "I'm all right now. It was just the shock," she said. "You hadn't told me you were going steady. Who is this girl? What's her name?"

"Gloria Bunshaft."

"You don't know what you're saying. When you say it will make no difference between us you're wrong. It always does. Well, get rid of that, and then come back and tell me all about her."

I did, investing Gloria Bunshaft with qualities I was not such a fool as to imagine she possessed, bathing her in the rosy glow with which we must all obscure our better judgment if things are to be kept moving along. Romantic ardor is in basic principle Lethean. Its purpose is temporarily to blind us to one another in order to bind us to one another; make us forget the low esteem in which we really hold one another, and in which we quite deserve to be held; the anesthetic administered to reason without which the race would not go on. Coming out of the anesthetic is never pleasant, and I quite appreciate the impulse to rush right out and make the same mistake over again with someone no better, and then someone else again — the system of serial polygamy toward which we seem to be groping — but in the end I tend to favor the Spartan policy exemplified by my parents, one dead and the other half-dead: to stick with what you're stuck with. What you're stuck with could be your offspring as well as your mate, of course. Procreation is potluck. After all none of us is a bargain, and we have only our own word for it that we are more worth perpetuating than weasels or mealybugs. If you can wake up in the morning and look over at somebody who doesn't make you retch, you have got about all that can be expected in this world. When we see what is embraced in a railway station we know man wants but little here below. My only excuse for this rather depressing and I suppose sophomoric digression is the point I want to make: in calling the woman I was going to marry nothing to write home about, I don't want to appear to be considering myself anything better. Far from it. I might be a pill as a husband, as very possibly I already was as a son. Gloria could herself a tale unfold, but this isn't it. This is my story. And at the heart of it must clearly lie my central philosophy: guarded pessimism.

I promised to bring Miss Bunshaft around for tea the following Sunday, and that settled, we tried to get our minds on pleasant things. Things at least as pleasant as the sunshine in which we basked. Mother leaned her head back and closed her eyes, and I knew she was basking also in the old satisfaction of resting among her beloved souvenirs. In the cramped plot to which she was reduced there seemed so much more of them than in the rambling house on Sunflower Street. They were the living embodiment of her past, as precious to her as the connoisseur's possessions are to him. She could remember the vacation on which each treasure had been acquired, even the wayside stand at which it had been purchased.

Sensing that she had been safely delivered to their contemplation, I returned again to the scholastic problem with which I was wrestling. Aristotle's aesthetic approach to the problem of laughter, and his consequent view of the ludicrous as a subdivision of the ugly, was going to be the toughest nut to crack, of the three views in which I hoped to synthesize my exegesis of the Goldsmith scene. Perhaps the two travelers' mistaking the house for a public inn could be analyzed as a sort of "spiritual disfigurement" of the truth? . . . I was struggling with the problem when an incident occurred that not only disrupted my train of thought but spoiled the afternoon as well.

A car slowed at the curb and drew to a stop. It had an Indiana license plate, and its passengers were a rather provincial-looking middle-aged couple who sat conferring in the front seat a moment, scanning the knick-knacks scattered about the yard in, as I say, great profusion. At least the woman did, the husband nodding in mechanical agreement. At last they climbed out and walked toward us.

"Look around?" said the woman, a Humpty-Dumpty

type clutching a bag by the strap. She smiled broadly, by way of greeting, and began to browse.

The man, who was rangy and wore a sport shirt decorated with palm trees, followed a pace behind this woman. "Ha-da-do," he said. He stood a moment viewing the contents of the yard, unsticking his clothes from his skin. He kept bending and jerking his legs this way and that in order to free them from the oppression of summer in a manner lending little grace to a situation already drained of dignity. At last, leaving his wife to her grazing, he came over and sat down in an unoccupied chair.

"Can't expect the womenfolks to go on a trip without picking something up," he said with a laugh, as though great humorous insight must be credited the observation.

"That's right," my mother replied. "I'm the same way myself."

By now I had recovered from my first surprise without, however, believing the testimony of my senses. These people thought this was a wayside souvenir shop and that the objects around it were for sale! Mother's house was not only on a fairly busy street, but on a stretch of local highway leading to a nearby turnpike.

"Am I to understand," I said, speaking with great deliberation, so there could be no doubt about my intentions or the asperity of my tone, "that you are stopping here to buy one of these things to take home?"

"Could be," the man said. He laughed again, as though now acknowledging a joke I had myself made, about womenfolks and their acquisitive ways while on holiday. A joke of underlying ironic intent. "A souvenir of good old Illinoise."

He sat well down in the chair, his hat shoved forward over his eyes. It was a limp white hat in the visor of which a length of green isinglass was incorporated. From beneath this, or through it, he cozily gazed at the street while engaging my mother in conversation. She sat next to him.

"I never see the beat of that woman for picking up mementoes," he said. He pronounced it "miminto," only another detail to set one's teeth on edge, alongside the audible *s* in Illinois. "I don't believe we ever come home from a trip, no matter how small, without the back of the car crammed full of stuff. You should see our place over to Valparaiso. Why, it's . . ."

Words seemed to fail him, but I quickly completed his thought for him.

"You mean," I said, leaning out of my chair to look past my mother, "you can't tell it from the places you picked the stuff up from?"

"Yeh-heh-heh-heh-heh," the man laughed, as though he had never thought about it in quite that way, and showing a row of teeth far from uniform in either length or color. " 'Bout the size of it. That's rich. You can't tell it from the oh heh-heh-heh," and threatened to explode in convulsions.

Stunned outrage, however, continued to be my portion, who failed to see the humor of the situation. There was nothing funny about one's mother being taken for a poor old woman forced to eke out her last days on the proceeds of a souvenir stand, and that stocked with the accumulation of a lifetime now being liquidated!

"Well, it so happens," I said, leaning still farther out of my chair, "that that is exactly the situation into which you have blundered. But if you think for one minute that my lady mother has to —"

She put out her hand to stop me, a motion lost on the customer, lolling as he was in the sunshine. The galoot waggled the foot of a crossed leg and said, "just wisht you'z selling snacks too, so's I could down a hot dog and some ice cold pop while waitin' for the old woman. She can take a long time to decide."

Fortunately today was an exception, for the woman called over, "How much is this pink stork?"

"Three dollars," my mother said.

"I'll take it."

This was really too much. I could not let it go.

"This is all a ghastly —" I began, but again Mother stayed me with a gesture. Again the protest was lost on the tourists, who were between them now engaged in producing the right moneys for the transaction. The creatures had in fact driven off with their purchase, waving as they went, before I quite understood my mother's motivation. She contemplated the bills in her hand with a wry expression before she thrust them into her apron pocket, and, with an accusing glance at me, said, "It may come to that."

The mood in which I took my leave can be imagined. She was punishing me. It was a wretched mood, that not even immersion in my work could clear. It persisted into the next few days, when suddenly all the to-do seemed for nothing. Before I could get Miss Bunshaft over to my mother's for tea, she broke off the engagement.

We were lunching at a campus restaurant famous for its pancakes — which she pronounced "pangcakes." She chattered on in a charming way about some of her habits and fancies, freely, as she did about her opinions and convictions. She prided herself on being an open book — and speaking of books, she said that in a brief attempt to become a model, it had been a principle of hers never to balance on top of her head a volume with the contents of which she was not familiar.

It now developed that she was mad about waterfronts and could not resist a departing liner. "I get a bang out of them," she said. Whenever in New York she would consult the *Times* shipping news for sailing dates, and between engagements or when she had nothing to do, she would go over and "catch" a departure. It seemed an innocent and endearing enough habit until something about it began to strike an ominous note: *there was no evidence that she got the same bang out of incoming vessels.*

Why not? Was there some pleasure here in the sheer principle of departure, in mass scenes of human separation? Rather a paradox in one so garrulous on the subject of intercommitment! I began to brood about it. Since I planned to marry the girl, the least I owed myself was to try to get to the emotional bottom of all this. So when we were lunching in the same coffeehouse, a couple of days later, I raised the subject again.

She was not a cooperative witness. She had a way of clamming up when questioned, or probed, on matters about which she was voluble enough when not prompted. So I hammered out an explanation of her conduct that satisfied me, and submitted it to her for approval. I spoke of the feverish, slightly delirious excitement of the docks, with their thousandfold destinies momentarily intertwined, the wanderers doubled over with their luggage like so many Groucho Marxes bent on unnamable adventures, the ravishing moan of the whistle as the anonymous hordes were committed to their liquid wilderness.

"Is it something like that?" I said. "Does that about say it?"

"I guess. Eat your pangcakes."

"Why do you stand there and wave at total strangers?"

"I can't stand to see people dwindle in the distance."

"Do you pick out a face?"

"Sometimes. Once I spotted an old man who wasn't waving, obviously because nobody was waving at him. He was dark and wizened, and I imagined he was a Greek going back to his homeland with the earnings of a lifetime of frying hamburgers in some greasy joint. So I picked him out to see off, so to speak."

"You never meet incoming ships?"

"If they happen to be coming in."

"But you don't check the paper for arrival times, or go out of your way to catch them. Because it's not the same thing."

"You know best."

I leaned across the table, chin in hand with an air of thoughtful evaluation.

"The real thrill then is in the voluptuous, almost promiscuous poetry of farewell."

"It is?"

"Yes. You sound like a kind of libertine of the emotions." I leaned back and wiped the syrup from my lips. "You like to say goodbye."

It did seem a faintly sinister summation of the behavior under review, especially when taken as a key to the personality of someone you were contemplating spending the rest of your life with. I was revolving these thoughts in my mind when she broke the silence with the surprising statement that she had just been dealt another damaging glimpse of the man she had hoped to marry.

"How so?" I asked quietly.

"Not even the object of one's affections is to be exempt from this um jaundiced intellectualism that you view the world with. No, you're incurable. Analysis is your life."

I replied that it was not only my life, it was my living; was, indeed, the means by which I would have to support her. She answered that that would not be necessary. She could not be happy with a man who drew no line on the skepticism to which he subjected human relations, skepticism from which apparently not even the beloved's little ways were sacrosanct. It offered no basis that she could see for a lasting union. This was goodbye.

I had the illusion that I was fading steadily from view, backwards, across a widening interval at whose other edge she stood seeing me off, on a voyage in which she would have no share. She went on to insist that it would never work. To each his own was the sum of all that could be said, but she wanted to warn me that if I went on stewing in my own juice, I would wind up in that final isolation whereby the cheese stands alone.

I moodily ate my pancakes and watched the late-comers queuing up for theirs outside the restaurant door, such was the fame of this specialty. Finally I said: "At least come and meet my mother. That's been arranged."

"No. I might like her, and that would make it worse."

"There's no danger of that."

"No, we'd better leave it this way. There'll be less to regret. And now kwee eat in peace? Kwee finish our lunch in that?"

When I called on my mother alone on the day appointed, she was standing at the front porch with her back to the street, wielding her stick in a mysterious fashion. She seemed to be dealing the house a sound thrashing. I dismounted my bike, on which I had pedaled over, propped it against the fence, and, pocketing my ankle clips, came over. Then I saw what she was using the cane for. She was nailing up a sign reading, "Stop and browse."

This was to continue my punishment, of course. But I said nothing about that. I paid this childish performance not the least mind. I simply announced that the engagement was off, and that there would now be no threat, real or imagined, to her financial well-being. I assumed this gave me leave to remove the ridiculous sign and tear it up; which I proceeded to do calmly and without further comment. Then we went on to tea.

Then a week later I ran into Miss Bunshaft again, quite by accident on Mulberry Street, and after exchanging a few words we had an impromptu dinner at a nearby spaghetti house run by an Italian named Mario whom we both liked (the hard-working sort who give a lifetime of devotion to a place and then retire to their homeland on the profits, like the imaginary Greek Miss Bunshaft had seen off). Over some good food and a bottle of red wine we patched it up. This was a blow to Mother again, but this time I decided to *drop in* with my fiancée, and surprise of surprises, they hit it off very well. They even seemed to like each other. Which goes to show again that there is no accounting for tastes.

Gloria's visits with my mother continued into the early months of our marriage, when, having quit her job in the alumni office, she was free to broaden her social horizons in the unoccupied hours left by her somewhat limited duties as housewife. It pleased me to think of the two of them sitting together over teacups every Wednesday, as tradition soon had it, and then more frankly over the relaxing cocktail prescribed by Dr. Wilmot for my high-strung mother, and I would fondly imagine the scene in the house as I shot by on bicycle.

Then one day as I pedaled past I saw another sign on the front porch, this one reading, "If U Don't C What U Want Ask 4 It." Flinging my bike against the fence I marched into the house without removing the clips from my ankles.

"What is the meaning of this gibberish?" I demanded, flourishing the offending shingle which I had of course wrenched from its moorings.

"It means that maybe there's something in the house I can show them, or get from the attic."

My mother was sitting in her window chair, her feet on the needlepoint stool, a sherry decanter and glass by her side indicating her to be in a state of relaxation far greater than that envisioned by Dr. Wilmot. Her flushed expression and bellicose manner cleared up any doubt on that score.

"Of course I know what it means in that sense. I mean what's the idea of starting up all this nonsense about going into trade again? That's what I mean."

"I might as well get rid of it piece by piece while I'm still alive and can use the money. Better than leaving it for others to throw out. They might feel some gratitude for *that*."

"You're doing this to me," I said. I glanced angrily around. "Where's Gloria? It's Wednesday."

"Good question. She hasn't been here for three weeks." She twitched her nose, giving a satisfied sniff.

"Have you sold anything?"

"A string of ducks."

"The little terra-cotta ones you brought from the Dells?"

"That's right."

"How much?"

"Five dollars. I paid eight, twenty years ago." She drew a bill from her apron pocket to show me. "Why not?" she continued in the dramatically flat tone people adopt when bent on a course of self-destruction, taking others with them. "Besides bringing in a little money, it also helps pass the time when nobody comes to see you any more."

"Why should they come to see you when you don't even look at them?" For I had had to maneuver about to stay in Mother's line of vision. Now she looked at the floor and then at the ceiling in a large display of indifference to my reactions, which were of course precisely what she was trying to provoke. "To say nothing of the trouble you can get into this way. You have no license to run a business. You're violating zoning regulations and God knows what all. Now let's stop this nonsense once and for all, shall we?"

I was improvising objections as a means of diverting even my own mind from the real problem, Gloria's activities. Why had she been deceiving me about her calls on my mother? Where was she spending the time when she was supposed to be here?

I pumped homeward through a steady drizzle, to find the car in the garage. I hung my clips on the handlebars and went into the house. Gloria was at the range, frying chops in a tweed suit. She was all out of breath, as

246

though she had preceded me into the house by minutes.

"Where have you been?" I demanded. "You haven't been at Mother's for weeks."

"I never said I was," she answered cheerfully enough, though stooping to regulate the flame under the skillet. Was nobody going to look me straight in the eye today? She turned with an air of girlish delinquency and said, "All right, I'll tell you what I've been up to. I've been playing the market."

"What are you talking about? What with?"

"The five-thousand-dollar bond my grandmother gave me when I was fifteen. It's matured now."

"I'm glad something around here has."

"I cashed it and um invested the income. It's worth fifty-four hundred now, besides earning nearly five per cent. A company with a machine that cleans by electronic bombardment. Furniture, ovens, even cats and dogs."

"What's that got to do with where you spend your time?"

"I go to the broker's office. It's fun watching the tape. Gets into your blood. I'm sorry about your mother, but I haven't said that's where I was, or promised to keep up these visits. But let's drop in on her tonight if you'd like by all means. It's O.K. with me."

Such gestures of tribal loyalty atoned for sins other than those I was intended to suspect, I soon learned. It was not monkeyshines with money that turned out to be most in need of concealment here, nor was gambling her besetting sin — as I began to suspect when I saw her lunching with the broker who first handled her account at the office where she played the market.

For Gloria Bunshaft had not exaggerated her capacity for the communion inherent in the lyrical concept of the Pair. Indeed marriage could not begin to accommodate it. I doubt whether she was selective, but I must be here, like the gospel writer forced to content himself with an illustrative smattering of Our Lord's works, a full account of which would have filled the world. So one example will have to suffice. Which brings us to this Joe Sandwich character with whom I have promised to acquaint you.

three

I HAD first run across him as a freshman in my Basic Sike class several years before. I regularly conduct those experiments aimed at demonstrating the highly personalized nature of sensory responses in moments of surprise or crisis, and hence the unreliability of much eyewitness testimony. I have people rush in the door as I am lecturing and stage a fracas. There is a confusion of wielded knives and drawn pistols. Shots are exchanged, with blanks of course, and then as suddenly as it all began the melee ends. The participants rush out the door clutching simulated wounds and shouting at the tops of their voices, and what not. I then have the class write out detailed reports of what they have seen. Naturally there are as many versions as students. Sandwich's prowess as a prankster having come to my ears, I rang him in as one of the "assailants." However, at the last minute he double-crossed me with variations of his own. At the height of the gunfire he exclaimed, "Oh, my God, Pepperrell, I said to put blanks in that gun! You've loaded it with — Oh, my God, you've — you —" and drawing from his shirtfront a hand stained crimson, courtesy of a confederate in chem lab, he dropped to the floor with a sickening thud right in front of my desk. I was frightened out of my wits, and later could scarcely give a coherent account of what had happened. Proving the whole point I was trying to make, you see.

It was with mixed feelings that, come September, I again saw Sandwich turn up at my feet, this time in Advanced Sike. It is in this course that I try to isolate for intensive study some basic human element and take up in historical order the theories and hypotheses purporting to explain it. Being interested in humor, I generally choose laughter.

Lecturing, one day, on the Platonic thesis that laughter is a way of enjoying the misfortunes of others, I touched on practical jokes as an obvious example of the hostility, and even cruelty, to which mirth gives expression. Sandwich promptly raised his hand to protest this, reeling off a list of notables given to pranks who were not notoriously cruel. There was Mencken, perpetrator of the famous bathtub hoax and other mischiefs; F. Scott Fitzgerald, who when not engaged in such formal ventures would enliven parties by gathering all the ladies' compacts into a kettle and boiling them in tomato sauce; and his friend Ring Lardner who often joined him in these tittups. I dryly asked him whether he were familiar with Lardner's blistering excoriation of the practical joker in the story "Haircut." He said he hadn't read it yet, his feet had been giving him so much trouble, but he knew a story *about* Lardner. How Lardner let a bore at the Lambs Club go on and on reciting a scene from a play he was in, only to tell the poor ham, who thought he was going over big, that he, Lardner, had misbehaved the night before and was doing this for penance. I said that in that case I must believe the artist's life confirmed his work.

With the alacrity with which students can spot a chance to sidetrack you and waste valuable classroom time, Pepperrell switched us onto the mystery of artistic motivation in general, and the contradictions posed by that most polarized of all creatures, the writer. Sensing this to be worth ten minutes or so I gave the beggars their heads for that long. At which time Horton, who wrote a little verse, said that "In the end, whatever sets the artist in motion remains a mystery. Not even the psychoanalysts can tell us. We'll never know what makes Sammy run."

"Or Saul Bellow," piped up Sandwich, causing a burst of idiotic laughter. Analyzing humor can be difficult with a clown in the class.

Still something of what you are trying to do rubs off. You do get through to them. I think I grabbed them with my elucidation of Bergson.

I see Bergson as the philosopher of creative evolution

for whom the ludicrous is always some failure of adaptation. You should have seen the banana peel and walked around it. Having goofed on your obligation to be "with it," society punishes you by bringing down the lash of laughter. Bergson reacted against nineteenth-century materialism which held the universe to be matter and man a mere automaton. "No!" he said in effect. "That is what we viscerally reject when we laugh — the spectacle of somebody *being* mechanical, instead of alive and vitally responsive." Thus inherent in every comic situation is the principle of dehumanization. That is roughly the poop on Bergson.

Having put it in a nutshell, I invited the class to cite anything funny and we would try to analyze it according to this thesis. "Fire anything at me," I said. "A situation, a joke, any joke. Old or new, good, bad or indifferent."

Up pipes Sandwich: "When they saw how tight his pants were they thought they'd split."

"Very well. Now it's interesting to note that Bergson applies his theory even to language, which in behaving rigidly and absentmindedly produces the pun. Here a pronoun's faulty adaptation to its grammatical environment — in this case a confusion over the antecedent of the third 'they' — sends an entire sentence sprawling on a syntactical banana peel, with consequence most amusing."

"What about the pants?" Sandwich said. "What ever

happened to them? They seem to me the seat of the problem. The words only set up a sight laugh in your mind. Like the milkmaid who was upset when she sat down in the butter."

"What?"

"It put her behind in her work."

"Oh, yes. You want to shift the emphasis to the man. Fine. Here again we have the element of dehumanization, a person at the mercy of inanimate clothing. Remove the pants and he'd still be funny, because, further, anything that reminds us of our body makes us comical by producing this reduction in status. But the important thing is that the man's pants *simply don't fit him*, this lack of adjustment again, you see, this failure of adaptation. The comic figure *is always out of touch with his environment*."

"Like the milkmaid sitting in the butter."

"Precisely."

Tooling home from school on my bicycle a few days later, I stopped for a red light, and as I did so a hearse crossed slowly by in front of me in the intersecting traffic. It was an old gray one, quite a vintage affair, with a bas-relief of imitation tasseled draperies flanking a window through which could be glimpsed a casket. Not a burial casket, but one of those carrying baskets made of wicker. As it glided past, very close to me, I saw the lid slowly open and an arm appear. It fluttered weakly in midair a moment before dropping back out of sight, as though its owner had just enough strength to protest feebly that it had a spark of life remaining, and must under no condition be interred. It was an SOS. I was horror-struck, as were several others who had seen it. The vehicle was gone before any of us had the presence of mind to look for an undertaker's name, but a couple of us did get the license number. I pumped for home as fast as my legs could carry me, repeating the number aloud to myself. I rushed into the house and telephoned the police.

"I assume you can get the undertaker's name from the license number in a jiffy?" I asked the officer who answered.

"What is this, a gag or something?"

"Would I be likely to make a joke of something like that?"

"No, you don't sound like the type. Yes, I can find out the owner in two shakes from the Motor Vehicles Department."

"Then do so, and for God's sake, man, call him instantly and head him off. They've apparently picked up someone who's still alive. Those things happen."

"They do. I remember last year — "

"Hurry! They may be getting ready to embalm right now. There's not a moment to lose."

I can testify to police efficiency in this instance. It

wasn't fifteen minutes before they called me back from headquarters and asked whether I were an undertaker. My license number had been reported on a vehicle containing a living body — by myself of course. I hadn't recognized it, as so few of us would our own number. I ran out to the garage to find what I fully expected. The plates had been removed from my car. Borrowed for the duration of a certain jape, no doubt? They came back in the mail the next day, by which time I had analyzed the facts from every angle and arrived at a theory that seemed to me airtight.

Our wag either worked for an undertaker or knew someone who did — or someone of like mentality who owned a hearse, as people own old fire engines and police cars. Some kind of auto buff. In either case there would have been no mortician's nameplate on the side of the vehicle, even if we bystanders had had the presence of mind to look, or at best a false one.

I acted perfectly normally in class the next day. Completely deadpan. And, deadpan, assigned them their weekend reading, with oral report Monday from Joe Sandwich. It was W. H. Auden's essay in *The Dyer's Hand*, which brilliantly demonstrates how the practical joke, indefinitely escalated, leads on to Iago. I thought that would give our merry-andrew something to chew on.

One other assignment from those days stands out in my mind.

I told the class to submit a piece of original comic writing. It could be fiction, a humorous essay or reminiscence, anything they pleased, three thousand words in length.

Well, never have I seen *carte blanche* so brazenly abused as was this by Joe Sandwich. What he handed in was a string of funny names. That was all. "M. I. Weary, Iona Ford, G. Whillikers, Gerry Mander, Art Nouveau, Gail Wind, Major Powers, Baron Gain, Lord and Lady Wobleigh . . ." On and on they came, three thousand strong — or fifteen hundred, if you allow for each having two, a given and a surname. There was not even a word of preface, or any explanation whatever. "Willy Maker, Woody Dare, Izzy Abel, Betty Kant, Justus Well . . ." Seeing which way the wind blew I did not even finish this piece of "comic prose," but disgustedly scribbled an F on it and handed it back without comment.

Then a curious thing happened. I couldn't get the damned thing out of my mind. Had my snort of disdain been justified? Nothing would do but that I try my own hand at it. Here is certainly a fatuous occupation for a grown man to let himself get sucked into, one bucking for an associate professorship at that, but intellectual integrity demanded it. One is not entitled to contempt for something to which one is not equal (should that turn out to be the case).

So after dinner I settled down with pencil and paper

and went to work. A good hour's eraser chewing yielded nothing. Then came my first inspiration: "Rose Bush." Very good. In due course "Pete Moss" and "Herb Garden" followed, no doubt through sheer horticultural association, and after that — nothing. I was stalled cold. Still I couldn't get the damnable business out of my mind. I lay awake half the night racking my brains for fit companions to the above. It must have been then that I first realized how this Sandwich customer had begun to degrade and demoralize me. About three A.M. I reached groggily out of bed and scribbled "Hedda Lettis" on the notepad with which I had retired, slipping it in readiness under my pillow. Not certain on second thought that I hadn't heard that somewhere before, and was therefore not stealing garbage, I snatched up pad and pencil and hurled them against the wall. Sometime in the pre-dawn hours I awoke from a fitful sleep long enough to write "Gerta Dammerung" and then fling the whole rotten business out the window.

So then that was the present scholastic kettle of fish: one was not up to something that was beneath one. Or one must look up to something one was above, whichever way you wanted to put it. This is a highly disagreeable sensation, like the anger a woman might feel at not being invited to a party she wouldn't be caught dead at. Yes, Sandwich had got his hooks into me.

I was glad to find him in no more of my classes after

257

that, and glad to see him graduate two years later. In schooldays he was said to have called a classmate "a latent cab driver," a description that fit himself to a T, for my money. But that sort always land on their feet. We presently heard that he had married some boss's daughter or other, and settled down somewhere on the outskirts of Wilton. The suburbs are beginning to have suburbs of their own, like those fungi that are said to grow on other fungi. Well, no matter. I made a few cursory inquiries about him without learning any more than those bare facts. Until our paths suddenly crossed again. On, of all things, my honeymoon.

four

WE honeymooned on Lake Superior, in a snug hotel perched high on a bluff above those waters of Mediterranean blue. I am sure it went well enough as those things go, for there is inevitably a period of accommodation, about which one must be reasonable and resilient. One night I awoke to find Gloria sitting up in bed against the headboard, her expression glum. She had been watching me sleep, my resemblance to a camel suddenly depressing.

"Well, anyway, we're over the hump," I said, making a joke of it, and instead of laughing she answered, "It certainly looks that way," with a sardonic force indicating she hadn't got it at all, or was putting a construction on my words not intended at all. There arose some byplay about a pet name for me, and she finally said she thought she might call me Christmas, since it comes but once a year. Whatever that meant. But then my sweet was not a model of clarity, and I had given up trying in every instance to explore her meaning.

I went into the bathroom where I sat on the edge of the tub to eat a banana sent up by the management and reconsider my position. Evidently it takes some doing to get one's sex life straightened around to where it is running on an even keel. The important thing was undoubtedly to get settled down at home in the real world as soon as possible, to the business of daily living. Paradise is too rich for anyone's blood. It is impossible to sustain it. We have got to come down out of the clouds.

By the time these views had been hammered out in my own mind my bride was herself asleep, her resemblance to a half-grown kitten very beguiling. I sat at the desk to jot down some notes on the *double entendre*. I was working on Kant at the moment, and had packed in my bag a volume elucidating his definition of laughter as *an affection arising from the sudden deflation of a strained expectation into nothing*. It was tantalizing to try to correlate this with the kindred Schopenhauerian view of laughter as a sudden expression of "the incongruity between a concept and the real objects which have been thought through it in some relation."

Shortly after midnight I wandered out to the balcony, taking an apple from the bowl the management kept replenishing at its own expense, a largesse evidently par for the bridal suite. I stood there nibbling on it and watching the water far below. A perfect half moon hung low over it, like the blade of an executioner's axe. The waves spread a gentle froth along the beach as far as the eye could see. Just below our window, and to the right, was a Lover's Leap, so named because of some legend connected with it about an Indian brave who had dashed himself to pieces on the rocks below for love of a maiden.

We did a lot of bicycling, but for trips of any length we took the car. One Sunday afternoon I found myself driving behind a motorist with a sticker on his rear bumper of which I couldn't make out the words. I speeded up in order to get close enough to read what it said. I was curious, and obscurely frustrated. Bumper stickers usually indicate either how you vote or where you've been. I shot through traffic in a series of spurts and dashes that finally fetched me close enough to read what this one said. It read: "Bumper Sticker." I shut my eyes and gritted my teeth. This sort of thing gives me a headache. I had had to slam on the brakes to keep from smacking into this citizen when he stopped suddenly for a red light, and as a result very nearly snapped my neck off, and my bride's into the bargain, for she was riding beside me. We rocked forward as a pair till our noses grazed the windshield, sat poised a moment, and rocked back again. "Jesus Christ," said Gloria, who had taken up profanity, partly out of boredom I think, almost as a kind of hobby. For whose driving the expletive was meant as a rebuke, mine or the cretin's up ahead, I didn't know and didn't ask.

The next lane being free of cars, I whipped out of ours when the light changed and shot around his right flank, my curiosity now transferred to the kind of man who would plaster his means of transportation with such feckless truck. As I drew abreast of him I recognized Joe Sandwich, and had to change my glare to a smile of greeting, or at least something more closely resembling neutrality, in the twinkling of an eye. He recognized me and waved. Then ducking his head forward to look past me he spotted Gloria, and his smile broadened, as from fifty watts to a hundred, in fact an expression of great delight crossed his face. She waved back and called out to him.

"I didn't realize you knew him," I said when we had lost him and settled down to something like normal driving.

"I don't really. We were in school roughly at the same time, and I remember seeing him around. He's a pistol."

It developed that the pistol and his wife were renting a cottage half a mile up the beach from our hotel. Gloria was instantly for calling and asking them for a drink. "Christ, let's see some *people!*" she said. I saw no objection, though it's the sort of thing that can be carried too far — as witness Sandwich's ringing us up to ask us for a drink before we could them. One's whereabouts are easily determined in a small town like Ishcanaba. It struck me as a breach of protocol though: I should have called him. But no matter; anything to get out of this paradise.

So it was that, come Sunday, we found ourselves slogging through the beach sand, shoes in hand, up to Eagle's Nest, there to be greeted by Joe Sandwich, looking brown and fit in Bermuda shorts. There was the same shock of red hair, now already thinning, the same green eyes and somewhat crooked smile, always in evidence except when a joke was being cracked or a stunt pulled. He slapped me on the back, apparently completely unaware that I was on a honeymoon, and said he was glad to see us. Then falling in between us, he led us up a steep flight of stairs, or rather several, to the bluff on which the cottage was perched. I was soon puffing, but Sandwich found the wind to grind out a story that I must say took what little was left in my sails.

He said it was especially good to see us because he had just been appointed to the Wilton faculty himself, so he and I would henceforth be colleagues. This came as something of a shock, since he had been no great shakes even as a student (that he might have tenure in that capacity being one of his own more germane jokes in undergraduate days). In making her own "inkwearies," as Gloria pronounced "inquiries," she had learned that he was now a stock broker for the man whose daughter

263

he had married, so his statement that it was economics he would teach lent a chilling credibility to this introductory palaver. Then he said it would not be a mere professorship he would occupy, either, but the chair.

"Chair?" I panted as we scaled the final escarpment to the cottage, feeling that rope and alpenstock should be provided here for the convenience of guests. All the resentment of a mere instructor bucking in vain for so much as an associateship welled to the surface as suspicions of financial pull darkened my thoughts. Was his father-in-law a trustee?

"Yes. Someone's endowing a chair in memory of the late Dean Wicker." (At the unveiling of whose portrait I had met Gloria.) His father-in-law was the donor! "It'll be known, of course, as the Wicker Chair of Economics."

Some astute probing on my part revealed this whole thing to be made out of whole cloth. There was nothing to it whatsoever. But instructions to secrete adrenalin into my bloodstream had already gone out, and they are not easily revoked. Thus my heart banged away in superseded anger as we were led, puffing like steam engines, up to a very attractively plump young woman in black shorts and blouse, with a red ribbon woven through her hair, who stood awaiting us at the back porch.

Mrs. Sandwich was called Naughty, a nickname from her single days as Betty MacNaughton. Soon we were drinking cocktails outside. It presently fell out that we

264

were on our honeymoon, and then nothing would do but that we have some champagne, as soon as Sandwich could lay his hands on some, possibly sometime later in the week. As we chatted away, I found myself resuming the game I had privately played all through his student years: wondering what made him tick.

I would say that he was one of those people who cannot take reality neat, whether out of anxiety or its second cousin, self-consciousness, and who must therefore knead it continually into nonsense shapes. They *seek*, they *cultivate*, the gap between abstract and conceptual reality, the recognition of which, we have seen, leads according to Schopenhauer to the nervous discharge known as laughter. Speaking of the white tidies left everywhere on chairs and sofas by the owners from whom they rented the cottage furnished, and about which he and his wife argued constantly whether to remove or leave them on, he said, "She's pro and I'm antimacassar." Then the phone rang, and he said to her, "You get it will you, dear? I don't have many shoes on." When at last I protested that we must be going, Mrs. Sandwich wouldn't hear of it; nothing would do but that we stay and get better acquainted. She even laid a hand on my shoulder and forcibly thrust me back into my seat. I sensed a hunger for rational discourse here, an hour's respite from the tomfoolery that was her downsitting and her uprising.

"I'd ask you to supper, but I'm a lousy housekeeper on a vacation," she said. "I couldn't even rustle us up a snack. We're completely out of staples."

"And there isn't a stationery store in town," quacks our nonesuch.

I thought Gloria would burst. She had to turn away to hide the tears that were streaming down her cheeks. She held her aching sides. It was one of the happiest developments of the honeymoon. Again I had the sense of something irresponsible in this remorseless chaffering of Sandwich's with absolutely every subject that came up. He could take nothing straight.

In the end we all moved on to dinner at a local fish house called the Sea Urchin. We had to stand in line even to get into the place, and while waiting outside the restaurant, leaning against a picket fence, Joe and I recalled the courses he had taken with me. He said he had always found my lectures stimulating, and had never taken notes for fear of missing something. Which I thought rather handsome of him. It was Joe and Wally now, and Gloria and Naughty.

Joe took over as host, getting us the promised bottle of champagne to wash our lobster and scallops down with. The effect of his clowning was as interesting to watch as the clowning itself, and I had a time comparing the reactions of the two women. This was of course old stuff to Naughty, and the smile with which she listened as the dutiful wife was something she wore, as she wore her lipstick. Gloria was a fresh audience, and he made the most of it. One of his routines was apparently an existentialist bit with headwaiters who came over to ask whether everything was all right. "Is everything all *right*," he returned with mock incredulity when ours did. "Are you mad? I've got two mortgages on my house, chronic tonsilitis, and tickets to a flop. The war between the sexes is escalating everywhere. There are no new Wagnerian tenors, the whooping crane is practically extinct —"

We were rewarded in this case with more absurdity than even he had bargained for. The proprietor, sensing the to-do from the cash register over which he presided, and believing a scene with a genuinely irate customer to be brewing, hurried over and asked whether anything was the matter.

"*Matter*. Where have you been?" Joe said. "Man is trapped in a biochemical riddle about which he was not consulted, and through which he is hustled to the same oblivion from which he was summoned. That is his lot. He cannot win. He spends a billion years hauling himself out of the primordial slime, another billion dragging his misbegotten guts across dry land, sometimes in pouring rain, goes up into the trees, comes down again, puts on coat and pants, staggers at last into Philharmonic Hall — to find Bruckner a bag of wind. And you can tell the chef that for me!"

"Yes, sir."

Gloria, turned again sideways in her chair, seemed locked in a convulsion that would not let her breathe, in or out. At last a gasping paroxysm appeared to free her from these hysterics, and she wiped her eyes. At such times it was the mirth itself that became the center of attention, and many were the smiling glances Naughty and I exchanged while Joe prepared his next onslaught.

"God, let's see a lot of *them*," Gloria said as we struggled homeward through the beach sand, again carrying our shoes, and this time by moonlight. I was nothing loth, and so see a lot of them we did, continuing to do so when summer was over and we were all back home in Wilton. It was there Joe worked in the only suburban branch the Chicago firm of MacNaughton and Blair had. He eventually wrote their weekly Market Letter, or at least typed out what wiser heads had decided must be said, but in those days he was still one of their brokers and had not been kicked upstairs yet — if such it was. I took little interest in how well he was doing until, having learned from Gloria that she had been giving him her bit of inherited money to invest, I made a few discreet inquiries. It developed that he was rapidly making a name for himself in his native tradition, only here the humor was unconscious.

"Do you know that the stocks Joe Sandwich recommends are known in the trade as laughing stocks?" I said to Gloria at the conclusion of this espionage.

"The ones he told me to buy have gone up, Wally."

"Everything's going up, and will keep doing so until it goes up the way it always does — in smoke. I wish you'd take your profits and get out."

"It's my money. I don't want to make an um issue out of it, but I think anybody's foolish to let a gravy train like this go by without getting a piece of the ride. I'll get out in time. Now don't be such a drag, Wally. Do you intend to check up on me?"

"You're darn tooting," I answered fondly.

I had no doubt Sandwich constituted a breath of fresh air in a profession sorely in need of comic relief, but one didn't want his wife helping foot the bill for the entertainment on the proceeds of her dowry. Not that I hadn't enough on my mind without worries over money matters. The president of the college called me in to say I wasn't doing any too well. What he meant, I believe, was that I was doing too well in far too many directions for my own good. I was supposed to be teaching psychology, but my very obsession with my specialty had me spreading myself thin. The psychology of laughter led one into the philosophies of comedy, and that in turn into studies of literature, till nobody could tell *what* I was teaching. I asked as tactfully as I could what had happened to the Renaissance man. Freud had addressed to lowly jokes and gags the same titanic genius that gave us the interpretation of dreams (see his *Jokes and Their*

269

Relation to the Unconscious). The president said he agreed in principle, but he had not invented the present academic system ordaining that one know more and more about less and less.

Then Mother remained a headache, continuing to hang on her gatepost punitive signs reading "Clearance" and "Everything Must Go" whenever she felt too long an interval had elapsed between our visits. I would shoot past the house with head averted, whether by bike or car, to spare myself these miserable and demoralizing sights. And it was at this time I got another dose of our Joe Sandwich in his customary vein — proving again that if you have a friend you don't need an enemy.

Oh, that is too strong. But let it stand as evidence of the strain on one's equanimity during that period. I suppose it was my own skill at charades that made them single me out as the butt of a trick of which Sandwich was, of course, chief architect. It was at the home of some friends named Weems, who were always entertaining. Joe said they had hearts of artichoke. After dinner we played these charades, and when it came my turn to act out a song title, he thought it would be amusing if there were collusion between both teams along the following lines. I, who had been guessing quotations and titles thirteen to the dozen all evening, would be given the simplest possible song to act out, only under no circumstances would anybody guess it. "Row, row, row your boat," was the assignment whispered into my ear, by which time, you understand, the whole thing had been cut and dried behind my back. But to work I went.

I sat on the floor in the middle of the room, ringed by traitors, and strained at imaginary oars till my joints creaked like rowlocks and the perspiration ran down my face, while my teammates, which included Joe, screwed up their faces in thought and exchanged looks of feigned consternation. This is hardly my idea of humor; it is a bit primitive for my tastes, but anyway. "Volga Boatman?" someone guessed. I shook my head, and with shut eyes continued. "Michael, row the boat ashore, hallelujah?" cried the double-crossing Sandwich. Again the terse headshake.

It had grown quite warm in the room. I rose to remove my coat before once more squatting down in my imaginary skiff and bending to the oars in shirtsleeves. "Inspirations" flowed thick and fast. "Up a lazy river." "Over the wave," "My bonnie lies over the ocean" — all but the right answer. Finally somebody got one "row," also by prearrangement, and then stalled cold, affecting perplexity at the burst of corroborational mugging from me. This is always something to behold in charades, I must say objectively. I worked head and eyebrows and hands in that everything-going-at-once pantomime by which we try to tell a teammate that he is on the right track — come ahead with more of the same. To no avail. Wearily

271

I let the air out of my lungs to indicate that a fresh start was to be made, and then, drawing a long breath, stabbed the air with one finger.

"First word is 'row.' "

"Right!" said the silent nod that wrenched my collarbone. I then thrust two fingers at the speaker and elaborately described ditto marks in the air to say that the second was the same as the first. Blank looks. With a sigh I sat down amid the hooked rugs and went back to work.

By now I was sweating bullets. "Roamin' in the gloamin'," said the mastermind of this lark, namely Joe Sandwich. Something made me turn instead to his wife.

Naughty was bent forward in her chair, leaning toward me with the most sympathetic expression on her face. She wore a kind of yearning smile, that of someone trying to communicate something by telepathy, in this case the fact that my leg was being pulled. It's easy to say that in retrospect now, yet the fact remains that it was a moment after this that I tumbled I was the butt of a hoax. I rose and returned to my chair, wearing the good-sport smile that is among the most tiresome of human chores.

When Naughty saw me thirstily polishing off a bottle of beer later, she disengaged herself from the group with whom she'd been talking and crossed the room to me. "You probably need that," she laughed.

"I could use a shower too."

"It is hot in here. Let's go outside on the porch. It's cool there."

We sat on the bannister looking at the moon, and talked of everything and nothing. But this inconsequential chatter was the first of several party conversations that Naughty chose to let grow in intimacy, as though discretion were a thermostat she deliberately turned down as acquaintance between us deepened — and as she probably sensed discretion to be what I was the soul of. I think from her point of view she saw us as two people who could feel sorry for each other, given sufficient decline in their respective fortunes.

The general theme at first was the plight of the woman who wakes up to find herself married to the life of the party, when the life of the party goes on playing the role at home. "He puts lampshades on his head *there*." Nor was that anything but the beginning. Neither of the Sandwiches drank heavily as a general rule, but at intervals one or the other of them would tie one on, Joe for the Saturday-night hell of it, Naughty because she was in the dumps. I once tried drowning my sorrows, till I found out they could swim. It was one night when Naughty was in her cups that she introduced another complaint than the life-of-the-party-at-home one, and here she really let down her hair.

"Look at him now, dishing it out for Vinnie Wright.

She sits there smiling like the queen beloved of a jester, but does she know the cap and bells act is for only one thing? Some night when the king is off on a hunt."

"Oh, now, Naughty."

"Cut it out, Wally. I'm not all that pathetic that I'm the Last to Know. He'll never stop prowling. And it isn't to Prove Anything either. He's just a glutton. He can't pass anything up. He can't be housebroken."

She took a drink, and then gazing into her glass pursued another of the associations that made her conversation seem disjointed whereas she was tipsily following connections perfectly logical in her mind and in the circumstances.

"Do you know he goes around the house naked as a jaybird all the time?"

"Well, that wouldn't be generally realized."

"The first thing he does when he gets home is take his clothes off and leave them off."

"Free spirit."

"He'll come down to dinner in the raw, sit around afterward in the raw, watching television or whatever. He'll even play chess in his birthday suit, shifting from ham to ham like Eliot's Sweeney in his bath. And as for hope of any literary discussion such as this! Once I asked him to please put something on because my mother might drop in, and he went downstairs and came back up dressed in a roll of linoleum."

"The original Dadaist," I said, to put the best possible face on all this for her sake, and because I knew what she was going through, though fully suspecting the impossibility of salvaging any human dignity for this boojum creature. I did not recognize him as a Wilton product. No, I disclaimed him utterly. I washed my hands of any responsibility.

I watched anxiously as Naughty looked into her glass again with the dreamy recklessness that prefaced her decision to pull out another stop. I steeled myself, nervously glancing about in hopes of interruption. I did not want any more information about the Sandwiches, if you please.

"At breakfast, when one can scarcely look an egg in the face, he'll come down whistling and twirling a cane, all dressed up in a derby hat. Or a scarf which he'll wind around his middle, or hang on his whatsis and invite me to ring for service."

Though chills were running up and down my spine, I said as steadily as I could, "You knew he was a load of laughs when you married him, my dear Naughty."

"Not this many laughs, which they finally aren't anymore, is what I'm trying to tell you. I mean hasn't he heard of the law of diminishing returns? He's an economist. Can't he ever knock it off? Oh, God, is there to be no respite? This queen-beloved-of-a-jester stuff he's pulling with Vinnie now, I even get *that* at home. He'll try anything on for size with anybody. Anything in skirts that is. Don't you give a thought about Gloria?"

"Naughty, I really think this has gone far enough."

"No, I meant her money." But I sensed her checking herself, swerving her reckless vehicle to one side, after having really meant what I'd thought. "Get her to pull out before the market goes to hell." Naughty's eyes raked the room till they found Gloria, away at the other end. Persisting in what I knew had been her original meaning I said, "They've hardly spoken to one another all evening." At which she rolled her eyes at the ceiling and said, "Jesus. What would be the first thing two adulterers would do?"

Well, I refuse to holler till I'm hurt. My wife's lunching with a freebooter didn't make her one. Joe remained the object of interest, the focus of my horrified curiosity. He belonged to that class of miscreants who fascinate while they appall, and the glimpse I had been vouchsafed of his household haunted me for days, giving rise to all sorts of kindred imaginings of which I was powerless to purge my head. I thought of my old pupil capering about his roost draped and daubed as told, like the primitive savage of whose crude bedizenments and disfigurations his own were a suburban echo, grotesqueries so evoking the aboriginal lurking in all of us that nothing would do but that I give them an experimental whirl myself.

I locked the door, one evening when I was home alone, Gloria being out to an adult extension course at the local high school, and went upstairs to the bedroom. I stripped to the skin. Then, selecting a bowtie to knot on the organ to which Joe Sandwich was known to affix such haberdashery for hacks, I stood in front of a full-length mirror to survey the results.

Never have I seen anything so dismal. I was trying to understand what made such a person tick. I was sincerely trying to gain some insight into the mentality that found diversion in such antics, much less thought he could indefinitely amuse a woman with this kind of buffoonery continued ad infinitum — without success. I was at a total loss. I could not identify with it. I put a tam-o'-shanter on my head, without making the total effect noticeably more palatable. It was perhaps not my speed. At any rate, all I could do was shake my head at the sorry result, dismantle it, and return the components to where they belonged.

I dressed and went downstairs, where I mixed a mild bourbon-and-soda. That nursed away, I lit a cigar and wandered outdoors for a breath of air. I wound up at the high school where Gloria was taking this course in amateur investment, along with a couple of housewife friends also putting a little money into things in search of modest adventure, to find her not among the class when it filed out at dismissal time. The evening being a total loss anyway, I thought it as good a time as any to pay a call on Mother.

For that I returned for my bicycle. It was now mid-autumn, with the garden gimcracks safely stored in the cellar till another spring, so no distressing legends awaited my gaze as I propped my bike against the porch and removed the clips from my shins. And the cottage was cheerfully lighted. There was no answer when I rang the bell, though, and that aroused some apprehension, till I went round to the side of the house and found the bathroom window lighted. Water was running in the tub. Pacing about the lawn with my cigar, I remembered Mother's obsession with daily bathing, scrupulously observed "in case something happens and I have to go to the hospital." She would then be found clean by anyone passing judgment on that score. Of course something did happen to her. She slipped on a cake of soap and had to be taken to the hospital for a spell of traction — which she felt justified her constant fuss on this point. A piece of circular reasoning if I ever saw one.

Vague shadows behind the window told me when she was out of the tub, and after another few minutes of pantomime with the towel I again punched the front doorbell. She admitted me wearing her bathrobe and carrying her stick. I pitched my cigar into the bushes and followed her into the parlor.

"Have you seen my gallstones anywhere?"

There are times when one wants to chuck it all. To

throw down the whole shooting match and call it quits. You will no doubt recognize the crotchet of some people for keeping mementoes of their operations, especially when these involve the removal of organs or parts not wholly repugnant, and preserving them in formaldehyde. Or perhaps it was a jar of alcohol the doctor gave my mother hers in, some years before, to take home and keep on a shelf — in her bedroom, the sewing room, sometimes even on the mantel.

"You may have moved it into the spare room when you had that housecleaning service in last month," I said. I went to look myself, and there was the missing souvenir. I carried it back into the parlor with me.

We set a spell, as they used to say in Mother's day, sipping the port she trotted out — a vintage bottle I had given her myself the Christmas before. We chatted of a number of things. Then she felt her left side in a gingerly way and said, "I've been having these twinges here lately, and a kind of tenderness. Right there. What side is your appendix on?"

"On the right, Mother, but you can have sympathetic pains on the opposite side," I said, not to bar her too abruptly from the hope of a companion commemorative for the mantel. So it went until we had finished our port and I rose to leave.

Naughty told me she got home one time from her shopping rounds to find Joe had marked his body off into zones, like the zones on the charts one finds hanging in the butcher shops, that illustrate the cuts into which dressed beef is divided. He had used iodine, tracing the lines with the stopper of the bottle. The chart was remarkably detailed and accurate, allowing for some adjustment from cattle to human. It was Naughty's view that he had consulted the carving section of one of their cookbooks. The cuts were not only marked off but designated in printed letters — Brisket, Shank, Loin End, and the like. "How would you like to sleep with somebody like that?" she said.

Knowing the question to be rhetorical I did not answer, but instead, in the silence into which this intelligence plunged us both, I reviewed the stage to which this latest example seemed to bring the career of one dedicated absolutely to the practice of shenanigans.

Joe Sandwich would seem to have come a long way since high-school and even college days, if the tricks he played on me and others then were any gauge. He was like an artist who has outgrown work of an earlier and more conventional sort, to which exception might be taken and on the strength of which final judgment ought not to be rendered, and would seem to have entered an obscure, but richer, phase, one demanding application of the viewer but also rewarding it, as the gallery catalogues say. "Replete with savage surrealist overtones" might be said of this latest period, certainly this newest effort.

Some kind of symbolism might even have been intended by the manner in which he had ringed his reproductive organs in a zone left purposely undesignated as to "cut." That our thoughts were running in the same channel was indicated by the remark with which Naughty now broke our silence.

" 'Is the idea the emasculating wife?' I asked him. 'The castrating female, and butchering marriage and all that? Am I to go in and win?' "

"And what did he answer to that?" I asked.

"He said to cut off his allowance, but not to go any farther than that. He had already gone on to some other monkeyshines."

"What was that?" I asked, again fascinated in spite of myself, too mesmerized by these disclosures to remember my decision to acquire no more information about the Sandwich household, if you please. I had had quite enough, thank you. I wished to be privy to no more. "What was he doing now?"

"Oh, I don't remember. Yes I do. You know he has absolutely masses of props, picked up from God knows where. Jumble shops, second-hand stores, white elephant sales. He bought a naval uniform for a dollar, a Prince Albert coat for twenty-five cents. One thing he got somewhere was a stethoscope. He wandered over with that and put it to my chest. I was a sick actress who had canceled a matinee, and he was the doctor sent over by the producer to see whether it was really true I couldn't go on. 'What are you playing these days, Miss Pliquid? Is it a taxing role? Camille? Oh, in that case you definitely can't go on. Not with that cough.' "

Any pleasure in this little fancy, amusing enough in its way, is then promptly dissipated by the spectacle next visited upon our poor Naughty: the spectacle of Joe jigging away into the bathroom singing, "Let's get stinkin', said Abraham Lincoln," snapping his fingers as he goes, and revealing rump steaks not to have been neglected in the overall charting.

I don't know why I'm telling you all this, but for the fact that according to my recollection of what happened to Naughty, it was about then that he proposed the idea that we go halves on the purchase of the cottage they had rented when we had first run into them in Ishcanaba, and regularly summer with them there. The aged owners had died, and it was now up for sale by the estate. Joe said it had charm, but that a few thousand bucks or so in repairs would make it livable.

I am not such a fool as to go halves on anything with the Sandwiches. Images of Nature Boy coursing through the rooms in the altogether, or wearing his sincere jockstrap, or trailing seaweed or whatever, came inevitably to mind, and I wondered how Naughty could think anybody given the benefit of the facts in my possession would even entertain such a project. But in any case they bought it for themselves (with the usual leg up from the MacNaughtons), and since Gloria and I continued to vacation in Ishcanaba too, we saw more and more of them. We stayed at the resort hotel where we had honeymooned, not in quite that early splendor of course, but in fair enough style in one of the light-housekeeping cottages behind the main building where our senior counterparts rocked themselves to death on the breeze-swept and capacious porch, overlooking Lover's Leap. Not to write the elderly off, because the most excitement was provided one summer by a partially infirm old gentleman who drove around the grounds and even the town in a mechanized wheelchair, wearing a crash helmet.

I have said I am no fool. Yet a certain vagueness linked in the popular mind to intellectuals of an academic stripe must be admitted. Your absentminded professor type. Gloria has even called me a bumbler, a term I cannot conscientiously disclaim. I sometimes pedal off into town on some errand or other, spend an hour window-shopping or browsing in bookstores, and return home on foot, completely forgetting that I rode down. I have lost two bicycles that way. "That fog you go around in is going to be fatal some day," Gloria said. Prophetic enough words, I'm afraid, though that's again anticipating the story.

Our union bore no fruit, as we say, and that proved a

source of keen frustration to Gloria, frustration of the sort from which we often seek relief in food. Since her tastes ran to special and spicy tidbits as well as being unpredictable, I was often sent out in the small hours for the herring and pickles and strawberry ice cream for which the husbands of expectant mothers are more normally dispatched. One evening as we were having cocktails in our cottage, she asked wasn't I also sick of hotel dining room food, and didn't I think something from Mann's would hit the spot. Mann's was one of those delicatessens where they specialize in those huge three-decker sandwiches that are named after personalities of stage and screen whose favorite combinations of meats and cheese they are. We were happily washing our Mary Martins down with cold beer when there was a furious scrunching of gravel on the path outside our cottage, as of someone skidding to a violent stop, followed by a loud banging on the door. I opened it to find quite another kind of Sandwich, wearing a ballplayer's cap with the peak switched about and panting with a flushed expression.

"The abercrombies are running! They come in with the tide to spawn the first July full moon every four years between Presidential elections, as you know! Tonight's the night! Hurry! They're thrashing on the beach by the millions!"

"Where did you get my bicycle, Joe?" I said. I could

not help noticing where it lay flung down on the door-step. He had clearly been riding it.

"In front of Mann's. Wally, why don't you get your-self a horse? They'll come back without you."

"I appreciate your trouble, Joe. Thanks a lot. But how did you know it was mine?"

"It rang a bell. Like this." And he stooped to jingle the one on the handlebar. He became more serious. "Actually, we had dinner in that new restaurant next door to Mann's, which was how I saw it when we came out. But the thing is, guess who with. The Harrisons! They're in town for a couple of weeks." This struck no more responsive chord in my bosom than the news that the abercrombies were running, but I managed to con-ceal my lack of ecstasy at the prospect of spending any time in the company of Fido Harrison. "And the Wilsons are around somewhere too. We're trying to round everyone up for a party at our place later. Can you come?"

If you promise not to spell fuchsia, I thought to myself.

It was a little act of his, a bit he did when the hour was late and the guests well-oiled. "F," he would begin, then, "U," the laughter building till he would reach the "C" and then appear to hesitate, or falter, at which point they would be rolling on the floor. I couldn't for the life of me see what the hilarity was all about, except as evidence of the taste for the offbeat, the calculatedly meaningless, according to the mode of the day. Part of the humor no doubt lay in the way he would bite his lip, uncertainly, as he groped his way along like a schoolboy in a spelldown, a poor speller not at all sure he wouldn't make a mistake somewhere along the line. Then there were interpolations about being a weak character, often prey to impulse and beset by temptations. Some such folderol. I was not in the mood for any party, but Gloria, of whom he had obviously been trying to catch a glimpse over my shoulder, appeared, clapping her hands enthusiastically and exclaiming, "A great idea, Joe! When does the orgy begin?" She pronounced it to rhyme with porgy, I'm afraid.

"Nowish! Right awayish!" And he got back on my bicycle and disappeared at breakneck speed into the twilight, calling over his shoulder, "I've got to warn the rest of the countryside! There's not a moment to lose!"

My mood toward him mellowed as Gloria and I again walked the half-mile up the beach toward Eagle's Nest. I found myself shopping for approval for Joe among the poets. "Much madness is divinest sense," Emily Dickinson has written. "There is a pleasure sure in being mad which none but madmen know." Dryden. Then there was the famous line, "Born with the gift of laughter and a sense that the world is mad," a view eminently borne out by the fact that the authorities at Yale once had it

286

inscribed on a building in the mistaken belief that it is a translation of some ancient classic, whereas it is from no higher a literary source than Rafael Sabatini. It was the kind of story Joe himself loved, and collected, like the one about the electric chair in the southern state that had been condemned because it was unsafe. Or the huge Texas auditorium in which the air conditioning was on such a scale that condensation caused clouds to form on the ceiling, which in turn gave rise to a modest precipitation and corresponding rainfall on the occupants.

I gazed up at the sky as these thoughts drifted through my head. It was in any event clear, without even any of the northern lights that often made those summer nights sensational. The stars were like a belt of whiskey. I was carrying a flashlight, and occasionally pointed its beam upwards to indicate one or two that were of more interest than others. Our bare feet made a steady hissing whine in the sand, here so golden pure that one sometimes thought he could eat it for breakfast, like farina.

When we arrived at the cottage, Joe had already clustered around him a group of guests whom he was giving a mock garden tour. "There's some dandelions, there's some rocks that date from the eighteenth century." I squeezed Gloria's hand because an owl had flown out of a tamarack. "There's our Pontiac, which we're thinking of adding onto." As we traipsed in his wake I noticed that Joe was wearing a pair of those colossal outsize shoes that are used for display in shoe-store windows. They might have been size thirty or forty, if you want to look at it in that way. He kept them on inside the house, where he also lighted people's cigarettes with those twelve-inch-long matches used to start fires with. They kept a box of such tapers on the hearth, and every time a woman would get out a cigarette he would waddle over in his monster shoes and strike a monster match on the side of its monster matchbox and extend the flame to her, sometimes from halfway across the room. The effect became a little phantasmagoric, as though we were characters in *Gulliver's Travels*. Some of us began to get a bit woozy.

When this stage of matters had run its course, I rose from where I was and went over to join Naughty.

"How are you, Naughty?"

"Fine, Wally. And you?"

"Never better. That shade of blue becomes you."

"Slenderizing."

"Oh, don't start that nonsense when a man is trying to pay you a compliment. I mean it's just right for your skin, which I regard as one of the features of these parts. That creamy pallor. Your skin reminds me — and you may not like this simile — like that coated stock the better magazines are printed on."

"I like it fine. Tell me more. I need it. I also need a good set of exercises."

We slipped into our usual confidences, though this time there were no hair-raising revelations of the sort that studded our tête-à-têtes — only a report that, in a wicker picnic hamper that served Joe as a strongbox, she had come upon his will. It stipulated, for funeral arrangements, a service to be held at four A.M., in the woods, with the mourners perched in treetops being harangued by whichever of their number had lost in lots drawn for the purpose. She shook her head. I told her I thought it a rather good burlesque of the elaborate instructions for being ignored that are often in fact left behind by egotistical types, and that are so much more of a nuisance than conventional observances would have been.

In the midst of this brief, its subject was heard across the room, where he was amusing Gloria and Gertrude Harrison with some tale about a local painter. "He's by far the dirtiest in the colony. What he draws best is flies. Yich!"

I never decided whether Joe was intelligent or not; my opinion on that score was subject to such wide fluctuations. I remember his once saying in a serious discussion, about whether Red China should be admitted to the U.N., "You can't housebreak a dog in the yard. You have to bring him in." But saying it, he wielded one of the numerous pipes with which he would parody precisely such sententious conversation. Once when the topic was music and the discussion got around to Ravel, he said Ravel was a nectarine. Which I suppose has some dim sort of meaning. His reference to the ostensibly divergent Communist camps as in fact "birds of a fetter" was another example of a point of view very possibly adopted for the sake of the quip.

And yet it occurs to me that he may have had a secret fascination with the subject of Communism, now that I recall a stunt he once pulled with a tape recorder, that made fools of all his guests. It was at a Halloween party at his house at which at least twenty people were present.

He had taped half an hour or so of recorded radio music into which he grafted a fake news bulletin read by himself in a disguised voice. The tape recorder was concealed behind the radio, and further masked by several pots of house plants, and so we thought, as we sipped our brandies, that we were listening to after-dinner mood music from the local station. Indeed we paid no attention to the music at all until it was suddenly broken into by a galvanizing voice saying: "Ladies and gentlemen, we interrupt this concert to bring you a special news bulletin. Nikita Khrushchev has defected to the West. We repeat: Nikita Khrushchev has defected to the West. This astounding fact has just been confirmed by the White House, where the deposed Russian premier has been given asylum."

We sat open-mouthed, no doubt a sight to behold as we gaped at one another in stunned amazement. Fido Harrison began some expostulation but we all shushed him in order to listen to the bulletin.

I don't know by what sort of manipulation of recorder and radio Joe managed to expand this hoax, but, diving for the latter with some hanky-panky about "Let's get another station!" and with his back to us, he seemed to get one, where a talk on local sanitation problems was interrupted by a second bulletin "absolutely confirming" the first. "The former Russian premier is definitely a guest at the White House. A statement by the President will be issued within the hour, according to our Washington correspondent. We will bring you any fresh developments the instant we receive them. Now we return you to our regularly scheduled broadcast."

We made asses of ourselves according to our various lights. One woman wanted to go to church to pray. Another to telephone her father who was a retired political science teacher in Oregon. Fido Harrison said: "This is the greatest event since the birth of Christ," a remark for which he never forgave Joe. Naughty spilled the beans when she thought things had gone far enough. She later announced with a laugh that she probably felt mellow toward everybody because she was going to have a baby.

Fido left in a foul humor, supported by Gertrude in

the style to which he was accustomed whenever he drank too much. Joe seemed surprised to find people resentful, and defended himself by insisting he had played fair by giving everyone a sporting chance: the selection interrupted had been *The Merry Pranks of Til Eulenspiegel.* Naughty tried to change the subject, getting back to her old obsession about exercise, twice as important now that motherhood threatened her figure.

"Get a bicycle," I told her, unaware that on that proposal our joint fates hinged. "Joe too. He's getting a bit thick in the flitch. Gloria and I enjoy it. It's great fun, as well as healthy. We'll all go."

Thus was born that wheeling foursome in which our strange friendship found its next metamorphosis. Dressed in tweed coats and caps and fluttering scarves, we filed down North Shore byways or, come summer, along the bluff from which could be seen the waters of Lake Superior, boiling among the rocks far below. Or we wandered inland among back trails leading into stretches of northern forest standing mute since the birth of time, a rumination solemnizing some, but giving Joe the abercrombies. When we paused to gaze our fill, he would buck to be on with the business of turning fat into muscle and whittling down his paunch . . . So passed a summer, then another and another still, till suddenly those placid rambles gave way to a somewhat more exciting and even dangerous pastime among Ishcanaba's bicycling set, particularly its younger members.

You wheeled at alternating breakneck and snailpace speeds around a mile course circumscribing our hotel and a small common, or park, beside it, these two together comprising what was called the Square — and square was he who feared it. It is really more rectangular than square, and so circling the Square can best be pictured by imagining a large envelope with yourself starting at the point where the return address would be. The first leg was a short block of Michigan Street, which pitches at a steep angle down to Superior, named of course after the lake on which it fronts. Lover's Leap lies at the foot of this grade — a small lookout point actually with a pay telescope cemented into a brick parapet. You gathered as much speed as you safely could, braked violently at the last possible fraction of a second before you would have crashed into the parapet, made a skidding, slewing left turn, pedaled to the next corner with what remained of your momentum, made another left turn, and pumped as fast as you could up Water Street, turning left again at the postage stamp and streaking for home, your starting point. Someone discovered this to be an exact mile, records were chalked up, and doing it in two minutes came to be the thing among the boys. The crucial legs of the trip were of course the first and third, the sides of the envelope. The one took guts and the other stamina, for Water Street naturally goes up as steeply as Michigan does down. The difference between failure and success lay in the extra seconds you could pile up going downhill — time in the bank the youngsters called it, or "gravy time." Some with speedometers claimed to clock speeds as high as fifty miles an hour downgrade. How much of this you could preserve for the turn without a rear-wheel slew that cost you your balance and a nasty spill was the pivotal point in this challenge to courage and skill. Many a patch was laid, and many a tire blown that summer. And of course the stores did a brisk business in stop-watches.

I was eager to try it, but not in broad daylight before spectators. So one night when Gloria was washing her hair, her head well in a basin of water, I stepped quickly outside, unlocked my bike from the tree to which I kept it chained, and went to the starting point.

Though it was only a little after nine there were few people or cars about, the weather having been what Joe called "nasty as a budget." It had rained but the streets were now dry, so there was no hazard there. Naturally I had ridden around here innumerable times but never to circle the Square with a stopwatch. I had one of those in my pocket. I saw instantly as I poised myself for the takeoff fling that clocking yourself lost you time, besides being inaccurate, but all I wanted was a rough estimate of what I could do. So I clicked the watch in my pocket and shot away.

The first sensation was exhilarating. I had no speedometer but I guessed I was doing forty as I approached Lover's Leap. I was bareheaded, and my hair flew in the wind. The cold air on my cheeks was intoxicating, and over the crest of the parapet I could see the lights of a ship. I felt I could whirl straight off into the night and land on her decks, or keep deliriously going among the stars, provided they came out. One *can* become drunk with speed.

But it was time to check that, as well as my fantasies, and so I jammed on the brake with my right foot. It was a good calculation, if slightly on the conservative side as befit one's maiden heat. I made the turn easily with just enough slew but not too much, and streaked for Water Street. That was where the trouble began.

I had never actually ridden up Water before, and now I realized how steep it really was. She was a bastard, as the boys said. I ran out of my gravy halfway up, and from there on it was Work. I panted and I groaned and I gnashed my teeth. My legs ached from a strain for which not twenty years of normal cycling had prepared them. My calves felt as though they would burst, my thighs as though all the muscles and tendons were being slowly torn from the bones, and the bones from their sockets. It was like being put on the rack. I could see that this was the real test, not the turn — the test, when all was said and done, of youth. It was there, that night on Water Street hill, I knew I had run out of that gravy.

My wheels slowed, and slowed, and at one point, just as I reached the crest of the hill, stopped. So that for one anguished moment I stood poised in midair, standing erect on the pedals like a horseman in his stirrups. Straining with every ounce of strength I had, I gritted my teeth and pushed on. Slowly the bike inched forward, though kept upright only by my rapidly wagging the front wheel. At last with one supreme downward crank of the right pedal I gained the summit and turned left for the straightaway to the finish. Though that was level ground, not even it was easy now. My legs pumped like my heart. I was never so grateful to reach anything as I was that finish line. I dropped the bike and pulled the stopwatch out of my pocket. It had taken me three minutes and seven seconds. Bannister could have run it in less on foot.

I was so depressed by this that after I had chained my bike to the tree once more I strolled back to Water Street, still getting my wind. I dropped into a rather good lunch counter I had discovered there, for a cup of coffee and a slice of the apple pie for which it was famous. I was watching my waistline but I felt that tonight I had earned an indulgence. The cheese there was no good, and so I always took my own along when I went in there for this treat, a few squares of some excellent cheddar we kept in the cottage for snacks. When I had been served, I fished a few nuggets of it out of my coat pocket and dropped them furtively onto the pie, shielding the result from the counterman's gaze by cupping a forearm around the plate. As a result of this a rather nasty incident occurred, quite appropriately topping off a dismal enough evening.

The counterman was new, or substituting for the regular one with whom I had become quite friendly. He was rather morose, and after a few desultory remarks about how dreary the weather had been, he returned to wiping off the condiment containers all along the counter. There was no one else in the restaurant at the moment. I fell to gazing out the window, which was to my left. As I looked out, coffee cup poised in one hand while the other encircled my pie, I saw a man grinding up the hill on a bicycle. This was at the point where the grade was steepest, and he was having one hell of a time keeping in motion. In fact his grimaces interfered with my immediately recognizing him, but it was Joe Sandwich. His teeth were clenched in an expression of Herculean effort. He looked like a man who was cursing and swearing, though there would seem little sense in wasting valuable breath on such vain imprecations. He sagged from side to side and his front wheel wobbled as he lost and lost momentum. Would he make it? The suspense was agonizing even to me — perhaps especially to me who had barely managed to keep my own balance and stay afloat. Such was my excitement that I rose and went to the door to watch, leaving my pie unguarded. He had passed the restaurant, but I could see to the top of the hill through the window. Joe stood motionless for one split second, poised like a horseman in the stirrups, and toppled off. He caught hold of the tailgate of a passing truck and was towed rapidly from my sight.

I returned to my stool to find the counterman scrutinizing my plate. He resumed his cleaning chores while I once more fell to. I sat slightly forward with my forearm curled around the plate again, chewing with an innocent air. Staring at the wall ahead of me, I could just make him out on the edge of my vision, taking me in. He was wiping the neck of a ketchup bottle now, very slowly. I continued eating with nonchalance. When he turned momentarily away, I quickly reached into my pocket for another bit of the cheddar and dropped it surreptitiously on the last fragment of pie left. He turned back again just as I scooped up this final morsel on my fork and popped it into my mouth. He cleared his throat and spoke.

"I serve you that cheese with that pie?"

"Yes, I believe you did. How much is that?" I said, suddenly feeling the air to be charging up with something disagreeable, and preferring to pay for what I had not bought to explaining that I hadn't — and perhaps having to justify it into the bargain. But he was not to be put off.

"No I didn't. You brought that cheese in here with you. You been dropping little pieces of it on your pie. We don't serve cheese in little teeny pieces here, but one whole slice."

I didn't like the looks of this at all. I sensed a nasty incident brewing.

"And what of that?" I said, fishing into my trouser pocket for little teeny pieces of money. "It's my cheese and my pie, and I should imagine I'm at liberty to do what I want with them, in any combination that suits my fancy."

"I let somebody bring his lunch in here and just order coffee to drink with it?"

"That's not the same thing at all. There's no parallel whatsoever."

"Where do you draw the line?"

"I don't know. It's not my problem."

"No, it's mine. And if you ask me there's not that much difference, and I consider it a pretty petty thing for a customer to come in here and do what you just did."

"Not if he likes good apple pie and cheese. With the pie here I have no quarrel, but it deserves better than the processed cheese you serve, in which no flavor can be discerned but that of the cellophane it came wrapped in."

"A cheap thing to do," he went on, ignoring my apology in favor of the epithets churning to the surface of his own mind. "A *cheesy* thing you might say, and I've got a good notion to charge you for it."

"Little good it will do you, because I don't intend to pay," I said, withdrawing my earlier offer to do so. "I know apple pie and coffee are forty-five cents here. I've bought it many times from Louie, who by the way doesn't mind my bringing my own cheese. He quite understands."

I tumbled sixty cents on the counter and hurried out.

I went for a walk instead of returning immediately to the cottage. I felt distracted and at loose ends, after such a jumbled night, and wanted to clear my head. Seeing Joe Sandwich do no better than I on the Square Mile didn't take the edge off my disappointment with my own performance. He was still younger than I, and the good God knows there is always that when you have it. Doing better than someone years your junior is not a consolation sufficient to heal that gap. Then the incident had occurred when the summer was again drawing to its close, another summer put by and gone forever, with all the melancholy implications of approaching autumn. Soon we would pack our bikes into our station wagons along with everything else, all of us, and head back down along the streaming highways for home.

But before that happened another episode occurred far more permanent and disastrous in its consequences, as Gloria had foretold. It was another result of my infernal bumbling.

five

I SUPPOSE it's true that women talk too much and that, conversely, husbands never listen. All the magazines are full of articles at least on the latter, so there is probably in progress a national aggravation of this ancient problem.

Gloria and I were sitting in our cottage, late one evening, when I dimly sensed that she was discoursing at length on something that probably required keener attention than, through the fog of abstraction in which I listened, I was paying it. She was relating a dream she had had, but, like a late theatergoer who has missed an essential piece of exposition, I didn't learn that until it was too late. I thought she was talking about something that had actually happened to her that day, or maybe the day before.

"I was wearing my um new flowered slacks," she was saying, "and I was walking up Main Street. As I turned the corner and passed the library, I ran into Joe Sandwich. We stopped to talk a minute."

"Oh? How is Joe?" I asked, showing some interest.

"All right I guess. Why? What's that got to do with it? You see him as much as I do."

"Days go by without either of us seeing them at all. But go on." I didn't really care about this, or how Joe "was." I was only trying to keep the conversational ball rolling. "What then?"

"Well, suddenly he looked down at my slacks and started to laugh. He asked whether they were new, and I said yes, and he laughed again."

"Why, that son of a bitch," I said. "It's just like him though. Joe likes to think he's the answer to every woman's prayer, though often Lotharios like that don't really like women, as I keep telling you. They are simply a means to an end: their personal gratification. Affection, respect, these things aren't in it. So what happened then? What did you say?"

"Well, naturally I took offense, and asked him what he meant. He kind of looked away and said what he meant was that I was one of the few women who understood the art of dressing absurdly."

"That lout."

"He was trying to cover up, you see."

Did I see! My fists were clenching and unclenching. I saw another nasty situation brewing here, far worse than the contretemps with the picklepuss counterman. "He's a lout, yet at the same time mealymouthed. Then what?"

"Then I left him, and hadn't gone far up Main Street when I was glad to run into Gertrude Harrison, wearing stretch slacks too, and I told her what Joe said, and she was disgusted."

"I should hope!"

I shook my head in disbelief, or perhaps something both more and less than that. Because a man guilty of one thing, in this case libertinism, will usually display other major weaknesses as well, often unpredictably. Ostensibly quixotic chaps are frequently the reverse of what they seem, since their surface admiration of women is only a means toward their casual possession of them, which is itself a form of insult. Why be surprised when a gallant mistreats a woman openly since that is all he is doing secretly anyway? It was up to me to show the chivalry in this case. He had insulted my wife, and I must demand satisfaction. Not a very pretty prospect — indeed things were probably going to get a little messy — and therefore my search for extenuating circumstances was understandable.

"He wasn't drunk?" I asked, hopefully.

"Your guess is as good as mine."

"Because he's always saying things like that when he's had a few too many. You've heard him at parties. One too many and *bzoom*, the foot in the mouth. The next morning he's filled with remorse."

My wife had gone into the bedroom, where she occupied herself in trying to locate a magazine. There was a fashion feature in it about slacks, which were apparently transcending their casual beginnings to the point where they were now acceptable for dinner wear in many splendiferous varieties of fabrics and styles. It was entitled "The Pants Explosion," as I saw when Gloria found the magazine and handed it to me to read.

I had other things on my mind! I slept uneasily that night, and after breakfast the next morning I went for a solitary bicycle ride in order to sort things out and think through the next important issue: whether to seek Sandwich out or wait till I ran into him. I would certainly not make a scene in Naughty's presence, for that would make me the boor he had been. I had not thrashed this problem out when events solved it for me. I ran into him on Main Street myself.

He was coming down the steps of the local grocery store clutching a bag of purchases. He did not look very good. His eyes had the bleary look customary after a night of dissipation, and I again sincerely clung for his sake to the hope that he had been three sheets when he had insulted my wife; or I should say that I merely wished it were true, since she had made it clear that that construction could not be put on his gaffe. Well, why do we always try to bale out the guilty, I thought. To hell with it, and strode resolutely forward to confront the culprit.

This consisted principally in crossing the street (the

ritual of rival gunmen in Westerns here crossed my mind) and accosting him as he approached his station wagon, parked at the curb near the store.

"Oh, hi, Wall," he said.

"Hi." I returned his greeting curtly enough. He must have seen which way the wind blew even then. Appraising me, he gave a long snuffle: one of his famous summer colds was upon him. One is not at his best then. I checked a twinge of compassion. What must be done must be done, and if I had to punch his drizzling beak in broad daylight on Main Street, he should have thought of that sooner.

"How's by you?" he said, shifting the sack of groceries onto his hip the way a woman will a child.

"Look, fellow," I said, "I take exception to that crack you made to my wife."

"Who?"

He was seized with a fit of coughing, very conveniently I thought as I saw him reach into his hind pocket with his free hand for a handkerchief, which he put in a rather wadded version to his face. He really looked like something the cat dragged in. His complexion was gray. His eyes were like stubborn stains. Both were bloodshot. At last the barking stopped.

"Who? Gloria of course. How many wives do you think I've got? Do you think I'm a Mormon or something?" The nightmare of such a man with a dozen wives having to defend all their honors against the Joe Sandwiches of this world flared briefly in my mind. I tried to strike an attitude of composure despite my dander's being up, suggesting that firmness need entail no loss of the civilized amenities. I crossed one foot over the other and leaned one hand on the roof of what I thought was his station wagon, but which turned out to be someone else's. It was started and driven off almost immediately, pitching me into the gutter. Luckily I wasn't thrown off balance enough to be flung to the ground, so that I merely stumbled partway into the street on my feet. I stepped back onto the curb, and opened my mouth to say something else, but he spoke first.

"What crack? What are you talking about?"

"You know very well what I mean. The slacks. That seem to refresh your memory, Sandwich?" I deliberately reverted to the surname of schooldays, which would remind him who had been originally in the position of authority.

His face was again something as he hacked into the handkerchief, not yet pocketed. He looked away in puzzlement. "When was this?"

Here I again opened my mouth several times to answer before a lull in his coughing permitted. The whole thing was like some dream. "Don't stall," I brought out at length. "It doesn't become you, Sandwich, and hardly serves to dignify this whole thing, would you say. You know very well when this was, and what it was. It so happens that I think my wife looks good in slacks."

"Why, none better, man, buh whah —?"

"Soft soap will get you nowhere. We don't behave toward women that way. That's the long and the short of it. I demand an —"

"Wait a minute. Let me put this in the car."

He walked past me a few steps toward where his own station wagon was. As he opened the door to set the bag on the front seat, I remembered that I had been on my way into the grocery store myself for a few things, such as the soft drinks and snacks we kept in the cottage, so that we had very nearly met when we were both carrying bags of groceries. Perhaps as the challenged party he would have chosen the contents as weapons, and so I had a brief, surrealist vision of two vacationers flailing one another to death with domestic provisions — *reductio ad absurdum* of the Age of Togetherness.

He returned in a fresh paroxysm of coughing. "You say —"

"I've said enough to make my point clear, I think. I demand an apology."

"Why, of course, if I've said something I didn't mean when I had a few too many. I don't even *remember* it, which shows you I must have been three sheets. So I apologize."

"Not to me! I'm afraid that won't be enough. You'll have to apologize to Gloria. It's on that that I must insist," I said, and added, tapping him on the chest, "and I insist on it by tonight."

With that I turned on my heel and walked away.

The only good the entire ill wind blew lay in the satisfaction a man could take in having met the demands of chivalry for the woman of his choice. Which is a keen satisfaction indeed, and I relished it despite the bad taste left in my mouth by the overall incident. But it was a satisfaction I was not to enjoy long, for the episode was not closed by Joe Sandwich's apology. He made it by telephone before I got back to the cottage, where I found Gloria waiting for me in the doorway with arms akimbo.

"What — in Christ's name — have you done now?"

"Why? What have I done now?"

"Joe just called —"

I gave a snort. "As damn well he might! I buttonholed him a while ago and demanded an apology."

"For what?"

"For that snide remark he made about your slacks. What else?"

"That's what I thought." She heaved a long sigh, and said, "Now, look. Are you listening very carefully, for once? Will we not go around in a fog, or bumble or blunder, for one second while we get something straight?

308

That was a dream I had, a *dream* I was telling you about the other night, not something that happened. Joe didn't say all those things. I just *dreamed* he did. Now have you got it straight?"

"Oh, good God," I said. "I'm sorry. What a mess. Poor Joe. And you too. I'm terribly sorry. I must call him right away and apologize."

"I should hope."

I could say that we all had a good laugh over it and that was that, and it would be true as far as it went. It would only be an expression for something with subcutaneous elements and longer lasting results. Joe had been given a bad shaking up in a way that permanently affected his attitude toward me and mine toward him. Gloria said my misunderstanding revealed a subconscious wish that Joe *had* ridiculed her. I wanted to believe that he had wronged her, or would. I asked her when since the days of our courtship she had reversed her opinion that we all analyzed everything too much, and also what could be said of my misunderstanding that couldn't be laid to her dream as well. And Naughty, when told of the mixup, wished it *hadn't* been straightened out. Joe was guilty of so much for which he went scot-free that getting a few lumps for what he hadn't done would have restored the balance a little, besides sobering him. What he needed above all else was to have a good scare thrown into him, and having dealt him a dose of this much-needed medicine we had promptly negated it out of regard for the "truth." "What's that?" she asked, Pontius Pilate-like. "There would have been a kind of Pirandello justice in it," she went on one night at a party at the Harrisons', the last party of the summer. We were sitting on the beach, side by side on a piece of driftwood. Behind us could be heard the tinkle and laughter of rising gaiety in the house. Soon Joe would be spelling fuchsia, or something of the sort. "As it is now, he's the underdog, milking Gloria for all the sympathy he can get out of her. And God knows where that will end."

"Oh, I wouldn't say that."

"You wouldn't say it, but you see it."

It was only too true. Full-time amorists probably turn everything to sexual account, and he showed no signs of knocking off the hurt expression he had worn the day the mixup occurred and Gloria and I had hightailed it over to the Sandwiches to explain what had happened and straighten the muddle out and "have our good laugh." The homeless beagle eyes he turned on her were so mournful that she seized his hand in both hers and said, "Oh, poor Joe!" He had been wronged, and he was not about to let it be forgotten where it could cut some ice. She did her best to comfort him, and there was every evidence that she had managed to do so by the time the first snow flew.

It was one evening that winter, as it lay freshly blanketing the ground, that I built a fire and tried to amuse Gloria by recalling the episode in terms of what scholars will tell you about the full facts behind the fairy tale of the sleeping maiden who is awakened by the kiss of a true lover.

"She marries him all right," I said, poking the fire, "and they live happily ever after, but that's not the real ending. There's more to the story in the original version, which scholars have unearthed in Nuremberg. Every night after dinner she talks to him. And she talks and she talks and she talks. And at length his head nods on his breast, lower and lower, and one night he falls asleep, and he sleeps forever, and ever, and ever."

She was not listening. Or she was only half listening, as she smiled to herself. It was an absent smile, the faraway, secret, woolgathering smile of a woman with a lover.

six

AS late as the end of October, and sometimes even into early November, there are still a few roses around, and, of course, a few reprieved houseflies as well. I was picking the one and swatting the other when Mother called to say that I had not been to see her since the last time.

I looked in that afternoon, bringing a bouquet of our lingering Paul Scarletts and a box of chocolates. Gift-bearing put her in mind of Christmas, and what to give one another. She is a thorny problem. She has every-thing, including arthritis, and so has little use for any-thing. She was then not far from the time when you would yourself have to untie for her all the packages you had so painstakingly wrapped. I told her that, like a boy at Christmas time, I wanted a new bike, and could be made happy by a ten-dollar gift certificate at the sporting goods store where I had my eye on an English Humber.

I had noticed that the cyclists who made the best time

circling the Square rode English bikes. They are lighter, and the brakes are hand-operated, which gives the rider a slight edge in competitions of this sort. On the likes of my American Schwinn, you have to take time to stop what your feet are doing and reverse their action to slow down, whereas with the English system the hands are always independently free and ready for the job, thus putting at your disposal two sets of reflexes instead of one.

I liked the new feeling of lightness and freedom my new Humber Pegasus gave me. I liked squeezing the brake calipers on the handlebars. They gave you a completely new sensation of *throttling* something, of slowly strangling a friend that had turned enemy, in other words speed, with your two hands, when occasion required. I also relished the increasing ease with which I could battle upgrades, knowing that I was toughening muscles already tougher than Joe Sandwich's. No one likes the role of cuckold, a word the very sound of which makes you ridiculous. Joe had by now become an absolute incubus to me. I can use the term even in its medieval sense, for he was a spirit whom in dreams I saw literally descending on me, a demonological weight oppressing me as though he were sitting on my chest. As people do of whom we dream, he became to me correspondingly altered in waking life. That Gloria dreamed of him too, as attested, began in turn to change her subtly in my eyes, till finally nobody was himself any more, leastways I. The town where I lived was alien, and so was Ishcanaba when we got there — quite apart from the new crop of girls looking like boys and boys looking like Old Testament prophets. The old summer-time regulars were strangers, so do one's private dramas infect the backgrounds against which they are played. More than strangers, they were inimical, even Louie the fat counterman who had amiably condoned my bringing my own cheese to eat his pie with. I decided to put a stop to this deterioration by ringing up the Sandwiches and suggesting we resume our picnics. Nothing is ever lost by being civilized about something.

We took an old and favorite route, wheeling along the cliff for a mile or two and then heading on a byroad into an evergreen forest with a clearing in which to unpack our lunch. *Der Schweinhund*, as Joe entertained us by calling himself, avoided pairing off with Gloria too obviously, as though wool could any longer be pulled over our eyes. I managed myself to fall back with Naughty for a fresh installment of the Sandwich saga. Her accounts were no longer blood-curdling as of old, but curiously objective analyses of what had already been deplored.

"It came to me in a flash what he does," she said. "After a long time of knowing what you know without ever having quite put your finger on it before? You know that experience. What he does is *pretend to do what he's doing.*"

314

"What do you mean?"

"He plays in a mock way at being exactly what he is, don't you see, in hopes that you won't realize it's perfectly true. He pretends he's a stinker, a lech, thriftless, inefficient and tardy, laying it on so thick you think it can't be true and laugh, forgetting the shoe really fits. Slovenliness he feigns by leaving his clothes around, improvidence by being overdrawn at the bank, and lechery by — well, look for yourself. We all do it with our faults to some extent, but he's developed it into a fine art. Do you know what I mean?"

I did indeed. Dubbing himself *Der Schweinhund* was a case in point. It was done in a humorous disclaimer that any such term could be seriously apt, when it jolly well was. Like the counterfeiter laughing, "Just made 'em" as he pays his restaurant check with fake new bills, beating the cashier to the joke. It is intended to divert and disarm you — and often does.

"How about the running around in the raw?" I asked. "How's that coming?"

"Better. He can't do that so much any more now that little Ham's able to sit up and take notice." The Sandwich *fils* had been so named, no less. "It's time to start setting an example. Not that he hasn't bred another version of himself all over again. Doesn't Nina make that complaint in *Strange Interlude?* That sons just pass through their mothers to become their fathers?"

"A cute nipper though. The spit of the old man, with

that red hair and that crooked little smile." I remembered a story that Joe had convulsed her into labor when she'd had him. "He's bright as a dollar. You know that, Naughty."

"No modesty on that score. He's great. Well, here we are. Time to start unpacking the calories."

I observed Joe in the light of her observation. As we dismounted, he pretended he had been tooling along beside one's wife and for corrupt reasons. He was an unsavory character, he pretended. "I know you're an eminently reasonable man, sir," he continued with this hanky-panky as he spread a cloth on the grass, "appreciating that reason may not be the ruling force in the lives of men less wise and prudent who are at the mercy of passions for which they had not bargained. But this much honor remains to me, that I shall not add hypocrisy to skulduggery by pretending that I am not guilty, nor entirely debauch the code by which we live. I mean, sir, that if you require satisfaction, I am at your service."

"I'll send my seconds round in the morning," I said, falling in with this chatter.

Oddly enough, my spirits began to rise, even well before the rosé had been uncorked and begun to flow. It was like old times. The rocks and trees and fields kept their ancient places, in a world from which all clouds in time blew away. Everything was all right, or in the end would be. It would all come out in the wash, as my father used to say. I suppose there is always some satisfaction in having an adversary's number. Naughty's observation helped me put my finger on exactly what Joe was like. He was none other than the darkey heard thieving in the henhouse, who, when the farmer called out, "Who's there?" answered, "There's nobody here but us chickens." A good parable of the universal human pretense to innocence. Who of us does not us-chickens his way through this life?

The conversation had somehow gotten round to existentialism. Our *Schweinhund* leaned negligently back on one elbow and said, "Well, a man's got to believe something, and I believe I'll have another drink," and held his glass out to the fractured Gloria, who knelt bottle in hand. He was pretending to be a wastrel. Tilting the bottle over his glass, Gloria said, "Just exactly what is um existentialism in a nutshell?"

"That depends what you mean by nutshell. If you mean a long-term historical perspective with reversible features at no extra cost, why, yes, dollars handed out one a minute since the birth of Christ would wipe out the national debt. But if you want to look into the future, the fact is that if the world's population continues to increase at its present rate, six hundred years from now there will be only one square yard left for each person on this earth, which means that nobody will be able to lie down anymore and we shall all have to replenish it standing up."

Here I experienced an apocalyptic twinge or two. I wondered whether the antic improvisations known to enhance his mating at home distinguished it in general; possibly even enlivened life under my own roof when I wasn't there.

I sat up and said, "Who wants to circle the Square when we get back?"

"Nothing doing," Gloria said. "You're not going to break your neck."

"Of course I'm not. Who's game?"

"I'm not going whizzing around that dragstrip just because a lot of crazy kids have decided that's the thing to do."

"My God, they don't do that anymore! They're surfing now. To us they've thrown the torch. It's fun."

"You mean you've done it?" Naughty asked.

"For the hell of it. Not in par by any means. That two-minute-mile stuff. More like three is my speed. And then some."

Joe, whose curiosity was obvious despite his attempt to conceal it, now looked at me and said, "You mean you've been trying that caper?"

"Sure. Haven't you?"

He hesitated just long enough before answering to hint that he might have been secretly weighing the suspicion that he was seen plodding up the Water Street hill that night. It was even possible that he had caught a glimpse of me watching from the lunch-counter window, though unlikely. At any rate, he had everything to lose by deception and nothing by adopting my own offhand attitude. "Yeah, well, once when I was in town I tried it on for size. Not that I clocked myself. I don't think I can even make that Water Street grade."

"I couldn't, really, till I got that English bike. They're lighter, you know. Well, if nobody else is game the devil with it."

"No, let's try it. After a little siesta, that is."

It was nearly four o'clock when we filed back into town. Seeing me lead the way toward the starting line, Gloria said, "You need a stopwatch."

"I've got one in my toolbag."

When we forgathered at the upper corner of the Square — the return address on your imaginary envelope — several idlers drifted over to watch. They included the old man in the power-driven wheelchair, wearing his crash helmet, now at an angle that gave him a rakish air.

"I see you young fellows do this so much I've got half a notion to give her a whirl myself," he said.

"You could probably beat us," I said.

"Where you folks from?"

"Chicago. Where you?"

"Grand Rapids. Well, let 'er rip. Want me to watch Water Street?" Sometimes a monitor was posted there to make sure a contestant coming up the hill didn't get off and run his bike up the rest of the way (or hitch a ride from a passing truck), a service this man liked to perform.

"No, thanks. We'll use the honor system. Nobody here's going to make the Two Minute Club anyway. Thanks just the same."

I went first. Joe and I were to hold the stopwatch on each other, the honor system prevailing here too. I poised for takeoff in the usual fashion, left foot on the ground to shove off with, right foot on the pedal at its summit. By now there were so many onlookers, drifting over from checker games on the Square, that I began to wish we'd picked a more deserted hour. But there was no calling it off now. The size of our audience was apparent from the "He's off!" cheer that sent me on my way.

This heat was about par for me. I reached the first turn at my customary speed of about forty-five, braked just right and just in time to make the first left turn with a wide, looping slew that saved me momentum without costing my balance, and streaked toward the next turn up Water Street — rightly known among the slangy younger set as Sonofabitch Hill. It was the usual grueling ordeal, for which I had developed a technique that seemed right for me. Instead of trying to maintain a steady rolling rotation, I drove myself forward with a series of alternating downward jerks. Each leg was called on for a pile-driver blow while the other rested. You hugged the curb, of course, which was possible because the streets were one-way all around the Square and no parking was allowed. *Jerk* went one leg, *jerk* the other, driving like pistons while the usual grimaces contorted my face and my breath was reduced to a series of labored pants. I slowed to the inevitable creep, but I reached the final turn well in the saddle, and pumped for home.

"Two and a half minutes!" Joe announced, as, panting, I dropped my bicycle to the ground. I could tell from their faces what my own was like.

"You're *gray*," Gloria said. "Do you want to kill yourself?" And Naughty told Joe, "You're not going to do it." Guaranteeing, of course, that he would.

He handed me the stopwatch and walked his bike to the starting line. He pointed its nose downhill and straddled the seat. Then he hesitated a moment and looked over at my bike.

"You say the English ones are lighter?"

"Yes. Lighter and sturdier. Want to borrow mine? I don't want to take undue advantage of you."

Nursing her elbows, her shoulders huddled forward as though she were shivering, Gloria laughed and said, "These guys talk as though it's the Olympics or something." Naughty, also with folded arms, nodded at her and smiled.

Joe changed to my Pegasus and once more got on his mark. At the last moment he switched his cap around, which gave him a daredevil look, and everyone laughed again.

"Goodbye, Mrs. Witchingauer," he said, and shoved off.

It was a good getaway — better than mine, I thought. He picked up speed instantly, calling over his shoulder something delightedly complimentary about the bike. You always made sure there was no auto traffic in sight before you started, and he had the hill completely to himself. He flew down the middle of it like a streak of lightning, bent over the handlebars in racer fashion. He very quickly reached the point at which anyone going at that clip should begin to think about slowing for the turn. Several small fry running down the hill shouted at him to that effect. A moment more and I knew that if he didn't cut his speed he'd be going too fast to negotiate the turn, and be in for a nasty spill. But still his feet flickered around and around.

Then a dreadful suspicion swept over me. From this distance, it might be impossible to tell whether he was pedaling forwards or backwards. When he approached the actual corner, with the parapet of Lover's Leap looming just ahead, and no sign of a letup in his downward plunge, if anything his feet seeming to fly faster than ever, the suspicion was confirmed. He didn't know brakes on an English bike were different from those on an American.

"Squeeze the calipers on the handlebars!" I screamed at the top of my voice, but it was no use. He was too far away, with the wind whistling in his ears. We were as helpless here as he was there. He back-pedaled in an antic dream, frantically trying to make the brake catch in an axle mechanism where there was no brake. Sensing he couldn't stop, he swung as far as he could to the right of the road before veering left, in hopes of describing a wide enough arc so that he would hit the parapet a glancing blow. But he was now going much too fast to cushion the impact in any such way. Between the street and the parapet was a narrow sidewalk with a low curb, no more than a couple of inches high. He bumped over that with a light bounce, and, still giddily back-pedaling in a fantasy, headed for the waist-high wall that over-looked the hundred-foot drop beyond. Striking the curb must have fouled the turn he was trying to make, be-cause he hit the wall almost head-on, sailed over the handlebars and then over the wall, and vanished into Lover's Leap.

He disappeared in his dramatic crouch, like a jockey, retaining to the last instant the hard-riding derring-do in which he had descended the hill, so that his departure had a certain style to it, a valedictory vainglory, an undeniable dash. He seemed to be riding when he no longer had any mount under him, in a wild, free apotheosis that was the last image of him we had. In his green shirt, he was himself like a wreath flung handsomely into space, into a summer air through which it would sail forever as we watched.

We looked at one another in blank incomprehension. Our minds not yet functioning, we did not believe what we had seen. It was a mere visual event, a picture not yet developed. This was as true of the idle onlookers as it was of our trio. We remained frozen in time for the duration of several seconds, figures ourselves having only visual existence. Then two or three youngsters rushed pell-mell down the hill toward the pay binoculars, fishing in their pockets for dimes.

seven

NAUGHTY took it very well. She bore up beauti-
fully. The pressure of immediate "arrangements" is
always a kind of godsend in the distraction it offers, and
she took it very seriously — to the point of even conscientiously pausing over some of the obviously facetious
stipulations Joe had left behind in his "wills," for there
were more than one. She recalled the provision once
related to me, for a memorial service to be held at four
o'clock in the morning in the woods, where by the
dawn's early light we were to shinny up into the treetops
to listen to whichever one of us had been saddled with
the task of encomium, after drawing lots. One could not
help imagining the scene if, say, Fido Harrison had
"lost," or oneself for that matter. When there seemed at
one point some danger, in her state, of actually entertaining the idea of holding such a service on the ground that
its antic nature would be appropriately typical of the
deceased, I asked her whether she would dream of

following through on some of his other specifications — that his brain be left to Channel 13 for educational purposes, that vegetables be planted on his grave instead of flowers — and she said no. "Well then forget them all," I said. "They're just jokes of Joe's that of course we'll always fondly remember him by. Part of the Legacy of Laughter, as we poor professors can only keep calling it." Reason finally won the day, and a conventional sort of service was held at the church.

Consolation must in this case be a two-way street, alas. As the man responsible for what had happened, however innocently and inadvertently, I felt that my life had been ruined. It, too, was at an end. More of that later, but for the time being Naughty was quick both to console and to absolve me, in the midst of all her other trials. Gloria was another matter.

That we none of us ever went back to Ishcanaba goes without saying. But Gloria seemed no happier to be back home in our apartment. She was reluctant to unpack her suitcase; when unpacked, to put it away. She spoke almost never, and played solitaire for hours, in fact days on end — a bleeding Madras game if I ever saw one. Finally I told her the situation was impossible, and that she must clear the air by telling me what was on her mind.

"Things can hardly be the same after what happened," she said. "That much must be obvious to you."

"Of course it is. What kind of fiend do you think I am?"

"That's what I'd like to find out," she murmured, looking away.

"What are you talking about?"

"You were responsible for what happened."

"In a cause and effect sense, yes. But not morally. Anyone insinuating that would be the fiend."

There was a silence in which each waited for the other to speak next. In a crisis, language is always a little like a game of Russian roulette, in which there might be half a dozen synonyms for the same thing, one of which could be fatal if chosen, while the remainder would leave you still open to further, if equally precarious, conversation. I chose a word that seemed to offer no surprises.

"I quite admit I'm a bumbler, if that's the way you want to put it. But I don't think being an absentminded professor is a sin for which anyone should be hanged."

"Bumbling like a fox," she again murmured, again glancing away.

"What are you jabbering about? What do you mean?"

"You didn't tell him the brakes were different."

"It never occurred to me. I assumed he knew, as I guess I would assume everyone would. We don't make a point of what is familiar to us, simply because it is familiar. It never entered my mind."

"Would you have told him if it had?"

327

"Of course! But it didn't. It just slipped my mind."

"Ah! Why did it slip your mind? Because subconsciously you wanted it to."

"And why would I want it to, my dear?" I asked gently.

I could afford a quiet tone, knowing I had her checkmated. She could not make her point without the forfeit of her cause. If I were guilty as charged, it must be only from a motive springing in turn from guilt of her own.

"Why?" I persisted with a little smile. "Or is there nobody here but us chickens?" — the parable of the darkey in the henhouse having again occurred to me.

"What?"

"Nothing. Skip it. Just answer my question. It must be answered before we can go on with this discussion. Why would I want harm to come to Joe?"

Whether the simple force of her reply was the product of rage at the loss of a lover, or something like that emotion toward the man responsible for his elimination, or a combination of both, I don't know. Perhaps she could not herself have said. But it was at least to her feminine credit that she made it a declaration rather than an admission when she said, "Because I was sleeping with him!"

Here some histrionics on my part were necessary if the present forensic framework was to be maintained; which was in turn essential if my position was to remain tenable.

"*What?*" I gasped. I pretended to be thunderstruck, to be absolutely floored by this revelation. Not making a very good job of it, I'm afraid, since I'm not much of an actor.

"Oh, for God's sake, Wally, stop this nonsense, shall we?" Gloria retorted angrily. "At least don't try to cover up your tracks by pretending you don't have a motive. That's too much."

"So that's the way it is. At least you didn't sleep with him subconsciously," I answered, attempting a tone of dry irony — rather difficult since dry was what my tongue was. "But what do you mean, cover up my tracks? You make me sound like a criminal. You mean actually and seriously to imply that I'm that?"

"Well, I hope I wouldn't do it any way but seriously. You played a subconscious prank on him. Or your subconscious played a prank on him."

She was sitting on the living-room sofa, against a mass of cushions of which she would periodically select one for special pummeling by way of gestures for emphasis — as though dealing body blows to an opponent. In this way she managed to avoid my eye at critical moments in the scene — which is what it now rapidly became. I rose from the chair in which I'd been sitting and stood over her, grasping the lapels of my coat.

"Let me get this straight," I said, quite deliberately. "You mean to accuse me of —"

"I'm not making an *accusation*," she said, giving the

329

pillow of the moment another right to the solar plexus. "I'm making a speculation. Or suggesting one that could be made, in the nature of the case."

"All right then, I'll put it that way. You mean to suggest, speculate, insinuate, imply, or submit as a possibility worth serious consideration, that I am a subconscious murderer."

"You said it, I didn't."

"I will not stay in this house and listen to such rubbish — especially from my own lips."

"You won't have to," she said, rising, and scuttling past me toward the door, as though an inadvertent malefactor might not be above dealing you a cuff or two in open awareness that he is doing so, or committing some graver and more conclusive offense. Which at least had its humorous side. I never quarrel, much less fight. This was our first quarrel (though I have listened to some brisk monologues) and our last. Strife between the sexes seems to me one of the pities of the world. People doing to each other what life does to both, and to us all, seems to me like the conduct of those two French noblemen who fought a duel on a battlefield on which enemy shells were raining.

Well, no matter. Where were we? Oh, yes. "I'm going — for good!" she said. "I'm not going to stay in the same house with a self-confessed murderer!"

"Nor I with an adulterer!" I called after her. Adding,

just as she slammed the door, "Correction — nympho-maniac!"

She opened the door from outside it just long enough to fling back, "How would you know?" before slamming it once again. It was, as Joe Sandwich said of shoulder chops, the unkindest cut of all. I heard her run down the stairs and outside.

It seemed, again, a good time to visit Mother. (You will recall my pattern of choosing, for these filial calls, those junctures from which no further decline need be expected. This certainly seemed nothing even she could make worse.) Leaving a note for Gloria to the effect that I would be gone for a couple of days, which would give her ample time to pack her things and be off for Reno or wherever else she planned to solemnize our rupture, I threw a few things of my own into a bag, flung that into the back seat of the car, and headed for Mother's.

It was the height of summer, and she sat outside rocking in the sun. A few aprons hanging on a clothes-line strung across the front of the yard partially con-cealed her from view. "I thought I'd sell off some of my house things," she said. "Including a few dresses I'll never wear again, but I want to launder them first. I can't move very fast anymore."

"Well, I can," I said, and whipped them one by one from the line, pitching the clothespins into a nearby

331

wicker basket along with them. I carried basket and all into the house, and while there poured out two glasses of sherry for us to sip outside. I wanted to get my news off my chest as soon as possible, but first I had to hear out her ailments. I listened with only half an ear; here, again, one did not want too much information. One wanted as few facts as possible. When she was finished, we gossiped a moment, and then I told her what was afoot.

I was surprised by her reaction. Remembering how upset she had been by my getting married, I expected to find her equivalently relieved (however secretly) at news of the divorce that would set me free once more, and make my society available accordingly. Nothing of the kind. She carried on in exactly the same way as when I had announced my engagement. She paled, then grew rigid, as though taken by some kind of seizure. Her head fell back and her eyes closed. She even began to slaver a little — that was repeated. It was the same shock as before. And, as in the first instance, I galloped back into the house for something stronger than sherry, brandy of course, uncorking the bottle as I returned. Her sherry glass was empty on the table beside her, and I poured it full of brandy and held it to her lips. I could not pry them open. She moaned faintly as her head rolled from side to side. At last I jerked her erect by grasping her hair, and without actually having planned to do so, simply seized by an impulse, I flung the contents of the glass into her face.

That revived her. She moaned a bit longer, in the manner of one regaining consciousness, and her eyes fluttered open. When I had calmed her down, I settled back in my own chair and as quietly as possible related the facts, those, at least, I thought she should know. I said Gloria and I had had a quarrel of an intensity that confirmed a degree of incompatibility we had long felt marred our marriage, and decided the best thing to do would be dissolve it. Mother kept interrupting me with deploring comments: we had never had a divorce in the family, the home was breaking up, the fabric of society was unraveling, and so on.

It was only one of many conversations we had on the subject, for having, indeed, no home of my own now, I visited Mother often throughout that fall and winter. Living alone after having been married was not the same as single life before that had been. It was a different kind of solitude. I often thought of vacating the flat, storing the furniture, and moving in with Mother. But always decided against it.

Gloria wrote from Nevada, to which she had indeed repaired for the divorce, but only enough to keep me advised of the progress of litigation and to discuss the terms of the settlement, really already decided. She wanted no alimony, merely a modest cash settlement, enough to keep her till she "got going" again; meaning, I supposed, another job or a new husband. Forced into response by a long letter from me, thrashing out my side

333

of the story once and for all, she advised me to leave Wilton and go somewhere far away. Somewhere I wasn't known, and could make a fresh start. "I would *certainly* advise this if you ever want to get married again, Wally," she wrote, "because no woman will ever marry you knowing the facts. No woman will marry you with this blot on your name."

There were hints and signs that she was not exaggerating. At least so I suspected from the way people looked at me, crossing the campus, in class, at faculty meetings, and at the college restaurants, including the hangout where we had eaten so many lunches of "pangcakes" and coffee. Conversations were broken off when I glanced over, whispers resumed when I turned away. Of course this had an inevitable strain of dark glamour to it. I was known as the man who had polished off his rival by sending him head-over-heels into Lover's Leap. No one had in the history of romance more adroitly dumped his competition. This hardly served to palliate matters — because I began to believe the story myself. It got to me. It ate at me. It gnawed at my vitals. It corroded my conscience.

Mother and I declined together — till I'm sure I began to look her age. I had no appetite, even for the drink that sees so many people through tribulations of their own. Once again I tried drowning my sorrows, to find them amphibious. One's sorrows are not a sack of kittens. I managed classes but that was all. I lost all zest for my subject and for the discussions to which my lectures sometimes led. I had no ambition for promotion, publication, or any of the other rewards and perquisites of my profession, such as one needs to spur him on. I tried to relax with hot baths, the hotter the better, soaking for hours, and lolling back in the tub with closed eyes, the better to imagine myself a licentious Roman under Hadrian. And I developed a compulsion.

The obsession that now laid hold of me was this. I absolutely had to look at every bicycle on the street, to see whether it was American or English. That is, what kind of brakes it had. Soon it was not merely a matter of checking those I happened to see, but of actually looking around for them. It swiftly became a hazard in driving my car — which was all I ever rode. I never got back on a bicycle again. Every time I stopped for a light I would look in all directions to see whether any was in sight, and I even kept glancing around when moving in traffic. It is an obsession from whose grip relief is promised only now that American makes are slowly beginning to adopt the braking mechanism of the English, and all distinction between them is destined gradually to fade away.

One afternoon in late spring, Mother and I were sitting outside when a tall, rangy man in a plaid suit and two-tone shoes approached along the sidewalk. He paused a moment when still a few steps off, and seemed to size us up. Then he came forward, drawing a notebook and pencil from his pocket.

"Good afternoon," he said. "Lovely day."

"Yes," I agreed listlessly.

"I'm the Inquiring Reporter. I wonder if you'd mind answering the question of the day."

"We'll see. What is it?"

"It's about marriage. You're married, aren't you?"

"We're not living in sin."

"Well, then, this is the question. What do you consider the secret of a happy marriage? What, in your opinion, is the most important thing?"

"Mutual respect," I replied. I slid lazily down in my chair, tilting my cap forward till this offender was blotted from view. "Sharing things fifty-fifty, especially the chores of daily life. Its fatigue duty, if you will. Going halves on that," I dilated as the cretin scribbled audibly on his pad, hurrying to take down these gems.

"Can you give an example?"

"Well, dishwashing for instance. I don't think there's a more important domestic chore than that for exercising this mutual respect that I'm talking about. Every night after dinner, my missus and I, we clear the things away together and then she washes half the dishes, and I come in and wash the other half. We each take out half the garbage. We divide it neatly into two piles, at the end of the day, wrap them in separate bags, and carry them out to the garbage can — *together*."

This seemed to satisfy him. After finishing jotting down my treatise which he said ran exactly the right length, he asked for my name and address. Noting which he thanked me and went his way.

I never watched to see whether this nugget was published. Evidence that it had been came in the form of a letter I received in response to it. It arrived in a blue envelope, in a vaguely familiar handwriting. I turned it over to read the return address. It was a letter from a totally unexpected quarter — none other than Naughty. I had not spoken with her, or heard from her, since the events that had brought our foursome to its abrupt end. It was both eagerly and apprehensively that I tore it open and read:

Dear Wally:

I saw your little contribution in the *Eagle*. Some people don't know when they're having their leg pulled, I guess. Quite a little philosophy, or I should say formula for marital bliss, but I couldn't help detecting a note of bitterness, Wally. I mean real sardonic, no-holds-barred bitterness. I think I can understand why, partly at least. I make it a rule never to judge or to take sides when people get divorced. I will never be lured into saying what I think of your divorce, or of Gloria's getting it. It is her business and yours. That's that. But there is probably another source of your state of mind, of which I can speak, because it concerns me too.

Wally, rumors of what you're like continually reach me. I think I would have written anyway if seeing your name hadn't prompted this. Wally, I'm disturbed by what I hear. I have only this to say. The time for brooding is past. It's over and done. But instead you apparently go on brooding

337

yourself into a deeper and deeper hole. Why? *It wasn't your fault,* as I told you then and told you a dozen times since. You couldn't *help* it. It's just one of those things. It simply never occurred to you to raise the point that might have prevented what happened. I don't think it would have occurred to me either. There, is that enough reassurance? Look. If I don't hold anything against you, then who has a right to? Then why hold it against yourself? Or is this the kind of self-flagellation that you once told me was an inverted form of self-indulgence?

I suppose I could have telephoned to say all this but I thought your reading it, being able to see it, would make it more tangible, and therefore more convincing. It's here for you to reread any time you want, or think you need any such reassurance.

It's too bad we don't see one another anymore, but it's not because I don't go out again, because I do. It's apparently you who prefer to crawl into a hole and pull the hole in after you. I have no intention of doing so. I keep busy at my work, plus a day a week volunteer work at the hospital, and I see a few friends. Little Ham is fine. He's going on six now. Can you believe it? Tempus keeps fugiting all right. Always repeating itself though, because his resemblance to his father, both in looks and manner, is such that he sometimes seems like a piece of plagiarism running around the house. You should see him.

Regards,
Naughty

The letter perked me up somewhat. Nor was its boost to my spirits temporary. I carried it around with me, rereading it whenever I needed bracing, so often that I finally had it memorized, recourse to it unnecessary save for the satisfaction of seeing and handling it. Then one day, yielding to the wish to see Naughty that the letter had generated, I telephoned and suggested I drive out the next afternoon, Saturday, to call on her. She said she was busy then, but Sunday was agreed on.

They lived in the same house on a quiet side street clear on the other end of town. The door was opened by a boy who was so obviously a Tom Thumb version of his father that he gave me a start. The resemblance had increased that markedly in the two years or so since I had seen him. It had been notable then; now it was almost eerie. He wore a tweed jacket as green as his eyes, and the red hair hung, in the fashion of the hour, in a thick mop around his ears and down to his eyes. Its luxuriance constituted the only difference from the molting Joe. He had a toothpick in his mouth, or perhaps a matchstick.

"Hello, Humperdinck," he said.

"Hello, Ham. I'm Wally Hines. Remember your old Uncle Wally?"

Naughty came smiling into the vestibule, making some kind of adjustment to a bracelet clattering with bangles and charms. "He doesn't remember you? Or do you, Ham? It must be two years since he saw you last."

"I remember him," Ham said. "Stealing shells off the beach."

"I got them for my mother, officer."

Naughty was no slimmer, and certainly no younger.

Her expression, when she saw me, was proof enough of how I had aged in the interval. She gave me some tea, on learning that I should prefer it to stronger drink. Ham watched television in a nearby room, from which he reappeared once to offer me a cigarette from a table case. When I tried to light it, it wouldn't draw. I sucked on it in vain, puzzled, until examination revealed it to have been perforated along one side with tiny holes, so small that I had to put on my reading glasses to see them. Ham had by now returned to the television room. Naughty had also absented herself, and now she came back winding a scarf around her head.

"Let's go for a walk."

"Is Ham coming along?"

"Oh, I think not. But —" She stepped to the side room and called through the open door, "Uncle Wally is nice enough to ask you along, but you'd sooner watch television, wouldn't you? Would you rather I called Eileen to sit with you? We're only going to walk around the block."

"How many times?"

"We don't know yet. We'll look in every time we pass the house if you'd like."

"Forget it," he said without turning around.

"Ham!"

He was sitting on the floor, as I saw when I drifted over to call out some word of acknowledgment about the manner in which the cigarettes had been tampered with. It was then, rather than in response to his mother's rebuke, that he turned around. "I don't know what you're talking about," he said. He held a can of Pepsi-Cola in his hand, and a flash of association recalled to mind Joe's sitting on the beach of Ishcanaba, one summer afternoon, drinking vichyssoise out of a can, the way one drinks beer — a whim certainly not to be counted among his indefensible drolleries. That was the afternoon he told us about the Chicago chiropractor of whom we had heard, who gave you a ninety-day guarantee on your back, after a course of manipulation. Joe had had some sort of affliction I never got straight. Something to do with imbalance. Pressed for details of how he had managed to avoid Army duty, he said he had some kind of trouble that enlisted the sympathies of the draft board.

Ham was in any event successfully brought to his feet to say goodbye to a guest, however brief might be the guest's withdrawal, or however likely to be one of a series. He passed a hand jauntily across his face in farewell as we made off.

Naughty told me laughingly as we went out, "You should have seen a questionnaire he answered to get into this rather good private school. One question was, 'What are your favorite television programs?' He wrote,

'None.' He likes them all, you see! It's all he does is look at it. But they were terribly impressed."

"It's easy to see he'll make out."

I called on Naughty the next Sunday, and this time we went for a drive, taking Ham along. He sat in the back seat reading a comic and eating gumdrops from a bag. Later there were drives we took alone, and then some dinner dates.

I had been seeing her more than a year in this way when I was moved to ask a question.

"Doesn't it strike you, Naughty," I said, "how much we enjoy each other's company, in a quiet sort of way?"

"Yes," she said. "We were always relaxed together, Wally. Natural. At ease."

I was certainly at ease now, rather than in any sense stimulated, or excited. We were walking along the lake front, bundled in heavy coats against the autumn wind. It was a heavy wind, coming in sudden violent gusts, so that even the gulls sometimes lost their grip on the air and were blown about among the leaves and scraps of paper that swirled about overhead. Occasionally a jet went by, ripping the gray sky in two.

She took my arm. This emboldened me to go on, but it was some time before I mustered the courage to say, "Then I was wondering, crazy though it may sound, why we couldn't make it permanent."

She let go my arm, without, however, breaking stride

with me. She plunged her hands deep into her coat pockets, and gazed down at the sand to answer, "We haven't even kissed."

"A sign of my respect. Even of my affection. You wouldn't find me much of a bargain in that department, I'm afraid. It would be mostly companionship."

"That makes us compatible. Well, if all bets are off in that department, I guess you can't either win or lose. There it is. You've already got it, and you know what it is you're getting."

I laughed in a nervously happy way. I remembered how Naughty had once quoted Nina, in *Strange Interlude*, complaining that boys passed through their mothers to become their fathers. I now recalled a speech of Charlie Marsden's, who when he gets Nina in the end, and all the rack of lust and toil and struggle are done, says, "God damn dear old . . .! No, God bless dear old Charlie . . . who, passed beyond desire, has all the luck at last!"

So it was that Gloria's prophecy that no one would have me turned out to be untrue. I broke the news of this engagement to Mother, brandy bottle at the ready. Again Mother went rigid from the momentary shock, closing her eyes as her head rolled back, and again there was the bit of slavering. But she was brought round in short order, to learn that there would be no marriage for another half year at least — a half year in which we also

343

heard of Gloria's remarriage, to a manufacturer in California. Naughty and I slipped quietly off to the local parsonage one Saturday afternoon — or as quietly as was possible with Ham in tow.

My bed was pied on the honeymoon — in which he also joined us. In the course of the two weeks we spent at Lake Louise I learned what would be required of me if I was going to realize the ambition on which I was determined — to be as good a father to Ham as I was going to be a husband to Naughty. Unable to lick the wits, I decided to join them. I became a practical joker.

"Nice job you did on the bed," I said, giving his hair a punitive rumple. "But I've got something cooked up for when we get back that'll really knock them dead."

"What's that?" he said.

The Sandwiches had had some next-door neighbors named Moses, whom I remembered from the old days when we had so often made a foursome, and whose acquaintance I had briefly renewed when I was courting Naughty, if you can call it that. But only briefly. They had recently moved to a small town some ten miles away, on Mr. Moses's being transferred by his firm. It was more like six or seven miles from the small house near the campus where we were going to settle on our return from this honeymoon. That is neither here nor there. The joke was this. I got the idea from a power failure we had had just before taking off. The next time there was another, whether due to wind or an ice storm, or to some utility mishap such as had plunged the eastern seaboard into darkness a short time before, we would telephone them and ask, "Where was Moses when the lights went out?"

Now, this was far from simple of execution. Many obstacles made doubtful its realization; indeed, the challenge posed by the mathematical odds against it was precisely what attracted me, and would lend its successful consummation rather more scope and substance than might at first blush appear, as I tried to explain to Ham when I told him about it. This was no small feat in itself, because I was lying on the bed and he was sitting on my stomach, bouncing up and down, causing a great many misplaced emphases in my account, when the wind wasn't knocked out of me altogether.

"It depends *on* such a number of factors working *out* just right, that is, just wrong, requires such perfect timing," I said, "that it is raised above *the* level of the mere gag. First, a utility blackout *of* such extent and duration as to plunge into darkness *an* area embracing our two *towns*, whether huh —" Here the wind was knocked out of me, and I had to pause. "Whether mechanical or meteorological in origin," I rapidly rattled off between bounces. "If meteorological, it will have to be pulled when falling limbs have broken power lines *but* not yet the telephone cables beneath them, *huh*. It

345

hinges on the Moseses and us *being* brought to the same pass sime- sime- simultaneously."

"The real gimmick," Ham said. Though we were indoors, he was wearing in its entirety a new outfit we had bought him, including a hat of the sort associated with Swiss yodelers, with a whisk protruding from the band, and pushed jauntily back on his head. He liked to wear a hat indoors for some reason. And I had recently caught him smoking.

"Precise*ly*. But there's another gimmick in this logical chain."

"What's that, Wally?"

"Mrs. Moses will have to answer the phone, not Moses himself, *huh*. You can't very well say, 'Where were you when the lights went out,' can you? The least thing going amiss, and everything is reversed. The absurdity backfires, and the humorist is the one with egg on his *fuhh*. Face."

It was two years before the necessary factors coincided. An ice storm began early one afternoon in December, sheathing the trees so quickly and so thickly that by nightfall cracking limbs had reduced power lines to spaghetti over a radius of fifty miles. Our juice was gone but the phone was still alive when I arrived home about five thirty, after a precarious walk, slithering about among fallen boughs and live cables threatening electrocution.

"Now's our chance," I said to Ham when he greeted me in the vestibule with a flashlight. I unwound my scarf and hung it and my hat in the closet, groping my way, for my eyelashes were coated with ice and I could hardly see. It was a moment before my glacéed face was restored to normal in a house in which, of course, the furnace had also gone.

"For what?" Naughty called from the kitchen, where she was making a selection for our dinner from the freezer compartment of the icebox, full of things on which we should have to gorge ourselves in the next few days to prevent their spoiling. The bounty included frozen steaks, cakes and pies, and several flavors of ice cream, not to mention a brace of frozen pheasant someone had sent us the Christmas before. She worked by candlelight.

"The Moses thing. You get on the kitchen phone, Ham. I'll take the bedroom extension. There's not a moment to lose."

With another flashlight, I bounded up the stairs two at a time, wild shadows fluttering on the wall. All this occurred in rather dramatic chiaroscuro. I sat on the edge of the bed and dialed Information. While waiting to get the number I wanted, I could hear Ham breathing on the other extension. Information broke in to ask, "Is this an emergency, sir?"

"My God! The entire Midwest is a shambles, woman, and you ask is it an emergency."

"Very well then. The number is 237-4086."

I dialed the area code and then that. There was a crackling sound for some seconds. Then the phone began to ring.

"We've gotten through," I said to Ham. "It's incredible."

The phone rang several times, and then a woman's voice said, "Hello."

"Where was Moses when the lights went out?"

"What?"

I squeezed the receiver more firmly against my ear. The connection didn't seem to be a very good one. "This is Mrs. Moses, isn't it?"

"Yes."

"Well then — *Where was Moses when the lights went out?*"

"In bed. He hasn't been at all well."

"Aw, gee, I'm sorry to hear that." I chuckled discreetly and said, "Then he wasn't down in the basement eating sauerkraut?"

"What?"

"Nothing. That old childhood rhyme, you remember. Why, what seems to be the trouble?"

"A slipped disc. Not one, but two. He's in terrible pain most of the time. We may have to take him to the hospital for an operation."

"One of those spinal fusions. They often work wonders."

"Who is this?"

"Mr. Hines. Remember us, and the Sandwiches, on Sycamore Street?"

"Of course! Mr. Hines, how nice of you to call. We think of you all so often. 'They were nice folks,' Moses said only last week. We heard you and Mrs. Sandwich got married."

"That's right. We're still living over here in Wilton."

"How's little Ham?"

"Not so little anymore."

"How old is he by now?"

I didn't know. I couldn't for the life of me remember whether it was eight or nine. But of course he could speak for himself, and so I said, "He's on another phone. He wanted to say hello to you, too, Mrs. Moses. Ham, are you there? Speak up."

His voice when he finally answered was faint, as though he were choking. "Hello, Mrs. Moses. This is me. I'll be nine in August," he said.

"Oh, that's fine. Getting to be a big boy. I'm certainly glad to hear all this. You know what? I'd like to put Moses on the wire. I could tiptoe in and see if he's asleep —"

"Oh, don't do that!"

"We have to keep him sedated and . . . It's so neighborly of you to call. Just the sweetest . . . We've been so —" Here Mrs. Moses burst into tears. Her voice trailed off into a high squeal, like the noise Stan Laurel makes when he starts to cry in the sequences in which he exasperates Oliver Hardy so. I thought she might have been going to say they were lonely and friendless out there where they now lived. I wanted to wind up this conversation as quickly and gracefully as I could, leaving her with her illusion about its motive intact.

"Well, we just had you on our minds, and wanted to wish you a Merry Christmas," I said. It was nowhere near the holidays yet, but it was the only thing I could think of. At least it was December.

"A Merry Christmas to all of you," she squeaked, "and God bluh — bluh —"

"God bless you too, Mrs. Moses. And God bless Moses. You tell him that, you hear?"

"Can you come and see us some time?"

"Love to."

"How about next Sunday? If the weather's nice."

"It's a date."

When I picked my way downstairs through the gloom again, it was to find the boy sitting in the living room. He had his fist stuffed in his mouth, and he snapped off his flashlight as I entered. However, I trained the beam from my own on him.

"Well, there's nothing like a good laugh," I said, fixing him firmly in the cone of light.

"That's right." He removed the fist from his mouth and said, "Mother wants to know what we want to eat. There's everything, including pheasant, that we have to eat in the next couple days, unless they get the power back on soon. Which they won't."

"Yes," Naughty said, coming in from the kitchen. "Thank God we've got a gas stove."

"Embarrassment of riches. Nothing like an emergency to make you live it up. Let's have the pheasant. I've never eaten it."

I found a bottle of white wine which, the refrigerator being what it was, I chilled by setting it outside on the doorstep while dinner cooked. Ham was still smiling when we sat down to eat in our coats and hats.

"You know those ballrooms for middle-aged people they have in Chicago," I said to Naughty. "They've just opened one that's a discotheque. For middle-aged couples. You know what they call it?"

"No."

"Tell her, Ham."

"The Slipped Discotheque," he said, shoving his hat back with his thumb.

So we banqueted by candlelight while outside the cold rain fell, and the coats of ice thickened steadily on the bending trees, till not only their boughs but even their trunks began slowly to crackle and fall like the rain itself, and the night was filled with the thunder of disintegrating hickory and oak and sycamore, and the world lay at last in crystal splinters at your feet, like a great glass bowl someone had dropped.

Thus do we stick around, never knowing when next we shall be pleasantly surprised . . . Because, death, you old folk remedy you, I'm not quite ready for you yet . . . Not quite yet.